The Optimist

Strewn along the beach were the corpses of eighty-seven sand sharks and a man.

The sharks had been trapped in tidal pools and asphyxiated. The man was about thirty-five. He wore a white linen suit and loafers with no socks.

A leather eyeglass case with a pair of horn-rimmed glasses was in the right inside pocket of his suit coat; in the left was a cashier's check for one million dollars.

"Could've been worse," Detective Derry said. "Could've been eighty-seven men and one shark."

JERRY OSTER
CALIFORNIA
DEAD

CHARTER BOOKS, NEW YORK

This book was previously published by
Harper & Row under the title *Rancho Maria*.

This Charter book contains the complete text of the original
hardcover edition. It has been completely reset in a typeface
designed for easy reading, and was printed from new film.

CALIFORNIA DEAD

A Charter Book/published by arrangement with
Harper & Row, Publishers, Inc.

PRINTING HISTORY
Harper & Row edition / March 1986
Charter edition / January 1988

ISBN: 0-441-70426-3

Charter Books are published by The Berkley Publishing Group,
200 Madison Avenue, New York, New York 10016.
The name "CHARTER" and the "C" logo
are trademarks belonging to Charter Communications, Inc.

PRINTED IN THE UNITED STATES OF AMERICA

10 9 8 7 6 5 4 3 2 1

1

"It's like screwing, murder: there's all kinds of ways to do it. A guy of your obvious experience, I don't have to tell you what I mean." The man had a purple blotch on his left cheek and a mouth that sucked intermittently at nothing. He kept his eyes on the pump as he filled the Celica with regular.

"You can push the guy off a building, but you got any real high ones where you are? I don't think so. You can go for a boat ride, throw him in the ocean, but some guys turn into Johnny Weissmuller at times like that—adrenaline, I guess. You can booby-trap his car, but why total a good set of wheels? What does he drive? A Benz, probably. You can sap him, stick him, garrote him, but you got to get intimate with him, and like the swimmers, some guys get real strong all of a sudden—it could be you who gets stuck.

"All of which is why the individual I represent prefers shooting. It's relatively quiet, you use the right equipment, pick the right time of day and shoot straight, which the individual I represent does. You don't mess up your suit, you don't have to see the guy's face up close, which he doesn't like to do. He's a human being like anybody else—wife, kids, dog.

"See that sign, 'No Free Water'? It doesn't make sense. I mean—what?—two-thirds or something of the planet's water and we're all going to die of thirst because a bunch of assholes in Washington gave our water to Phoenix. *Phoe*nix. Maybe you should save your money, wait for this, uh, friend of yours to die of thirst. Ha. You don't want to wait, the choice of method sits okay with your people, it'll be fifty large. I know we said thirty in our preliminary discussion, but, well, marksmanship is what it sounds like, an art."

"I don't have p-people. It's my decision."

The nozzle sprang off. The man lifted it carefully, tapped a couple of drops into the tank, and replaced it in the pump. He screwed on the gas cap and stood with his hands poised before him, a maestro without a band. "I can understand them charging for water, I guess; that don't mean they can't have a rag or something to wipe your hands with." He scrubbed them together briskly. "That'll be cash, no new bills, nothing bigger than fifties, half in advance. Oh, and, uh, another grand for expenses, also up front. I'm not going to account for what I lay out, give you receipts or anything. I save a few bucks 'cause I'm a good shopper, I keep the difference, call it a bonus. I go a little over a grand, I go a little over. It's only a little, I can absorb it, you know what I'm saying? I go over a lot, you'll hear from me. Fuck did I do? I should've got super, you're paying for it."

"I don't have the cash with me. I have to—"

"Right. You have to talk to your people, 'cause you've got people, guys like you always have people. Look. Mr. *Smith*. I don't care if everyone in southern California's in on this. I don't care why they're in on it or how they got in on it or what they want out of it. All I care is I and the individual I represent don't get fucked around, which is what you're doing by not being straight with me, pretending you don't have people. You know how to reach me. I wouldn't wait too long. There's a demand for the services of the individual I represent. He's one of the best, maybe *the* best. I mean, he's not doing a bit, is he? He lives in— Well, never mind that. Today Wednesday? I'd say you got till Friday. You going to pump some gas? There's something forgettable about a guy who drives into a self-service station, pumps some gas. A guy who doesn't, I don't know, the cashier might remember it, take it personal or something.''

"R-regular.'' He drove an incongruous Caprice.

The man pulled the nozzle from the pump and handed it over the trunk. "Good thing I didn't get super. I mean, I'm not working for you yet, am I? You got to talk to your p-people.''

2

Strewn along the beach were the corpses of eighty-seven sand sharks and a man.

The sharks had swum in pursuit of prey into pools formed during the high tide; when it turned they were trapped and eventually asphyxiated. A few gulls still snacked on the carcasses, but the delicacies, brains and eyes, had been eaten by earlier birds, who stood angled to windward, sated and stunned by their good fortune.

The man was about thirty-five, slight, with olive skin, dark curly hair and mustache, a prominent nose and a six-inch gash in his throat.

He wore a white linen suit, an off-white cotton shirt with French cuffs but no cuff links, loafers with no socks. A pint of vodka was in one pocket of his suit coat, a bottle of Valium in the other—both empty. The suit was from Turnbull & Asser, the shirt a Charvet, the loafers Hermès, the vodka Finnish, the Valium from Corwith's Pharmacy, Southampton, New York, prescribed by Dr. John Broughton for Mrs. Eugene Marston, Gin Lane.

In his right pant pocket were ninety-five dollars in bills, thirty-five cents in change, a New York City subway token and a Cartier tank watch with no strap; in his left, a stub from the Southampton Trio theater. A leather Mädler eyeglass case with a pair of hornrimmed glasses, frames by Ralph Lauren, was in the right inside pocket of his suit coat; in the left, a schedule for the Hampton Jitney and a cashier's check from a bank in Zurich for one million dollars.

"Could've been worse," Derry said. "Could've been eighty-seven men and one shark."

Branch squinted at him. "You counted the sharks?"

"Langley did. You know—he's new."

"Langley find him?"

"A jogger. Kid who works at the Yacht Club. Lives in Esperanza, runs up the beach every morning. He had to get to work and swab decks, so I let him go."

The sun hove up just then from behind the Arozbispos, sending their shadows sprawling across the sand, turning the spindrift golden. Five years a Californian and Branch was still taken by surprise; he'd been expecting a sunrise out over the Pacific.

Derry, a native, studied the surf from under the brim of his Dodger cap. "Nice curl."

"You call Strock?" Branch said.

"I didn't want to wake him up, Sam. Besides, Escobar's office can't get anyone here for an hour at least. There was a shooting in Madrid. Bikers."

"Wake him up. There's a reception tonight with a lot of people coming from down the coast. Strock'll want to keep this quiet as long as possible. Send Langley up to the Yacht Club to tell the kid to wait till tomorrow to start bragging." He'd surely bragged already, but the reception was tennis people, golf people, polo people; they didn't mix with Yacht Clubbers. "I'm going to make some calls to New York—and Switzerland, I guess." Did Swiss banks have secret phone numbers, as well as accounts?

"What do you make of it, Sam?"

Branch slipped off his blazer and hung it over his shoulder from a finger. "That the guy's a long way from where he's been lately; that Langley and the kid walked all over any tracks that might've been around the body if the wind didn't blow sand over them already; that the gulls aren't going to tell us anything, or the sharks." He was usually better at speculating. Perhaps it was the hour—or the year.

"I meant the million bucks. It's made out to cash, for Christ's sake. Anyone can cash it. *We* can cash it. The banks open at eight, by nine we can be in Mexico."

"Send me a postcard, Jeff."

Branch slogged to the car and tossed the blazer on the passenger's seat, unintentionally—but conscious he'd done it—hiding the discreet letters embroidered in scarlet on the breast pocket: *RMLP*—the same letters that were on each of the blazer's fourteen gold buttons and on the license plates of the otherwise unmarked BMW.

The *P* had been a bone picked clean: Some in Rancho Maria de la Luz hadn't wanted to admit that the community needed a police force; others had accepted the necessity but boggled at calling it that. Security Patrol, Community Guard Unit, Department of Investigations, Bureau of Protection, Public Safety Division—those had been some of the proposed euphemisms. Gendarmerie and Constabulary had each had its adherents among the xenophiles; a vocal splinter group from those favoring the latter had argued for changing the name of the building where whatever it was to be called was to be headquartered from Six Hundred North Beltway (a location conspicuously outside the rancho's walls) to Scotland Yard and for referring to its occupants by metonymy.

Rear Admiral Fletcher Christian Hawkes (USN, Ret.), chairman of the Board of Governors at the time, had prevailed. No lawman worth his wages, he asserted, would belong to a police department with a name that made it sound as though cops weren't welcome as members. If the rancho was to have a paramilitary force—which was what the police were, after all, damn it—call it that and let it be exemplary, its uniform an emblem of pride.

There the Admiral had been scuttled, for though the Governors yielded on the name (while omitting the word *Department,* which rang mundanely, and rejecting the alternative *Force,* with its implicit belligerence), they were not so insensitive to local paranoia as to turn loose in the community a band of men in garrison caps, tunics, Sam Brownes, jodhpurs and jackboots—the getup Hawkes had in mind and had had his wife, a semiprofessional watercolorist, sketch.

With due respect to a man who had worn his shoulder boards throughout his onerous seven-year captivity by the North Vietnamese Communists (who had winged his Skyhawk on a bombing run over Hanoi), the Governors (and *their* wives) were adamant that the members of the RMLP would dress in double-breasted blue blazers, gray pleated slacks, navy over-the-calf socks, brown wingtip shoes, blue plain-collar shirts and striped ties in the community's colors, royal blue and scarlet. Hats would be optional, but if the option was acted on they were to be gray fedoras in winter, panamas in summer. (Derry's Dodger cap, therefore, was more than an affront to Padres fans, in the majority locally—baseball being à la mode these days, after years of being *infra dig;* it was against the regulations.) Sunglasses—*not* the mirrored kind—were fine for driving, but were to be pocketed when afoot; prescription glasses should be framed in nothing outré. Finally, to ensure the respect of a citizenry that believed you are what you drive, the chief of the RMLP would be behind the wheel of a Mercedes, his men of BMWs (captains and lieutenants), Volvos (sergeants) and Honda Accords (patrolmen).

*   *   *

Branch watched the ocean for a while before turning the ignition key, watched it and thought what another fine hot day in an eternity of fine hot days it was going to be and what a fine start he'd made of it. First, he'd let the water run while shaving, disregarding No. 3 of the Ways to Save Water decal he'd put up on the bathroom mirror. Then, though he hadn't been at all tempted to skip with the cashier's check for a million dollars, he'd given an order to keep the murder of its bearer quiet. He would forgo some future shower to atone for taking water from an avocado tree; the cover-up was all in a day's work. He could bury the insignia on his blazer and pretend he was just another ranchero bound for his brokerage house, his law firm, his plastic surgery, eager to put in a traditional Friday half-day before repairing to the Racquet Club, Holly Hills or the Meadowmere, driving his fast foreign car with vanity plates; but he was one of the RMLP's finest, a master of priorities.

That was Megan talking across the years and miles. Not her diction but her sensibility. *Nothing's changed, then*, was how she would say it, and would go upstairs for a grand cry, leaving him to wilt under the kids' recriminatory stares. By *nothing* she meant everything—everything but him: he had dragged her and her children from coast to coast and gone himself from niche to niche; had bared their Irish complexions to an unforgiving sun and stayed himself in the shadow of his underhandedness. After six months of pointing out to him that worse than his unrepentance was his indifference, she flew back east with the kids, leaving him the car, the house, the furniture, the debts and the certainty of damnation. Four and a half years later, Branch had forgotten what she looked like, though not that she winced when he touched her breasts, as if they were bruises; her morality, an inquisitional spirit that haunted the house with an enthusiasm she had not been able to bring to living in it, was ineradicable.

The kids. They would be there in less than a week, pale and edgy from a winter held hostage by humorless nuns, hungry for their annual dose of fathering. Perhaps it was time to wean them from the usual junk food and feed them some pragmatism, to teach them that here, as anywhere, there was a scheme of things that God and Christ knew nothing of, that—just for example—a Rancho Maria reception was not just another party and that when it was one of Portia's there were to be no unscheduled surprises, such as the news of a violent death in the vicinity . . . even though the victim, for all his spiffy brand names, was a stranger and very probably a foreigner to boot.

As often, the thought of Portia spawned thoughts of Portia—Portia supine and Portia rampant, Portia at play and Portia in repose, cool and passionate, clothed and naked. Having undressed her, he had to cover her up or masturbate on duty—a depth to which he hadn't, Megan, plummeted. He tried to dress her for the evening, but left her in her periwinkle robe; they'd spent most of their romance in bed, or close by it, and he didn't know what she'd wear to a party.

3

The airline that forgot to load the movie and ran out of
Bloody Mary mix having also lost her luggage, Eve
Zabriskie didn't know what *she*'d wear, either.

"There're stores in Rancho Maria." Annie Buck tapped
the horn to plead for a place for her Rabbit on the Costa
del Sol Freeway.

"My Water Pik's in there, too. And my diaphragm.
What if I eat corn on the cob, or meet a man?"

Annie felt for Eve's hand and gave it a squeeze. "It's
nice to see you. You haven't changed a bit."

Eve put Annie's hand on the wheel. "Do you always
drive this fast?"

"Welcome to California."

Eve made herself ignore the cars at speed on every side
and take in the oil derricks and gas tanks. "It's beautiful.
New Jersey with palm trees."

Annie smiled. She had come west to put as many miles
as possible without emigrating between herself and the
tumultuous end to an otherwise passionless marriage, settling first in Carmel, where the sun shines only fifty-odd
days a year; the rain and fog had been the objective

correlatives of her mood and she enjoyed for a time pretending to be the heroine of an Ingmar Bergman movie. But when her law firm opened branches in the southern counties and offered her the one in Rancho Maria de la Luz, she was happy to trade in the role for one more sun-drenched. "The only time I get homesick is on New Year's Eve, watching the ball drop at Times Square. It's only nine o'clock here when it does, and waiting for local midnight's an anticlimax. The kids love it, so I suppose I'll stay forever, or until they grow up—whichever comes first."

"Sounds like there're no men in your life."

"A man. I guess. He's— Promise you won't laugh?"

"Why would I do that?"

"He's a cop."

Eve laughed.

"His name's Sam Branch. Do you know him?"

"I just got off the plane, Annie."

"He was on the NYPD for twenty years. He got in some kind of trouble. Maybe you read about it, or your father knew him."

"What kind of trouble?"

"Sam won't talk about it. He came out here with a wife and two kids; she left in less than a year, with the kids. She's a cop's daughter, too, and couldn't forgive Sam for disgracing her father."

Eve knew all about the wives and daughters of cops; she was one of the latter, hence Annie's "too," born of one of the former. "My father always says cops with daughters— Look, Annie, a fire."

Smoke, actually, billowing up from behind a ridge on their right, as dark and dense as a thundercloud until the wind got hold of it and knocked it about. A helicopter sashayed above the ridge, now dipping down out of sight, now rising up again.

Annie leaned over the wheel to see out the windshield

and stayed that way as the rubbernecking slowed the traffic. "It's a controlled fire. An avocado orchard. I should've warned you about the drought. Until recently, about half our water came from the Colorado River, which forms the border with Arizona. Most of it's been diverted to Tucson and Phoenix—by order of the Supreme Court, which in its wisdom failed to note our history of dependence on imported water. In the late seventies, a lot of retired people invested in avocados as tax shelters. Even though the Court had already decided and it was just a matter of time before the water got turned off, they overplanted. There was a glut that depressed prices for both the crops and the land. Now that the water's finally drying up, hundreds of groves are being bulldozed and burned."

Eve felt a long way from home, where water came from tanks, shaped like lunar landers and funny hats, on the roofs of buildings, and avocados from the basement of the Jefferson Market. "What about all the snow on those mountains I just flew over?" She felt very clever: NEW YORK GAL SLAKES CAL'S THIRST.

"There's a state aqueduct that carries melt water from the mountains around here; but it's not enough. A couple of years ago there was a proposition to build a canal to bring south the melt water that flows off the mountains up north into San Francisco Bay. It was defeated by a coalition of northern Californians who didn't like the idea of giving the south something for nothing, of environmentalists who thought the plan didn't have enough ecological safeguards, and of big San Joaquin Valley farmers who thought it had too many."

Eve had graduated from causes and college at the same ceremony, but she admired the glint in Annie's eye. "I'm glad I washed up on the plane."

Annie smiled, but stayed on her soapbox. "All the water around here's controlled by a public utility, Southland Hydro, that sells it to city and county water districts.

Southland's idea of a solution is to expand the state aqueduct, a very modest version of the plan that was defeated
at the polls. Some more farsighted people, who include a
number of my clients, are trying to raise private money to
build a dam on a tributary of the Colorado and sell water
to the county. Southland's afraid it'll be undersold; they're
spending money they could be spending on water for a
public relations campaign to turn people against the idea.
It's an emotional issue. Mark Twain said whiskey's for
drinking, water's for fighting.''

"Merle Haggard says water's for *tears* and whiskey's
for drinking.''

"Since when do you listen to Merle Haggard?''

"Since when do you read Mark Twain?''

"Sam reads him. What spark there is between us comes
from books. Most of the people around here have even
given up the pretense of having books; they have video
collections. Sam's house looks like a library.''

"That could be why he got in trouble.''

Annie punched Eve's arm—"You *haven't* changed a
bit"—then sat back in her seat and swung into the emergency lane to follow some cars that were getting off the
freeway at an exit up ahead. "This'll take us a little out of
our way, but I can show you Rancho Maria's beach.''

The glimpse she'd had of the Pacific out the 747's
windows before clenching her eyes for the descent had
tweaked in Eve a nostalgia for a time in her life when she
went to Florida every late winter and early spring, and at
Annie's last word the memory became full-blown, scented
and sonorous. She hadn't gone to vacation but to write
about (of *all* things, her mother always said) baseball for
(of *all* newspapers) the *New York Times*. It was harder
work than any of those who envied her could imagine—
prizing words out of laconic men who regarded her not as
a pioneer but as poontang, mining for subtext in the game's

mountain of statistics; but most mornings had been hers and the ocean's. "Does Sam have any interesting friends?"

"Meaning there're no men in *your* life?"

Eve supposed there were two, which was somehow worse than none. One was a stand-up comic—except that he didn't stand up, he sat on a basketball, which was surprisingly funny. The other was a venture capitalist, which meant he stared at his bedroom ceiling for hours at a time, then made a couple of phone calls and murmured large numbers; he'd loved the sixties and still had his hair in a ponytail and wore tie-dyed shirts. Eve called him the Allman Brothers. "Three thousand miles and a few hours and I'm already starting to forget what they looked like."

The beach road was only a little faster than the freeway, for there was the distraction of a trio of police whitetops parked neatly on the verge.

"That's Caliente Beach," Annie said. "I wonder what's up."

It was all so orderly, they might've been cooping; in New York, they'd've parked every which way, and had their lights flashing, to maximize the disruption. "Is your friend there?"

"Those're county cops. I hope it's not some kid. With school out, some of them get pretty wild. There's more drinking and drugs than makes a mother comfortable. Which reminds me—since when do you know anything about wine?"

Eve laughed. She knew less about wine than just about anything, but having given up the trammeled security of a paycheck for the penniless freedom of the free lance, she wasn't above taking an expenses-paid trip anywhere at all, especially to a place where a long-lost friend coincidentally lived. She had feigned oenophilia to get the assignment from a new magazine to do a piece on a couple of affluent southern Californians who were rumored to have concocted a champagne that was going to set the wine

world on its ear. Ignorance of her subject had never kept
her from writing a good story before, and in any case,
what was really wanted by the magazine, a *Vanity Fair*
knockoff whose editors only humored the suggestion that
there was intelligent life west of Fifth Avenue, was that
she do a number ("but *doucement*, Eve, *doucement*," her
editor added) on the fauna of southern California.

That her prospective subjects happened to be clients of
Annie's had helped Eve land the job, and since she was
also getting a free room at Annie's (which hadn't hurt
her), she wondered if the magazine would pay for the
clothes she was going to have to buy (she would use a
toothbrush and be chaste) to represent it as it deserved to
be represented; but when, on passing through the gates of
Rancho Maria de la Luz, she saw what Annie had called
stores—D. Cenci, Bottega Veneta, Giorgio, Tourneau,
Česká, The Coach Store, Gübelin, Petochi & Gorevic,
Bulgari, Fred Joaillier, Cellini, along with outposts of
Saks and Bonwit's and I. Magnin and Neiman-Marcus and
Lord & Taylor—she stopped wondering. "What do you do
when you just want a T-shirt and jeans?"

Annie laughed. "Go to the city, but it was in the
opposite direction. There're some less expensive places
around the corner."

"All these limos—none of these women has a thing to
wear?"

"Tonight's sort of special. Not that it matters. When
Portia gives a party, all anyone notices is what *she*'s
wearing."

4

A black dress with nothing underneath it, and no question about it.

The soft breeze that seemed to accompany Portia Beaufils wherever she went molded the crepe de Chine against her thighs and belly and breasts (though it dared not ruffle her burgundy hair). Like damsels of yesteryear, the spaghetti straps over Portia's ivory shoulders swooned occasionally from the excitement, slipping down on her slender arms until she took distracted note of her dishabille and shrugged them back into place. While awaiting such adjustment, her perfect breasts kept the dress from succumbing to gravity.

Green-eyed, high-cheekboned, high-waisted, long-legged, not so tall that she had to slouch but tall enough that men of average height stood straighter than usual before her, Portia was living testimony to God's beneficence—or, if you will, to Nature's stringent perfectionism. And she was no blank book Morocco-bound: she had a B.A. from Berkeley, a master's in French literature from Columbia, had studied viticulture and oenology at the University of Bordeaux and written a respected monograph on the wines of the Gironde; she was licensed to fly Lears and Falcons, drove her Porsche (yes!) like a member of the factory team, played golf to an eight handicap and, with the Racquet Club professional as her partner, once extended Tim Gulikson and Pam Shriver to a tie-breaker in an exhibition charity mixed-doubles match.

From her father, the aforementioned Admiral Hawkes, Portia inherited her bearing, her ambition and her command; from her late mother, Esmé Hubbell Hawkes, her hair, her athleticism, her scholarship and her money; from both her parents, her horsemanship and her jingoistic pride in Rancho Maria de la Luz, a community that had not existed until the Hawkeses decreed that it must. The first of the bulldozers that chewed up the desert and spat out an oasis had had Portia at the controls; her father, still pallid from his captivity, sat beside her in the cab; her mother, a hard hat on her head and a roll of blueprints under her arm, leaned casually out from the running board, like a Keystone Kop.

"She's something." Eve watched Portia stride up the marble stairs from the sunken living room two at a time and confront, hands on hips, a boisterous crowd of sun-burned men who had just come through the front door, silencing them with a look that pitied them for missing even a little of her party. "The face that stanched a thousand quips."

Annie laughed. "The portly gentleman in the corner there, the one who seems to be smoking several cigars, is her husband. I think I'll wait till it's quieter to introduce you."

Eve supposed it made sense that the legendary acumen that had won Felix Beaufils the nickname Midas of Mutual Funds should have brought him a wife who went with the furniture, but if Eve were a man it would rankle, for Felix was more than portly, he was squat. She snared a canapé

from a passing waiter and leaned against a handy wall.
"Who's everyone else?"

The men in Portia's thrall were the polo players, flush
from a few chukkers at the Meadowmere. The tennis
players were at the north end of the drawing room, which
gave onto the rose garden, beyond which lay the Decoturf
II courts—six of them, for Portia's idea of an afternoon of
tennis was a round-robin tournament; she had started a
ladder a place on whose rungs was coveted far more than
one on the Racquet Club's.

The golfers were a chip shot away at the other end of
the room, which had a view of the infamous fifteenth
green of the Holly Hills Country Club, whose annual
tournament the touring professionals had recently threatened to boycott if the hole was not mitigated. Just outside
the windows, which had been refitted with shatterproof
glass, lay a full-scale replica of the hole from pin to green,
commissioned by Portia out of a compulsion to master the
original and carved out of what had been the horse pasture,
Portia having lost her enthusiasm for equitation on the
death of her mother. She could be found there most mornings, playing ten or twelve balls at a time and now and
then getting one of them down in par from the ladies'—or
rather, lady's—tee.

Near the center of the room, within reaching distance of
the bar, were the sedentaries, suffered by the sportsmen
because they were punctilious spectators at one or all of
the contests that were the fare of a typical weekend.
Presiding there, she with a gimlet, he with a bourbon and
branch, were Rancho Maria de la Luz's mayor, Aura
Quivers, and chief of police, Tom Strock, look-alikes,
respectively, for Sophia Loren and Charlton Heston and
assured of their jobs for their lifetimes as a result.

Most of the outsiders were from down the coast, a few
from as far north as the Bay area—a tribute to the drawing
power of the host and hostess but more than that a mani-

festation of the fear that the rumor was true: that by some alchemy the Beaufilses had in their boutique winery transmuted the rather ordinary local *cépage*—Pinot Noir and Pinot Chardonnay—into a *cuvée* that surpassed any champagne produced in the Napa and Sonoma valleys or the Central Coast—and, the most refulgent version said, rivaled those of the *départements* of the Marne, Aube and Aisne. The vintners of the Champagne were keeping their Gallic distance, but emissaries had been dispatched from Domaine Chandon, Korbel, Hanns Kornell, Mirassou and Schramsberg.

A voice was pitched above the general hubbub and Annie turned toward it. "Uh oh."

"What?"

"The big man in the blue blazer talking to Felix is Warren Cable. He's the president of Southland Hydro. I told you about Southland, the utility—"

"The utility that doesn't want the dam built. Why uh oh?"

"Felix is a prime mover in the dam project. The two of them never just talk; they fight like wild dogs. Warren must've been invited for form's sake, but I doubt if anyone thought he'd come. I hope—"

But it was hopeless. In just a few seconds, the battle had been joined, and Felix Beaufils and Warren Cable were bright red with contentiousness. Out of decorum, they hissed at each other through their teeth, and few of the guests were aware of the altercation. One who was was the police chief, Strock, who got between the two men and used his stature and his office to quell the disturbance. An arm around Cable's shoulder—his other hand held Cable's forearm in a bouncer's grip—Strock escorted him from the room, and as quickly as it began, it was over. Strock returned alone in a few moments and clearly reported to Felix that Cable had gone home. Felix nodded his thanks and said something those around him laughed at, and laughed at it himself—a hearty burble that dispelled the tension.

"I'll have to call Warren in the morning," Annie said. "The last time they had one of these—it was a lot louder and a lot longer—the committee lost three members. It's a fragile enough coalition as it is."

"Fragile why?"

"Not everyone's convinced Felix is the altruist he makes himself out to be. He says he wants to build the dam to ensure water for the rancho, and since his wife's the founders' daughter that has the ring of truth to it. But some people can't help wondering if most of the water from a dam wouldn't go to Felix's vineyards."

"You're his lawyer. Would it?"

"I'm his lawyer. Don't ask."

The room smelled of Drakkar Noir and Giorgio, of Felix's Cuban cigar, of money and nerves and sex. In New York, only gay men generated as much heat, AIDS or no AIDS; heterosexuals, veterans of herpes and unavailability, kept their distance. But this bunch! There wasn't a neurotically retracted pelvis among them. The small talk was freighted with innuendo—and nearly inaudible in the din of body language. Breasts and thighs—it might have been a poultry farmers' convention—were not so much bared as paraded. In front of every window and the open French doors to the terrace stood at least one slim young thing in something sheer, hipshot and very conscious of the X-ray effect of the backlighting. The men, their virility swaddled (O inconsistent mores!) in yards of fabric—any one's lemon sport coat or madras patch slacks could have been easily made into dresses for any two of the women— were constrained to use their hands and eyes, which roamed unchecked, and now and then a tongue, which would follow a confidence into an ear.

"Promiscuity is the other local sport," Annie said,

seeing that Eve was getting the picture. "And you're being scouted by one of the leading scorers—Patrick Wade."

The man she tipped her head toward had had his eye on Eve for a while, which hadn't interfered with his palpation of the rear end of a girl, perhaps out of her teens, with snow-white hair. He was as handsome as any man Eve had ever seen, but his acute awareness of it made him ugly. "Where's your friend Sam?"

Annie blushed. "He is a cop, Eve . . . and he had a romance with our hostess."

"Really? So he's not a *cop*."

"I know only that it was brief, that it ended before Portia married Felix—they met in Paris, where Portia was visiting—that it left Sam bitter. He won't talk about *it*, either."

Eve squeezed Annie's hand. "There *is* an available man. I read about him in *Scientific American*. They've got him in a top-secret laboratory outside Washington and're going to breed him selectively in hope of passing on the trait."

Annie smiled. "When you meet Sam, Eve—you will; I've told him about you and he remembers reading your baseball stuff—please don't mention your father."

"Your *father*." Patrick Wade had blind-sided them, and put an arm around Eve, his fingertips close to her breast. "You're not a daddy's girl, are you?"

Eve slipped away. "Careful. My daddy's a cop."

Annie laughed. "Eve Zabriskie. Dr. Patrick Wade."

"Let me guess," Eve said. "You're a gynecologist."

His vanity made him gullible and he cocked his head in anticipation of her explanation. Close up, his beauty was defective, pocked and roughed.

"Your ears. They're all cauliflowered."

Annie went away, shaking her head.

Patrick Wade propped a hand against Eve's wall and looked without abashment down the front of her dress, a lavender jersey of polyester knit with a surplice top (The Top that Drove Men Mad, she had concluded after watching the Allman Brothers watch Jacqueline Bisset wear one in *Under the Volcano*) that slipped and slid over her breasts, continually exciting her nipples. A provocative frock to make a debut in, but marked down forty percent at the rancho's Bonwit's. "New York?"

"Where else?"

"You might be interested in coming with a few of us down to Caliente Beach, to see the scene of the crime. It'll make you feel at home. Afterwards, we can have a late supper, just the two of us. My houseboy makes an admirable sushi." He leaned away to take her all in. "But you look like a meat and potatoes girl."

Men were never indifferent to Eve's size; they were challenged by it, or threatened, or repulsed. Even those who found it attractive never failed to say that it was extraordinary for them to desire a woman like her. The ones with liberal educations jogged their memories and out came adjectives like Rubensesque; the others called her an Amazon, or a broad. Patrick Wade looked like one of the collectors—of anorexics and meat and potatoes girls and everything in between. "What crime?"

"The police aren't talking, but apparently some . . . Israeli got his throat cut."

"Some Jew, you started to say. And that *is* a crime here?"

"When it's out of season." He grasped her arm as she tried to turn away. "Don't act offended. You started it. And you're not Jewish. Your hips're too supple. You like sex."

"Let me go."

He did. "I hear you're writing a magazine piece. I can tell you some choice local gossip."

"It wouldn't be any use to me. Try *Hustler*."

"The wonderful thing about women like you," Patrick

Wade said, ''is the perfect balance you strike between ball-breaker and cock-teaser.''

''Perfect? My. Now excuse me. There're so *many* men here.''

Wade brushed a knuckle against one of those supple hips as she passed. ''Ask Felix how things are at Moneda Investing.'' He smiled as she faltered just a little. ''He'll know what you mean.''

5

Escobar did the autopsy himself, for though the man on the beach wasn't Rancho Maria de la Luz's first murder victim (the Latino hired help had passions their masters and mistresses were powerless to modulate), he was unique in having an assailant not compelled by *machismo* to boast of his deed and make detection a simple matter of listening to what was being noised about. Escobar moved like a matador on tiny feet, giving a play-by-play of his morbid *faena* into a microphone suspended from the ceiling.

Sitting on an examining table, his legs asleep from dangling, Branch shut his ears to the prattle, as he'd averted his eyes from the swordplay; he couldn't evade the overpowering smell of disinfectant and swallowed repeatedly to keep his stomach in check. He rarely attended autopsies, but a phone call from Megan had left him feeling sorry for himself and where better than a morgue to regain your self-esteem?

He ought to have known it was she; there was exasperation in the telephone's ring. But he'd been on a roll and had learned so much about a man who hours ago he'd only

known was dead that he half-expected the call to be from
the killer, wanting to confess.

"Is that yourself, Sam?"

Why did she talk like that? The closest she'd ever been
to Ireland was Center Moriches, where her parents had a
squalid summer house. "Hello, Megan."

"I just wanted to be sure you were expecting the
children."

And hoping he'd forgotten—or was too busy, lying,
scheming, covering his ass. "Of course I am. Tell Ricky
we're going to a Padres doubleheader next Sunday—against
the Cubs."

In her silence he heard her disapproval of a team whose
nickname made light of the clergy; she'd sooner root for
the Harlots. Or the Addicts. "I do hope you've scheduled
some activities that Kathleen'll enjoy, as well."

"We're going straight from the airport to the zoo. Then
on to Sea World." Then to an *exhibition* and a hanging.

"Do go easy on the hot dogs and ice cream, will you?
Kathleen's skin's starting to break out and Dr. O'Connell
says she needs lots of fruit and vegetables."

Dr. O'Connell, whose brother was a bishop and whose
prescriptions were filled by God. "We have fruit and
vegetables in California, Megan. We in*vented* fruit and
vegetables." And the Hell's Angels and the Black Pan-
thers and the Manson Family.

". . . You mentioned in your letter that you have a . . .
friend with children Richard and Kathleen's ages. Were
you intending . . . ?"

To photograph them in pornographic poses? Yes. Is that
all right? "I thought they might like to spend some time
together."

"Is she . . . ?"

"She's a lawyer, Megan. And, I regret to say, a Presby-
terian. Or maybe it's an Episcopalian. In any case, a
reprobate and the mother of reprobates."

". . . Have you been drinking, Sam?"

He suddenly wanted one—a margarita, with a señorita chaser. "I'm busy. We had a murder here this morning."

Megan sniffed at the pronoun. "Just one more thing, Sam. I'm sending along a recipe the children absolutely adore. It's for . . ."

For what, he'd already forgotten, so smitten was he with her unswerving predictability. Recipes were Megan's weapons against chaos; she cast them like oil on the world's troubled waters—or to put it another way, imposed them like dogma upon heathens everywhere. He could take her children from her for four weeks a year, but they would get their sustenance from her.

Escobar peeled off his gloves and sauntered away from the mess he'd made, tossing his conclusion over his shoulder. "Death by massive hemorrhage resulting from a severed trachea. A very sharp knife with a six-to-eight-inch blade. Maybe a hunting knife. Attacked from the front. A slight bruise on the left wrist that might be a defense mark, but otherwise no sign he put up a struggle—"

"Meaning he knew his killer? Or had no reason to think—"

Escobar sliced the air to cut off the hypothesis. "You always ask me what things *mean*, Lieutenant. I am competent to tell you only—and only to the best of my ability—what occurred, and when. In this case, death ensued between eleven P.M. Thursday and one A.M. today."

Branch wrote that in his notebook and underlined and starred it. He felt Escobar studying him and spoke without looking up. "I have a theory—"

"In the absence of a suspect." Escobar got full value out of the sibilances.

"—a theory why we don't get along."

Escobar folded his arms on his chest.

"We're both a long way from where we started—me

from New York, you from Miami. Men don't make moves like that at our age unless there's something they'd like to forget, as if moving were all it took. You've heard talk about me; I've heard talk about you; neither of us has heard the other's whole story, and neither of us wants to. If we did, we'd find out for sure what we already suspect—that we were both set up, that we're both as good at our jobs as you can get, and that we have a lot in common off-duty too. Hell, we'd become allies—maybe even friends. Only problem, if that happened everyone'd say it was because we're birds of a feather, a couple of crooked loners.'' Branch put his notebook away and hopped off the examining table, marching in place to get the blood circulating. "I say the hell with what everyone says—let's find out what we *do* have in common. At the very least, we'll do a better job—catch those bad guys quicker—and, hell, we might wind up with someone to drink with, instead of always drinking alone.''

With thumb and forefinger Escobar touched the corners of his mustache. The contempt that had been in his eyes when Branch started speaking had given way to puzzlement. The ball was in his court and losing momentum with every bounce; but rather than let it die, he scooped it up and flipped it back. "The Valium—your report mentioned that an empty bottle was found on the deceased. The lab tests will have to say it for a certainty, but it seems clear from a preliminary examination that he was not addicted—that he was, to *theor*ize''—Escobar smiled—"quite clearheaded at the time of death, having consumed only a small quantity of wine—a Chablis, I believe—and that, yes, he very probably did believe that no harm was about to be inflicted by the individual he confronted. Whether he knew him, I cannot say; but there was almost certainly an attitude of trust.'' He coughed artificially to displace his unease.

Branch nodded. "Thanks, Ray.''

Escobar turned away from the Christian name and headed

for the door, waving a hand at the corpse as he did. "If you care to take a look . . ."

Branch took a glance and was glad to have given a name to the dead man before handing him over for evisceration. He was beyond naming now.

In the lining of the dead man's linen suit coat they had found a key to room 303 at the Hotel Del Rey; it had fallen through a hole in the pocket and been missed on the first going-over. Room 303 yielded a passport and a Marley Hodgson Ghurka organizer that provided the name—Joseph Litvak—and specifications: age thirty-seven, height five six, weight one thirty, hair black, eyes dark brown, born Haifa, occupation consultant (on what and to whom unstated), resided Paris and Jerusalem, business addresses in both cities, habits meticulous (except that he drove recklessly; there were two speeding citations on his driver's license), tastes expensive.

The last two characteristics had come not from the passport or identification cards but from the credit card receipts tucked carefully into a pocket of the organizer, blazes on Joseph Litvak's trail: He had arrived in New York Wednesday of the previous week on a flight from Paris, and checked in at the Sheraton Centre, where he ate a room service dinner; he had Thursday breakfast at the Sheraton Russell, lunch at Joanna, dinner at the Quilted Giraffe, and on Friday (without checking out of his hotel) took the Hampton Jitney to Southampton, returning to New York on Sunday evening (having seen a movie Saturday night but eating and sleeping, it appeared from the absence of documentation, on the cuff).

Monday: the Ambassador Grill, Christ Cella, Le Refuge. Tuesday: the Carlyle, the Oyster Bar, Le Cirque. Wednesday (with misgivings, doubtless, at the prospect of airline food): a flight to Los Angeles on American Airlines, a room at the Beverly Wilshire and a case of left coast shock, for either he skipped dinner or paid cash.

On Thursday morning, Litvak rented a Camaro and drove to Rancho Maria de la Luz, checking in at the Del Rey in time for lunch. He ate dinner there, as well, his last meal.

Branch couldn't have given as good an accounting of his own movements over that time. And it all checked out: Yes, the hotel managers said, Mr. Litvak had been a guest; No, they said, there had been nothing unusual about him, no incidents, no embarrassments. The restaurant maître d's had said the same: Oh, it was *odd*, they supposed, that Mr. (sometimes Monsieur) Litvak ate always alone. But he'd eaten so well, and if anything, they'd pitied not him but his absent friends.

As on all rolls, all the phones were answered, all the right people were on duty. Even Eugene Marston of Gin Lane, Southampton, for whose wife the Valium had been prescribed, was listed in the phone book—maybe because that was how people knew you lived on Gin Lane. Or maybe because they were just folks, since Marston himself answered the phone.

"Yes, I know Joe Litvak. He's my brother-in-law. . . . Why?"

"I'm sorry to have to tell you this. He's, uh, dead." The particle was to soften the blow, but it came out sounding callous, as if there were still some hope that subject and predicate might not be joined.

Marston said, *"Dead?"*—as they all did. "How?"

"He was murdered." Before Marston could say *Murdered?* Branch added, "Any idea who would want to do that?"

Everyone has an idea who would want to murder anyone they know, but, as they all did, Marston said of course he had none, and how the hell did Branch get this number and where was he calling from, Rancho what? and how did he know Branch *was* a police officer. Branch said he'd hang up and Marston could get the number from information and call him back and Marston said he'd do just that; but someone intervened.

"This is Leah Marston. Joseph Litvak was my brother." She was cool—she'd gotten her tenses right—and didn't sound as though she needed Valium . . . or not often. Branch gave it to her straight and she took it without flinching audibly and he would have bet a lot that if she hadn't expected to one day get this call she was realizing that she ought to have. Adhering to the past indicative, she said her brother had trouble with jet lag and that she gave him the last of the Valium—three or four tablets, she thought. She ascertained that the body was free to be claimed, got Escobar's name and number, enlightened Branch on the wherefores of Judaic burial practices and, in general, put up a dense smoke screen of efficient calm.

"Your brother's passport says he was a consultant," Branch finally put in edgewise. "What kind of consultant?"

"Joe did a little bit of everything."

For example? Though he knew that someone who told his sister he did a little bit of everything didn't give examples.

"He represented Israeli companies doing business in Europe. Import-export, real estate, banking . . ."

A little bit of everything. "And what was he doing in the United States?"

"Looking for someone."

"Someone he wanted to give a check for a million dollars?"

"Yes." Leah Marston laughed and Branch waited for her to tell him what was funny. The laughter turned to tears and the phone banged and he was left listening to room tone. After a while, someone hung up the phone, which was what Branch would've done in the first place; but then, he knew there was no law that said you had to talk to a policeman who called you on the phone, long-distance or not.

He thought about calling back, for he'd forgotten to ask Leah Marston what movie her brother had gone to see and what she knew about one more item among his possessions—a bumper sticker promoting a Detroit beer and a New York City radio station, autographed by the station's morning man. He put it down to souvenir hunting, for Litvak had taken as well an ashtray from the Beverly Wilshire.

6

Portia materialized like a goddess, bearing a quivering mortal in a double-knit suit that was too big and too blue. "You're Annie's friend, the writer." Though Portia's voice was a cool stream, Eve noted from her handshake that she ran a little hot, not as if she needed a tune-up but preferred a high idle for the quick start it gave her. "Forgive me. I want very much to talk to you, but it will have to be later." She exerted a pressure that promised more than chitchat. "This is Howard Maddox, my husband's assistant. Howard, do tell Miss Zabriskie everything she wants to know about anything at all, will you?" She dropped Maddox at Eve's feet and flew off.

He had thick glasses and big ears and a haircut that on someone else might have been last year's punk chic but on him was just bad. He gave Eve an exiguous hand that slid away when she tried to grasp it. "Shall we step into the office? It's q-quieter there."

Quiet thanks to a soundproof door that shut on an air hinge. Dark, too, which made it even quieter, the only light coming from a couple of track lamps on the ceiling and from a dozen glowing computer consoles, whose cursors throbbed restlessly. The windows were curtained in a red that was nearly black and a dense carpet of the same hue covered the floor.

Maddox handed Eve into a black leather Eames chair, then sat in another behind a steel and glass desk. His pale face the amber of the computer screens, his glasses reflecting their displays, he looked like an office boy trying out the boss's chair. "Mr. Beaufils feels the best work is done in an environment from which the distractions of daily life have been b-banished. The telephone, alas, is a necessary evil, but those here glow rather than ring, which is less disruptive to the search for solutions."

Perched on the edge of her chair, not wanting to succumb to it, Eve thought she could use a phone like that. She could make love by it, in lieu of a fire, and not have to irritate her friends by taking the receiver off the hook or her lover by switching on the answering machine, then jumping out of bed to see who'd called while they were at it. "I'm really off duty at the moment, but I would like to ask—"

Maddox conjured a thick folder from a drawer and slid it across the desk. "Everything you want to know about Kallistos Enterprises is in here, Miss Zabriskie. It contains a history of the company, a biography of the founder and profiles of each of the divisions. It is not the sort of handout I'm sure you've seen far too many of in your career. It is t-tailor-made, the product of a software program that has read and analyzed a number of articles similar to the one you propose to write and has generated a series of questions that—forgive me for saying so; I don't mean to denigrate your professionalism, merely to congratulate my program—that I believe has anticipated most if not all of those you will have. The q-questions are presented along with their rather exhaustive answers."

Eve hefted the folder, on whose soft leather cover the letters *KE* were embossed in gold. "Does your program do

windows, too?'' She almost added *Or give head?* to see if
it would get a rise out of Maddox, who had his glasses off
and wiped at them with the end of his necktie. If ties can
be said to fit, it did so as badly as the suit, hanging nearly
to his crotch; it was some synthetic that made Eve's neck
hairs crawl to see handled, and a color whose name she
didn't know. His shirt was kindred, without a natural fiber
in it, short-sleeved. Doing a tap dance in the kneehole of the
desk, his shoes were Hush Puppies—gray, over dark brown
ankle socks with a beige pattern. Maddox was the guy who
in high school was on the audiovisual squad and had a ham
radio license. Where was his plastic breast-pocket holster
for pens and pencils?

"I started to say I want to ask something about you.
How long have you been with Kallistos? What did you do
before that, and before that? College, wife, children, pets,
hobbies?''

Maddox's stammer went into automatic. "I d-don't
d-don't—Why?'' He jammed his glasses on like safety
goggles.

Eve put an elbow on the desk and wagged a thumb at
the door. "I haven't met your boss yet, Mr. Maddox, but
I've been around enough men to know an eight-hundred-
dollar suit when I see one and a Havana cigar when I smell
it. This house cost—what?—two million? There're world-
class tennis tournaments played on worse courts than the
ones here, and as for the private golf hole, well . . .
There're one and a half servants to every guest and I saw
their quarters on the way in: they'd make a nice university.
I've heard about the stable of Ferraris and I've seen Mrs.
Beaufils; that's a very big diamond on her finger and a
Halston on her back, so to speak.

"The guests're of a feather: the kind of people who
have a Mercedes *wagon* to go shopping, only they don't
go shopping—not for groceries; who get a new Rolex like
I get a Timex, because I'm tired of the band. Those de

Koonings are de Koonings, they're not from some museum gift shop. I don't know anything about antiques, but the ones in this place're *old*. This is very high-tech equipment in here and I'm sure it's just the tip of the iceberg. The only thing that doesn't fit, Mr. Maddox—other than me, but I'm a journalist; we get to go all kinds of places we don't belong—is you, with your thrift shop clothes and your barber college haircut and your Latinate sentences. You interest me. How come there's no swimming pool?''

Maddox's feet had picked up the tempo, but his mouth curled at the corners. ''It's screened from the house. M-Mrs. Beaufils likes to swim *au naturel*.'' He said it with a perfect accent, and smiled more broadly, for he knew she knew he had. He found his watch—a Casio digital—somewhere up on his forearm, checked it and covered it up. ''We don't have m-much time—and you're off-duty. Briefly, I'm a graduate of MIT and the Wharton School. I know how to design computers *and* how to sell them. I worked for a number of companies on the so-called Golden Semicircle—Route 128, near Boston—all engaged in the same pursuit: creating more and more powerful computers and the software to run them. I didn't stay with any of them for very long. It's that sort of b-business.''

''Volatile,'' Eve said. ''Cutthroat. By the way, what do you know about the local murder?''

She thought he would hem and haw, but he made a small gesture of dismissal—and she noticed that his hands were elegant, like a croupier's. ''Caliente Beach is not strictly speaking part of the rancho. It lies well outside the walls and although its parking lot is restricted to residents, it is not in any way fenced off from neighboring beaches and is nearly, de facto, a public one. All our residents have pools, or live in condominiums that do, and in any case, the ocean is rather forbiddingly cold much of the year.'' Maddox took his glasses off again and sighted through them at one of the track lamps. ''Is your curiosity professional or . . . ?''

"Sociological. I like a town with a system in place that keeps rain off important parades—although there has been a little leakage. Aren't pools a little extravagant, with nor any drop to drink?"

Maddox giggled—not at the allusion, but at what he was about to say. "All the pools in the rancho are filled with water pumped from the ocean. The entrepreneur who came up with the idea has b-built himself quite a bustling little b-business on the side."

Eve didn't have to ask who the entrepreneur was. She tapped the folder. "And how's the rest of the Beaufils empire doing? How's, say, Moneda Investing?"

Maddox's eyes receded. "I'm not sure I know what you mean. Moneda is one of the most successful mutual funds in the nation, Miss Zabriskie—successful not by dint of speculating in small, fast-growing high-tech companies, as so many funds are doing these days, but rather by staidly emphasizing dividend and interest income and conservative stocks. The economy slowed down f-faster than expected and company earnings failed to meet the predictions of most market analysts. Funds that p-performed the best were those, like M-Moneda, that invested in bonds and the common stock of electric utilities, regional telephone operating companies, brewers and other businesses that benefited from the decline in interest rates. But I'm afraid I'm confused, M-Miss Zabriskie. I understood that you were more interested in . . . surfaces."

"I am," Eve said. "I absolutely am. . . . We left you on Route 128, near Boston."

Maddox popped his glasses back on. Late sixties . . . Silicon Valley . . . high technology and high finance inevitably bedfellows—*she* could've told *him* his life story. "Coincidentally, given the occasion for this evening's celebration, Mr. Beaufils first proposed to me that I work for him during a visit to a boutique winery in the Mendocino Valley, near Ukiah. He and Mrs. Beaufils stopped in Palo

Alto on their way n-north and invited me to accompany them for the afternoon. Their thought at the time was to buy such a small winery; they had no inkling—''

His watch beeped and he stood straight up. ''I'm afraid that's all for now, M-Miss Zabriskie. This is a moment I've been waiting for for years and I want to savor it.''

Eve stood, too, replacing the folder on the desk. ''I'll pick this up afterwards, if I may. You didn't say, but am I right in assuming there's no wife or children or pets or hobbies?''

He swept a hand around the room. ''These machines are as alluring as any woman, and as complex. They are as fulfilling as children, as diverting as any p-pets or pastimes.''

''And,'' Eve said, ''you can unplug them.''

And they don't have to pee. Nor did rich people, it seemed, for it took Eve a long time to find a bathroom—longer than it should have, for she passed it by the first time, her expectations still those of a New Yorker unaccustomed to a facility with an anteroom the size of some apartments she'd lived in, furnished with a leather couch and armchairs, big sand-filled urns for ashtrays, one wall hung with a painting of sinuous ladies by some Pre-Raphaelite in, she guessed, waning favor.

She stayed put for a while after she'd finished, for the heels she'd bought at Ferragamo hurt in direct proportion to their cost. The door to the hall opened and closed and Eve found herself for the first time since high school an eavesdropper on a rest-room conversation:

''How 'bout a quickie?''

''How'd you like a kick in the balls?''

The man chuckled. There was the sound of discreet scuffling.

''Cut it *out,* you big goon. This stuff *wrinkles.*''

''I can remember a time when it didn't matter to you *if* you got wrinkled, long as you *got* wrinkled.''

"Don't you read Ann Landers? Three out of four women prefer cuddling to fucking."

"Glad I got me the fourth."

More chuckles and scuffles. She giggled. Then the sound of hair being vigorously brushed.

"Was Warren very angry that I told him to go home?"

"Thought *I* told him to go home."

"Because *I* told you to tell him. Was he angry, goddamnit?"

"He reckoned he'd made his point."

"The fool. He has the tact of a billygoat."

"Speaking of which . . ."

"Get your hands *off* me. My nipples are standing straight *up*."

"They got company, sweetheart."

"Later, Billygoat Gruff. Later. I've got something you're going to like."

"What?"

She giggled.

"*What*, damn it? You can't do that to a man."

After a long beat: "Gloves."

After a longer one: "Kind of gloves?"

"Lace gloves. Naturally."

". . . Gloves. Damn. Gloves. Lord a'mercy. Gloves. I like it. Gloves."

The door to the hall opened and closed.

Gloves?

Eve tugged herself together and hurried to the door, opening it carefully and peeking out into the hall in time to see Mayor Aura Quivers and Police Chief Tom Strock nearing the corner, she slapping at his hand, he tweaking her ass one more time before they returned to public scrutiny and put on their trustworthy faces.

7

Portia was weary. She wanted these people out of her house, to get into jeans and a sweatshirt and flop on the rug in the den and watch a ball game with a beer and a bowl of pretzels. The Padres had a night game in Philadelphia and it would have already begun. At times like this, she wanted Sam.

Sam, Sam, Sam. He had taught her how to watch baseball, to feel the potential energy in its pauses, to understand that because it was played without a clock its rhythms were more like life's than any other sport's. That was what he loved about it. Then why had he imposed a clock on her rhythms, kept a timetable of her comings and goings, demanded to know why she hadn't called him then or had lunch with him then or spent the night with him then, since his surveillance told him she had been free to?

Because he was alone after fifteen years of marriage and felt scared and urgent, that's why. Okay, there was something to that. But there was more to it. He was a cop and to a cop everyone who is not a cop is a prospective criminal, a cheat, a welsher, a two-timer. (Baseball, he'd told her once, quoting one of his goddamn books, kept the

39

American melting pot from boiling over by teaching immigrants the importance of playing by the rules.) That she was promiscuous was beside the point; he reproached her instinctively.

How Felix was going on! It was only champagne, and even if it was as good as they hoped, it would be years before they could produce it at a profit—and then, Howard Maddox's machines projected, only by increasing their annual output from five thousand cases to twenty thousand, with the attendant risk of a decline in quality.

But Felix's motive was prestige, not profit. When you could buy just about anything in the world, and had bought nearly everything you wanted, acquisition lost its charm; it was no longer a measure of wealth but of impotence, for you couldn't, trite as it sounded, buy happiness. To be happy, Felix (whose name meant "happy," something else she'd learned from Sam, who had been president of his high school Latin Club as well as captain of its baseball team)—Felix needed to create what he coveted, which would be to truly possess it. That others would covet it, too, whatever *it* was—was an enhancement, though he was not, God knew, going to sell it retail, or at least not over the usual counters.

A Ferrari maven, he had naturally thought first of custom-building sports cars. But that would mean taking orders from dilettantes who would want automatic transmissions and wouldn't drive the damn things anyway, for fear of scratching them. Once a year they would have their vehicles trucked to a *concours d'élégance*, would stroke one another's fenders, and that would be that.

Tobacco, silk, gold, diamonds, kid leather—those were a few more of Felix's favorite things. But to grow, as it were, his own promised no excitement. Matters of climate and geology and technology aside, he would get no kick from seeing someone smoking a Felix Beaufils cigar, wearing a Felix Beaufils suit or gown or necklace, walking on

Felix Beaufils shoes—no kick because he would feel no
. .. domination.

But champagne!

"It was," he was saying now, in the accent that those
who knew him well thought of as not foreign but Felix,
"the perfect challenge. To begin with, I was told it could
not be done, not here, not in the south. 'Buy a boutique
winery up north, Felix,' they told me, 'if a boutique
winery you must have. There they have the soil, the
tradition.' I told them they didn't know wine and they
didn't know history. It is not the soil, it is the vine; the
vine, the climate, the vintner, then the soil.

"Tradition? What tradition? There is no tradition. Prohibition destroyed the tradition; everything is new, young,
fresh. And before Prohibition, the tradition was here. Just
a few miles from where we stand, at Mission San Diego de
Alcalá, the first grapes in California were planted by Father Junipero Serra more than two hundred years ago. The
first commercial vineyard was in Los Angeles. You can
see from the Santa Ana Freeway where it was—if you are
so foolish as to take your eyes from the road." Felix
flicked his hand at the laughter, and the jewelry on his
fingers, cuff and wrist sparkled. He used the hand to adjust
the big rectangular glasses that seemed to enable him to
see not only better but more. "Temecula, Escondido, the
Pomona Valley, Rancho California—sure, today there is
smog there, today there are freeways and franchise restaurants, but there are also wineries.

" 'All right, Felix. Sure. Okay. But look at the wines
they produce: White Riesling, Cabernet Sauvignon, Zin-
fandel, Petite Sirah, Chenin Blanc, Gamay Beaujolais,
Sauvignon Blanc, Fumé Blanc. But no sparkling wines, no
champagnes.' So? At one time in the Champagne there
were no champagnes.

"They become very agitated. 'You see, Felix? That's it.

Yes. The Champagne. Champagne, true champagne, is made only in the Champagne.' Bravo. Go to the head of the class. You know that much, but it is only a little. Dom Pérignon—he was a real person, you know that?—at a vineyard in the Champagne invented a way of making sparkling wine. Because he worked in the Champagne it is called *la méthode champenoise*. Had he worked somewhere else, it would have been called something else. Who knows? We might be about to drink"—he smiled over his shoulder at Portia, and gestured to indicate that she had prompted him—"bourbon."

Felix went on over the laughter. *"La méthode champenoise* is a tool, that is all, and a tool may be used anywhere. In the Champagne or in Rancho Maria de la Luz, the method is the same: the wine ferments until absolutely dry, between ten and eleven percent alcohol. When it is stable and bright, to it is added the *liqueur de tirage*, a dose of sugar that begins the second fermentation, which produces the *mousse*, the bubbles. The bottles are stacked *en tirage* until the yeast settles, they are shaken, they are stacked again. By now, the percentage of alcohol is about twelve.

"Then the *remuage*—in English, I am told, it is called riddling, but I have never heard that word. The bottles are placed neck down in *pupitres*, racks"—he made a steeple of his hands to approximate their shape—"and every few days they are turned—at first a sixth of a turn at a time until two full turns have been made. Then increase the angle of the bottle and another full turn, a sixth of a turn at a time. Then place the bottles nearly vertically—upside down, you understand?—then another full turn, a quarter of a turn at a time now, and the yeast will have settled on the inside of the cork.

"Finally, the disgorging: the neck of the bottle is frozen in brine, the cork removed, the plug of ice containing the sediment bursts free. Quickly, quickly, the void is filled with the final *dosage,* the bottle is corked and wired. *Voilà!* Wine made according to *la méthode champenoise*— champagne. . . . Mine will not be sweetened a second time, I told them. A bone-dry *naturel* is more suited to the American palate. The French, Americans are always surprised to find, prefer a *brut,* or even—the terminology is confusing—an extra dry. . . .

" 'Felix! How do you know all this? You are a businessman, a financier. A connoisseur, yes, of course. A gourmet, sure. A collector. But still . . .' " He had been turning slowly for a while, like one of his riddling bottles (except that he was the shape of a brandy snifter), keeping his eyes on his audience but extending a hand behind him toward Portia. Anticipating her introduction, and his revelation—though it was hardly that—that she had been his mentrix in these matters, the guests began applauding, tentatively at first, like first-time concertgoers, then with vigor.

Amputees would find a way to clap for her, Eve thought from the back of the crowd, where she'd retreated from Patrick Wade, who had ambushed her as she came out of the office wing, and had resumed his suit. Moving a little to dodge his latest leer, she planted a heel in someone's instep. Before she could apologize, her victim took her by the elbow and led her behind one of the pillars that formed a small alcove off the living room. To spank her, or to order her to give him fifty push-ups? His cropped gray hair, commanding eyes and unrelenting jaw told her he was military.

"Been noticing you." The jaw hardly moved as he spoke. "Nobody puts one over on you."

"Oh?"

Dressed more businesslike than the other men, in a gray double-breasted suit of tropical wool, a blue pinstriped shirt with buttondown collar, a maroon silk tie, black wingtip shoes polished to glassiness, he was as tall as she only because every inch of him was at attention. In his lapel was a tiny pin that Eve was sure denoted one of the nation's highest honors. "Hawkes." He thrust a hand at her in a karate-like move. "Fletch to you."

His handshake was surprisingly gentle. "Zabriskie. Uh, Eve."

"Bilge." His eyes moved just enough to let her know he didn't mean her or her name but the proceedings.

A navy man. "But a friend asked you to come?"

He laughed—a dry hack. "I'm her father."

That could be a burden, for Eve knew whose he meant, there being only one woman in the room who could be encompassed by a pronoun. "Uh hunh. And you're skeptical about this venture?"

"You ride?" Hawkes twisted a class ring down toward the knuckle, as if he'd punch her if she gave the wrong answer.

"Not for years"—and then only on a merry-go-round.

"One Loma Largo. Six's best. Still cool then. Got a real gentle mare."

"Six o'clock tomorrow morning?" It hurt just to say it.

"Got plans?"

"No. *Well* . . . No."

"One Loma Largo." He about-faced and was gone.

At least Patrick Wade would be impressed that she couldn't have sushi, or meat and potatoes, because she had a date for a dawn gallop with Fletch Hawkes.

The speechmaking at an end—Portia had said very few words, for it was Felix's day—the cynosure became a fountain in the middle of the living room that had a marble dolphin as its centerpiece. (A discreet placard assured the guests that the water burbling from its blowhole was being recycled.) Maddox had parted the crowd to make a path for a waiter, who pushed before him a silver and glass tea wagon bearing two silver ice buckets, each containing a bottle of champagne.

Someone, somehow, had rigged a silken rope from a chandelier and fashioned its free end into a harness. After offering a look at the label of one of the bottles to Felix—who got another laugh by lifting his glasses and peering at it as if he'd never before seen an F. Beaufils *Naturel* 1983, the waiter secured the bottle in the harness, then passed it to Portia.

Those at the inside edge of the ring of onlookers took a step or two back, and there was a moment of compensatory reshuffling. In the silence that followed, Eve heard the absence of a drumroll or fanfare, and Felix seemed to, too, for he gave Maddox a look that asked why he had hired only the string quartet that had sawed away mightily but unheard in a corner and was now being fed in the kitchen. In Maddox's meeting the look Eve read unexpected dignity.

Felix cleared his throat, tugged at his coattails and signaled to Portia with a bow of his head that the time had come. Rather casually, she swung the bottle at the end of the rope. It fell in a lazy arc and caught the adamantine mammal squarely in the flank, breaking apart in a shower of foam and glass. Portia turned her back on the debris with a carelessness that made Eve dislike her a little; she remembered hurling a glass into a fireplace after toasting herself on her divorce and how the joy had been instantly diminished by the reality of having to clean it up.

The crowd, though, loved it—all the more because of the appearance of a maid, who swept up the shards that had gone beyond the perimeter of the fountain, swept them with a silver-handled broom into a silver dustpan—both crafted by Tiffany for the occasion and inscribed with the date and particulars.

Taking a linen napkin from the waiter, Portia lifted the

second bottle from its nest of ice. Felix scooped two crystal tulip glasses from a silver tray held out to him by another waiter and stood expectantly, a parody of Justice with her scales.

Twenty more waiters clattered in with silver and glass tea wagons and wheeled them into a circle around the crowd, like settlers arranging a wagon train for the night. They were followed by still another twenty, balancing trays of glasses like circus performers, then whisking them onto folding serving stands.

(Eve wondered why so many similes occurred to her. Was it that the very rich *weren't* like you and me, and required figures of speech to make them familiar?)

Holding the base of the bottle in the palm of her hand, which she had draped with the linen napkin, Portia twisted off the wire and tossed it on the tea wagon.

The cork exploded.

Champagne foamed over Portia's dress and glistened on her chest.

The first waiter bent to retrieve the cork from where it had fallen at Felix's feet; he thought to present it to his master, but registered that his hands were occupied with the tulip glasses and stepped away to stand at parade rest, holding the cork behind his back.

It was as if the breeze the waiter made, though, was enough to set to toppling the house of cards that hindsight would make it possible to say Felix had become. He swayed forward and was saved from falling by the last of his reflexes, then began the backward tilt that became a pratfall that ended with him prone in the arms of Dr. Patrick Wade, the tulip glasses only then slipping from his fingers.

Wade had had no expert premonition that something was amiss, just happened to be standing where Felix fell. Not that he was dense: no one knew what the hell was going on. The very few who, had time been stopped and a

survey taken, could actually have said that the cork had
turned into a projectile were aware that it struck *some*thing
pretty close by. The likeliest candidate was Felix—it was
at his feet, wasn't it?—but the look on his face wasn't one
of distress or pain; his mien was as it had been long
seconds before—a mix of pride and humility, with the
former holding a slight advantage. Only after Wade had
caught him did it become eternally impassive.

8

"Got your kid gloves on Sam?" For a big man, Strock moved like a sylph. Like an insecure comic, he laughed at his jokes to indicate that's what they were.

Branch dropped the cork into a glassine evidence bag and signed to the waiter who had guarded it like a talisman that he was free to go. "You want to handle this, Chief?"

Strock put an arm around Branch's shoulders and steered him to a corner of the kitchen. "I don't know that there's anything to handle, Sam, but as long as you're here . . . Why *are* you here, Sam? Who called this in? *I* didn't call it in."

Branch shook his head. "It came through County."

Strock pursed his lips and sucked on the implications of that. "County means reporters and reporters mean a lot of tromping through the flowerbeds and mud on the carpets and I think we *all* owe it to Portia not to make this trying time all the more difficult by putting duty before friendship. We're not just cops and civilians here, Sam—we're family. You catch my drift, don't you?"

Drift was the closest thing in Strock's repertoire to an order. He commanded with the impunity of a Zen master.

"Reporters . . ." Strock spoke the word carefully this time, aware how bad it tasted. "Warren Cable was here tonight, Sam. The reporters should absolutely not find out he and Felix had one of their polite rassling matches. No sense pointing fingers at innocent people."

"Felix wasn't murdered, Chief."

Strock slapped Branch on the back. "Right, Sam. Right . . . You know what I'm thinking, Sam?"

The chief never said what he could get someone else to say. "That we should give the reporters the Caliente Beach murder."

Strock brightened: "Beautiful, Sam. Beautiful. Let them chew on that for a spell." Then darkened: "If only we knew what he was doing with that goddamn check."

"He was looking for someone who was owed the money."

Strock laughed, letting go of Branch and stepping away to let him see the full extent of his amusement. "If I were owed a million dollars, Sam, I'd be easier to find than tits at a strip show." Another laugh, for his rhetoric.

"I'll know more tomorrow. The time difference was against me on calls to Europe, and everything in Israel's shut down for the sabbath."

"Sabbath, Sam? It's Friday—Oh, right . . ."

"I did talk to Litvak's sister—that was her Valium in his pocket. She didn't say it in so many words, but I inferred that she didn't approve of whatever he did for a living. She did say that under Jewish law bodies have to be buried by sunset the day after death—unless it's the sabbath, in which case he'll be buried Sunday. I okayed flying Litvak to New York tomorrow night. His sister's paying the tab."

Strock wagged an admonitory finger. "You may not know this, Sam, being from back east, but it's the law of the state of California that a body to be flown on a common carrier must be embalmed."

"Escobar took care of it. A mortuary in the city."

"People move out here to die, Sam. There're more mortuaries than air-conditioning showrooms. *Which* mortuary?"

Branch resolved to get up earlier to work on the song he'd been trying for six months to write. If it was a hit, he'd move to a condo on Maui; if it was a flop, he'd get the picture and consider a different career change, like driving a Peterbilt. Anything would be better than police work, which was becoming just so much small talk. "I think it's called Dawson's."

"*Law*son's. Lawson's doesn't do very good work."

"Escobar had trouble finding one that'd do the embalming without any restoration."

That smile again—the smile of a man who suffers half-wits. "No restoration, Sam? The victim had his throat cut."

"They're not having a service, just a burial. I didn't see any point in their paying for embalming, especially since Escobar says there's no way to preserve a body indefinitely." Or maybe he could go on a game show, answering questions about the Talmud and inhumation.

The finger again, backed by the smile. "A properly embalmed body in a moistureproof casket of the highest quality will last thirty to forty years, Sam, certainly long enough that the survivors could hardly accuse a mortician of wasting their money." Strock hooked his thumbs in the vest pockets of his salmon-colored western suit and rocked on the heels of his Lucchese boots. "What I'd like to tell the reporters, Sam, about this Litvak, is who killed the son-of-a-bitch."

Branch surprised himself with his reply. "The man he was looking for. Or the woman."

Strock snorted. "To keep Litvak from forcing the million dollars on him?"

"Or her," Branch said. "Maybe he doesn't want people

to know who he is. Maybe he's not who his friends and neighbors think he is. Maybe he'd rather they didn't find out who he is. Or she.''

"If that's so, why didn't he lift the check? Without the check, Litvak's just another stiff, a stiff we don't ask a lot of questions about. I'm not questioning your police work, Sam; I don't care what happened back in New York—you're a good cop. But why didn't he lift the check, and Litvak's cash, and make it look like a robbery?''

It was a good question, if a book question, for Strock was a good cop, too, if a book cop, which, along with his amiability, made it all the harder for Branch to hate him; but hate him he did—for his reproachful finger and his condescending laugh and his arm around your shoulder and his way of making you an accomplice. And above all for his unrelenting forgiveness of old sins; like one of Megan's priests, Strock could remind you just in the way he said hello that he had granted you absolution. "I think he panicked. The body was found face down, which is probably the way it fell. The check was in an inside coat pocket, the bills in a pant pocket you couldn't get at without moving him; you can see it in the Polaroids. He slashed Litvak's throat—from in front, Escobar thinks, without any resistance, which would mean Litvak had to trust the killer enough to let him get that close. It was the first time he'd ever killed anybody. Or she—''

"Stop saying *Or she*, Sam. I get the point.''

Branch found that if he said something he kept his mind more open to the possibility of it. "It was the first time, the killer panicked, didn't have the nerve to touch the body, or maybe couldn't move it—or maybe had reason to believe that Litvak didn't have the check on him. Or maybe someone saw it—driving by or walking on the beach.''

Strock held his hands out helplessly. "Nobody's *called* us, Sam.''

"Chief, we put a lid on it, remember?" He wished he'd said *I;* he liked his complicity straight up. *Hunh,* Strock had said when Branch told him it had been his idea to keep the body on the beach a secret for a while. It was his highest praise, a snort of disbelief that someone had not only taken some responsibility but done the right thing. It echoed in Branch's ears like a rebuke.

Strock remembered the need for another lid. "You knew I was here tonight, Sam. Couldn't you've told County that and just let me handle it?"

"You're a witness"—he'd almost said suspect—"a civilian." He backed away as Strock swelled up to protest. "Just going by the book, Chief." Branch went out of the kitchen, leaving Strock impaled on his limitations.

"Sam."

"Hello, Annie."

"God, Sam. Poor Portia . . . Sam, this is Eve."

Branch nodded, but didn't offer his hand. "I'm afraid this really isn't the time . . ."

Annie stiffened. "I just thought Eve'd be a good witness. She's a professional observer."

"There doesn't seem to be any doubt what happened."

Annie felt like punching him. "Will you have dinner with us tomorrow?"

"I'm taking Hal Harper's nights this weekend. For when the kids come out."

His literalism continually defeated her. "Another night, then?"

Branch nodded, but didn't name the night. "Nice to meet you, Eve."

Having failed to get a nibble, Annie tried to hook his tail. "Sam, Warren Cable was here tonight. He and Felix had another argument."

"Felix wasn't murdered, Annie. I'm not looking for suspects."

When he'd gone, Eve said, "Pretty."

Annie said, "The son-of-a-bitch."

"A lot of men don't care for widows, if that's what you're worried about."

"A lot of men don't know Portia."

Aura Quivers leaned on the windowsill of Branch's car, toying with the gold chain around her neck by way of keeping her breasts inside her silk décolleté top. There was tobacco on her breath, but he'd never seen her smoke. "Hello, Lieutenant."

"Your Honor." He moved the wheel back and forth, like a kid playing at driving.

"I don't have to—"

"No, you don't."

She put a hand on his arm, and the breasts spilled into the car. "Oh, come on, Sam. Don't act put-upon. You have a job to do, and so have I. The ends aren't always the same, or the means. The Caliente Beach matter—sure, I want justice done. Felix, well, it's not a case of justice, is it? Accidents happen."

"And when they're fatal, we write reports on them."

She stood and shouldered her evening bag, which pulled her top out of her black silk pants enough to reveal that she wore a gold chain around her waist, as well. "I saw you talking to servants, Sam. Was it really necessary to get their pidgin-English version of what happened?"

"I speak Spanish."

". . . Of course you do. You took the trouble to learn it before you applied for the job here. I remember how impressed we all were when we saw that on your application; it made it all the harder to understand the— Well, we don't need to get into that. The Spanish comes in so handy, doesn't it, what with most of our crime problem being— Well, we needn't get into that, either."

"The servants provided some insight. The headwaiter

said the speeches started later than planned, and that maybe the champagne was on ice a little too long.''

She looked pleased that he would settle for such a simple explanation. ''Well, then. You'll probably finish up your report before you go home tonight.''

''Would you like a copy?''

Aura Quivers leaned down again and put a hand on his arm, then took it back and studied her lacquered nails. ''I apologize, Sam, for my manner. You probably didn't hear about it, but Felix and Warren Cable had another of their set-tos tonight. It was over as soon as it began, but it was just one more wedge between them. Warren and his people won't be able to help being happy that Felix is dead, because it could very well mean the end of the dam committee. I'm of necessity on the fence about the water issue, Sam; I want what's best for the rancho. My concern about what happened tonight is that Felix not be made into a martyr for his cause. You're smiling, but it could happen''—she touched his arm again and gave it the smallest squeeze. ''I've already asked Tom—that is, the chief—to see that I get a copy of your report. . . . I'm glad to see you're wearing your seat belt, Sam. It sets a good example.''

At the end of the driveway, Branch put his head out the window to let the wind wash his brain, unfastening the seat belt so he could lean way out. Martyrs weren't made by freak accidents, were they? They were murdered.

Weren't they?

Portia sat behind a big desk in the hospital administrator's office, which had been given over to her while doctors had labored vainly over her husband. She was smaller, shrunken. Her eyes looked down at nothing.

Howard Maddox came at Branch like a petitioner, holding out a stack of fanfold paper. ''Here're our figures on b-breakage, Lieutenant. Fermenting wine in the bottle from which it is to be served is the costliest and least controllable method of making champagne. The rate of f-fermentation—"

"Can we talk about this later, Maddox? I'd like to have a word with Mrs. Beaufils."

Maddox backed out of the room, hugging his statistics.

"Is there anything I can do?" Branch said.

Portia lifted her head just a little, but didn't raise her eyes. "Get this over with as quickly as possible."

"That was my only question." But he made no move to leave.

Portia looked up at him. "What?"

He shook his head.

"We've been to bed together, Sam. I understand your silences."

How quaint that she called it that, given her fondness for doing it out of bed. "I guess I do need to ask about breakage. I don't care about Maddox's figures, but the bottles do break, right? Corks explode?"

Portia shrugged. "The wine may've been too cold. It may've been handled too much. It may've been poorly corked, or the cork may've been defective. It's a small operation, Sam. We have the best people, but they're people, not machines." She snorted. "I understand the champagne was a success. I wonder who saw to it that the guests got served."

Dr. Wade, Branch knew. His specialty hadn't been needed, so he'd put on another of his hats. Branch moved to the door.

"I hear your children're coming," Portia said after him. She smiled apologetically when he turned. "Below-stairs gossip. You must be very excited."

Branch stood with his hand on the knob, wanting to say something. All that came out was a condolence of Megan's. "I'm sorry for your trouble."

*   *   *

Maddox was lurking in the hall. "These f-figures, Lieutenant—"

"I'll get a statement from you tomorrow, Maddox. Right now, I'm worn out."

Maddox struck a solicitous pose. "You *must* be, Lieutenant. Have there been any developments in the other m-murder?"

"Felix wasn't murdered."

Maddox gasped. "Of course not. I didn't m-mean . . ." He took a step closer, hunching his shoulders conspiratorially. "Surely it's just a coincidence; it can't p-possibly have any relevance."

Branch considered slamming him up against the wall. " 'It'?"

Maddox shrugged. "Well, I heard a *ru*mor that the man who was murdered at Caliente Beach was in New York last week. . . ."

Branch pulled a face at the suggestion the rumor mills were grinding that finely.

Maddox saw it and read it accurately. "All right, Lieutenant, I'll be direct with you. An acquaintance of mine is an employee of the Hotel Del Rey. I spoke briefly with him earlier today and he mentioned that you—that is, the police—had come across evidence that this Mr. Litvak spent some time in New York just last week. I was struck to hear it, because so did Mr. Beaufils." He spread his hands as if to say *There!* "That's it. A simple coincidence. And yet, for the two of them to meet the same fate on the same day, thousands of—"

"Felix wasn't murdered. In New York when?"

"Lieutenant, surely you don't . . ."

"When, Maddox?"

". . . Thursday before last through last Saturday."

Overlapping with Litvak, who was there from Wednesday before last through Tuesday. "Where did he stay?"

"Where he always stayed—the Carlyle."

"A business trip?"

"In particular, an attempt to pique the interest of New York restaurants in the new champagne."

"Felix went around to restaurants?"—of which Litvak had been a collector.

Maddox chuckled at the thought of Felix drumming. "The purpose of the trip was to enlist a well-known public relations agency to mount a publicity campaign. You're from New York originally, Lieutenant. Perhaps you've heard of Trager and Norman."

"Did Felix know Litvak, Maddox?"

"My immediate response is absolutely not, Lieutenant. On the other hand, most of us are components of what sociologists call triple chains. That is to say, since most professionals know at least two thousand people, and in the case of Mr. Beaufils the number was more like four or five thousand, and since the nation's population is—"

Branch just walked away. In the car, he rested his hands on the steering wheel and tried to understand why Maddox had told him what he had. It was as though he were establishing an alibi. But for whom? Felix? And against what accusation?

He wondered, too, how it was that Maddox hadn't stuttered during his recitation. What had he read about stutterers—that they often didn't when doing things that required more effort than ordinary speech—declaiming, acting, singing? And lying?

9

Strock was right about one thing: The dawn discovered a dozen reporters pacing like jackals outside the rancho's gates, imprecisely invoking the First Amendment and snarling back at the Rottweilers leashed to the guardhouse.

And wrong about another: They weren't sated by the tidbit of Joseph Litvak, even with the garnish of a million-dollar cashier's check; they wanted the main course of the *multi*millionaire felled by a champagne cork.

Branch used his beeper to roust Jeff Derry (in the background, the woman he'd been in bed with promised Derry blueberry pancakes if he'd only stay), and had him shoo the reporters to the hospital for a news conference. Branch was running on empty but he was saved from making a fool of himself by Escobar, who gave a virtuoso explanation of the thin ice on which Felix had been walking for a decade, thanks to his diet of cigars, cholesterol and Bombay gin and tonics (he hadn't really *liked* champagne):

"Atherosclerosis begins as an abnormal metabolic process of the arterial walls. Deposits of cell debris and lipid material develop into raised lesions, known as atheromas—"

One of the reporters, a cookie from the cutter that

supplies television stations throughout the land with personnel, interrupted to ask if Escobar was therefore talking about *lesion*naire's disease.

"—The disease is an aspect of aging and was hastened, in this instance, by the deceased's gender—an irreversible risk factor—and by his extravagant consumption of rich foods and tobacco. Focal fatty streaks eventually develop into raised pearly plaques that bulge into the vessel lumen until finally a calcified fibrous plaque, with variable degrees of necrosis, ulceration and thrombosis, progressively weakens and may rupture the vascular intima. This may lead to obstruction, hemorrhage or arterial emboli when plaque fragments are released into the lumen. In the case of the coronary arteries, obstruction of blood flow to cardiac muscle results in compromised oxygen delivery, known as ischemia—"

The reporter said he thought Ischemia was an island in the Mediterranean. His audience was not the coroner, or his peers, but a blond nurse who sat in a plastic chair along the wall of the hospital conference room, her starched uniform no disguise for the softness beneath it. It was no use; she was all Derry's, who stood against the wall across from her, her phone number on a tongue depressor in his pocket. She wasn't Branch's type—too breathy and made-up—but he wished she'd considered his maturity for just a moment instead of looking right through him at his partner. And he wished Derry would fail now and then, just to have some perspective. And he wished he could sleep.

"The brain thirsts for oxygen," Escobar continued, parrying the pun with a pathetic fallacy. "Comprising but two percent of the total body weight, it is supplied with about twenty-five percent of the oxygen exchanged in the lungs." Here he rose from behind a desk and on a blackboard drew a diagram that to the reporter resembled a freeway cloverleaf. "It is perfused with blood derived from the circle of Willis, a network of vessels supplied by two vertebral and two internal carotid arteries. But sometimes this supply is compromised. The most common cerebrovascular accidents—you know them as strokes—are often the result of atherosclerotic thrombosis: atheromatous plaques occlude the vessels of the brain, resulting in the ischemic death of tissues.'' Escobar replaced the chalk on the ledge of the blackboard and brushed his fingertips together. ''The cork that struck Felix Beaufils in the left carotid artery dislodged a piece of plaque that embarked on just such a journey. Rapid decline and death followed quickly.'' He flipped his hands apologetically and lapsed into English. ''That's it, ladies and gentlemen. Believe it or not. . . .''

''Believe it, hell,'' Rollie Ashburn said. ''A novelist wrote it, he'd be accused of unverisimilitude. And another thing—why weren't the servants doing the pouring? Felix'd survived, he'd've been hauled up in front of the Governors, charged with lifting a finger.''

On the tape loop, Merle Haggard sang ''Mama Tried.''

''It was a christening,'' Branch said. ''Like of an ocean liner. You cutting out the free peanuts?''

''Never seen one—or either ocean. Sure you don't want some eggs or something?''

''I don't know how that can be, since one ocean's ten minutes from here.''

''Ten minutes the way y'all drive.'' Ashburn got a tin from under the bar and poured some peanuts into a bowl. ''Ever tell you what Gertrude Stein said?''

''When was she in Nashville?''

''Nashville's got libraries and bookstores. Why it's called the Athens of the South.''

''And Athens is called the Nashville of the Mediterranean?''

Ashburn ignored him. ''Seems Gertrude'd read this book about a monastery in the twelfth century or something that the author said was on a fre*quented* road. Is that how you pronounce it, professor?''

"It's your story, Rol."

Marty Robbins sang "A White Sport Coat and a Pink Carnation."

"Anyway, she wondered what the hell, in the twelfth century, was a fre*quented* road. Did folks pass by once an hour or once a day or once a week?"

"Uh hunh. And that has what to do with living so close to the ocean and never laying eyes on it?"

"Everything's relative, that's all." A bell pinged and a light went on and Ashburn came out from behind the bar and went into the first-class cabin of the DC-8 that sat like a fish out of water on the Beltway within convenient walking distance of police headquarters. The flagship of the short-lived California-Nevada-Arizona Airways (whose acronym, Canariz, had been pronounced, with affection and some trepidation, *Canaries*), the jet had some years ago lost first its way, then its fuel, on a flight from Scottsdale to Fresno and made an emergency landing on the Beltway's westbound lanes. The crew and the half-dozen passengers were uninjured and the only damage was to the airline's reputation and Rollie's Country Music Bar & Grill, a Quonset hut knocked from its foundation when the pilot swerved to avoid an imminent overpass. Ashburn settled out of court for the plane and all its trimmings, renamed his establishment the Scene of the Crash and took some comfort that the muse who had deserted him, making him one of Nashville's most famous blocked songwriters, apparently had a relative who looked after restaurateurs.

Branch took a pen from an inside pocket and turned over a napkin. Weren't they the medium of the best songs, the ones that leaped nearly fully formed from the mind and went right to the heart? Maybe he had natural talent and had just been using the wrong tools—a typewriter and yellow second sheets.

I can tell from your voice on the phone when I call you

That your sensitive instincts warn you to beware.

Having dealt with the other customers who were drinking their breakfast, Ashburn sat on a bar stool and tossed some peanuts into his mouth. "Mind if I say something?"

"I'm doing it for fun, Rol. I know there's no future in it."

"There's plenty of future in it, you play by the rules, the rules being—there's only one, really—keep it simple. Take a song like 'Bye, Bye, Love.' Happiness, loneliness, caress, emptiness, cry, die, love, above, free, me—those're the rhymes. You can't get any simpler than that and still have a song worth singing."

I can tell from the way that you move when I touch you
That you still feel the pain of the bruises you bear.

"You were talking about christening ships," Ashburn said.

But Lord, Lord, Lord, you make good coffee.

Branch pocketed the napkin and put away the pen. "A woman usually—or maybe always—breaks a bottle of champagne over the bow. Don't tell me you never saw it in a newsreel when you were a kid. Only place I ever did, and I grew up a block from the ocean—not that it has a goddamn thing to do with oceans."

Juice Newton sang "Angel of the Morning."

"Where was that again—place you grew up?"

"New York City."

"Come on, Sam."

"Brooklyn."

"Sam, business is slow on account of the sun ain't a quarter up, we're having a friendly talk, all of a sudden you're clamming up."

"Manhattan Beach."

"Thought so, and the reason I'm going on about it is there's a town near L.A. called Manhattan Beach and Strock used to be assistant chief there."

"That's not exactly news, Rol. He has a picture on his office wall of him in his dress uniform—a toreador jacket and sombrero. He misses getting decked out."

Ashburn laughed. "But what *is* news is Manhattan Beach is where they just busted up that S and M thing. You read about it? Whips and chains and some prominent citizens in the madam's little black book."

"I'll have another beer."

"Ever been to Strock's house?"

"And some more peanuts."

"Strock"—Ashburn checked for eavesdroppers—"is a necrophiliac."

Branch laughed.

"Okay, maybe that's not the word. You're the professor—that's somebody who likes to put a lip-lock on dead bodies, right? Strock, well, he's into morticians, collects embalming equipment, has all kinds of books on undertaking."

"Probably a good investment. I'll have another beer."

"Correct me if I'm wrong, but aren't you the fellow who was just telling me about Strock going on about that autopsy, the same fellow's always saying Strock can't find his genitals with a map and a flashlight under a full moon and wishing the Governors and the City Council could see through his tap-dancing routine? Okay, forget about Manhattan Beach, even though this ring *was* operating for ten years and Strock was there part of that time and would've had to be blind not to know about it. What about this Caliente thing? I mean, why the cover-up?"

Branch closed his eyes and pinched the bridge of his nose. To keep his hand in, that's why: Every so often he went to the pistol range for target practice; every so often he practiced his duplicity.

"You feeling all right?" Ashburn said.

David Frizzell sang "I'm Going to Hire a Wino."

"Just tired."

"You want to try a Pauli Girl? Lot of folks're drinking it."

"Bud."

Ashburn went behind the bar, opened a bottle and poured some beer down the side of Branch's glass. "In your report on Felix, what'd you call the murder weapon—the bottle or the cork?"

"Felix wasn't murdered." Branch put a head on the beer and sucked it off. "That's another irony: Portia was meticulous about opening champagne. She said the problem people make for themselves is they put a hand on the neck of the bottle. That's the narrowest part, the part under the most pressure, and the heat of the hand increases it, raises the risk of blowing the cork and spilling champagne. She'd hold the bottle by the bottom with one hand and the cork with the other, keeping the bottle at an angle to reduce the pressure in the neck. The cork wouldn't explode; it'd just kind of ease out, with almost no pop, and she wouldn't spill a drop."

Ashburn toweled the bar. "Sounds like you two used to have a fine old time. How'd she take it?"

"She was wearing a black dress. An instant widow."

Ashburn's songwriting reflex wasn't dead, but the best he could come up with was: *An instant widow, in her cocktail gown/Ready to party, soon's you're in the ground.* "You reckon you'll . . . Aw, never mind. Felix ain't even cold."

10

Annie shuffled into the guest bedroom, her eyes nearly closed, holding a cordless telephone before her, looking like a modern-day Lady Macbeth. She put the phone on Eve's pillow and shuffled out.

"Evie?" said a voice near Eve's nose.

"Umm."

"Fletch."

"Umm."

"Reckon you reckoned I'd be in no mood to go riding."

"Umm."

"Well, I am."

"Hunh."

"Sending my car around. Be there in about ten minutes. Had breakfast?"

Eve put the phone to her ear. "Who *is* this?"

"Got to have a good breakfast. Who was it said the world belongs to those who get up early?"

"Fletch?"

"Think it was the Pope. Up early, a good breakfast, hell, you can lick anybody. Had Immaculata make up a tray. Shake a leg now."

How had he known where she was staying? And that she *was* a meat and potatoes girl. The tray bore a whole grapefruit, strawberries and cream, a tall glass of orange juice, roast beef hash with three poached eggs, four popovers, four slices of toast, pats of sweet and salted butter (stamped with crossed anchors), two jams, two jellies, a small pot of tea and a large one of coffee, milk and cream. No sugar—out of oversight, perversity or a token asceticism?

Eve was as insulted by the implication that she couldn't eat it all as by that that she would. She drank the juice, ate half the grapefruit, all the hash, one of the eggs, a popover with salted butter and had two cups of coffee, black. At the seventy miles an hour the driver, a lank young man whose right ear looked as if it had melted, piloted the Admiral's Coupe de Ville.

"That what you're wearing?" Hawkes scrunched his face till he looked a hundred years old. In his pressed chino pants, starched tattersall shirt, navy silk ascot and Frye boots, he looked like a model in a mail order catalogue for people who have only heard of blue jeans.

"This?" Eve slapped at her dress. "This is nothing." Although it smelled of tragedy, she'd had no choice but to wear the dress she'd worn the night before; the jeans she'd traveled in were still damp on Annie's clothesline and the two shirtwaists bought for the daytime were at the tailor's, having their hems taken up. They would be ready at noon, but she was one of those to whom the world belonged.

"I did say *rid*ing, didn't I?" Hawkes got even older, his scarred and weathered face flaccid with despair at his impotence to teach his countrywomen the lessons he'd taught three wars' worth of gooks.

"Look. Fletch. My luggage got lost and this is all I have to wear. I'm surprised I didn't use that as an excuse not to come, because last night, at least, I had no intention of coming. But here I am."

"What airline?" He tensed as if ready to scramble and shoot down one of its planes.

"I should've expected it," Eve said. "I mean, it's Amelia Earhart luggage."

They didn't ride an inch; they sat in a gazebo and drank a gallon of Bloody Marys, ate a second breakfast of chicken fried steaks, home fried potatoes, corn bread and iced tea.

From time to time, Hawkes broke up, hunching over and slapping at a thigh. "God, I love it. Why the hell'd they name it that? You wouldn't call something *Titanic* luggage, would you?"

"*Hindenburg* luggage," Eve said.

That got him going again and the laughter turned to coughing. Eve rang a ship's bell that hung in the gazebo. When there was no response—the servants clearly heard a mutinous hand on the clapper—she went to the rear of the house and through a door that led to a workshop. There was a small bathroom in it and she drew some water in a paper cup, ignoring the driver, who sat tipped back in a sprung swivel chair, reaming a pistol and watching a cartoon on a television with the sound off.

"Ever meet Pete Rose?" he said as she started to go.

Eve turned slowly, expecting to see the pistol trained on her. "Uh, yeah."

He'd changed his seat, straddling the swivel chair and resting his arms on its back. "What's he like?" His voice was as raspy as Rod Stewart's.

She shrugged. "Like what he seems. Charlie Hustle."

"Come you stopped writing 'bout baseball?"

"There's only so much you can say."

"Come you're writing 'bout wine?"

Come you know so much? "You really want to know?" He looked offended, and she was sorry. "Ever hear of the MacArthur Foundation?"

He didn't pretend he had but couldn't remember where,

just shook his head, which she liked. She liked, too, that he listened. "They give grants—genius grants, people call them—to artists, writers, academics. They can do anything at all with the money. No strings attached, nothing to have to show for it. After baseball, I wrote some about music—rock, jazz, country, including a piece on a composer who'd written an opera about the Iran hostages. He got one, a genius grant, in part because of my piece, which I'd intended to make him look ridiculous. I decided to write about inanimate objects. Wine's a good subject; people always think there's something more they should know. . . . Were you in Vietnam?"

He lowered his eyes.

"A POW?"

He craned his neck as if still feeling some pain.

"What's the story around here? Why isn't Admiral Hawkes at least a little bit upset that his son-in-law's dead?"

He looked up, first at her breasts, then at her eyes. "Ever meet Steve Garvey?"

Eve pushed open the door. She couldn't shmooze any longer with someone who didn't give as good as he got and whose heroes were white bread. "He's very clean."

It wasn't the biggest house she'd ever seen (she was a reporter, after all), but it was one of the most unusual. There was the moat, for starters, as broad as a small river and meandering for miles around the perimeter of the estate, its surface patroled by scale-model ships of war. As they rocketed over the swing bridge that was the only access to One Loma Largo (there was no Two or Three or anything else), the driver had explained that the ships were equipped with transmitters that recorded any disturbance of the water and sounded an alarm. He warned her that the water was deep and that though he'd only *heard* that the Admiral kept pet sharks, he *had* remarked the way the horsemeat in the spare freezer (where he stored the fish he caught on his day off) had of disappearing.

The house's lines were inspired by an aircraft carrier's: on the flight deck were a tennis court, a putting green, a covered exercise pavilion with equipment that lifted weights for you when you strapped yourself into it, and a swimming pool. The sail was Hawkes's private aerie, with an office on the first floor, a study on the second, a sauna on the third and an observatory on the fourth. The hangar deck comprised the living room, dining room, kitchen and servants' quarters. Below it, right at ground level, were the bedrooms, and below them the underground garage and the fallout shelter.

Hawkes was gone when Eve returned to the gazebo and she sat and drank the water herself and considered the possibility that she was still asleep. But he returned in a moment, wearing a pair of half glasses and squinting through them at a magazine. "Have a look at this, Evie." He stopped and looked at her over the tops of the glasses. "Kind of name is Zabriskie, anyway?"

"Polish."

"Polish Catholic or . . . ?

She waited, but he couldn't say it. "Polish atheist." It sounded like the beginning of a Polish joke. "It's an old husband's name."

He waved a hand. "Don't matter. Just wanted to know if this was going to shock you a little or a lot." He laid the magazine in her lap as carefully as a grandfather showing baby pictures—which they resembled in that the two women arrayed on the several pages of photographs, one pale, one dusky, wore only their birthday suits—unless you counted their jewelry, the flowers and ribbons in their hair and some scraps of lingerie. By the standards of such periodicals, the photographs were chaste; for all the women's acrobatics, their limbs and lips never touched and their tongues never tasted.

What to say? Disgusting? Exploitative? Out of focus?
Tiresome? Eve was with those who thought there was
entirely too much skin and innuendo abroad in the world—
not just the most egregious examples, *Captured Women*
and *Seka Does Secaucus,* but songs like "She's a Man-
Eater" (Hall and *Oates,* for God's sake), and Calvin
Klein underwear ads and Jontue commercials and *Sports
Illustrated*'s annual bathing suit issue—but keeping her
consciousness ever raised made her weary. (For another
thing, she was starting to like lingerie, of which the Allman
Brothers was a connoisseur, a collector of catalogues from
Victoria's Secret, a frequenter of shops like Come Again;
she had spurned his gifts for a time, for she was uncomfortable with luxuries, hers being David's chocolate chip
cookies, herring on pumpernickel with aquavit and beer, a
new John Le Carré, a Checker cab, 1 Fifth Avenue, a
sunset over water, a *New Yorker* with a Roger Angell
baseball piece, *To Have and Have Not* in a theater, not on
television, towels warm from the dryer—and cotton under-
pants. Then she'd slipped on a Sami silk charmeuse camisole and matching bias-cut tap pants and felt . . . different.)
She took her cue from the pout on Hawkes's face. "I hope
it isn't . . ."

"Some runaway daughter? Shit, no. But it's her, all
right. No doubt in my mind, even though this so-called
pic*tori*al calls her"—he moved to read over Eve's shoulder—
"Pe*tu*lia. Shit. She look like a Pe*tu*lia to you?"

Eve somehow knew he was talking about the darker
girl. "A Carmela."

"Close. Real close. That's Maria."

She waited for a surname, then made an inspired guess.
"Maria de la Luz?"

Hawkes slid the magazine off Eve's lap, rolled it up,
and stuck it in his hip pocket. He walked to the railing of
the gazebo and stood with his arms folded and his legs wide
apart, as if on a bridge in a blow. "Long story, the short

of which is Maria's mother worked for me and Esmé, my better half, doing housekeeping and the like, when we first came to these parts. I was just an ensign at the time, fresh out of the Academy. . . ."

Something about his manner—or was it the setup?—made Eve not want to listen to his story. It was a huge cliché, to be sure: no father . . . mother's fingers worked to the bone . . . having had Portia, Mrs. Hawkes unable to have more children . . . thought of Maria as their own . . . bright, pretty, perky . . . blah, blah . . . yawn, yawn.

A saint, a heroine, a fiction—Eve hadn't given any thought to the rancho's eponym. Thinking it about it now, she guessed she would have guessed that Maria had lived in the days before statehood and had died that her bandit— *bandido*—lover might go on marauding, a Mexican-American version of Bess, the landlord's daughter, the landlord's black-eyed daughter, plaiting a dark red love knot into her—"Fletch?"

"She was fifteen by the time I'm talking about now, not a woman yet, but not a child, either—"

"If you could just stop for a sec—"

"She had a kind of beauty that—"

"Fletch, heave *to*, goddamnit."

The nauticalese got through to him and he turned to face her.

"What am I doing here, Fletch? Your son-in-law died last night; your daughter's in mourning—and in need of a lot of reassurance, I'm sure, that accidents *do* happen; the community you helped found has lost one of its leading citizens. And you're drinking vodka only slightly cut with tomato juice and reminiscing to a total stranger about some . . . some Chicano chippy."

Hawkes chuckled. "Reckon it looks a mite strange—"

"It doesn't *look* strange, Admiral Hawkes. It *is* strange. For one thing, where'd you get the magazine?"

Hawkes pointed accusingly toward the house. "Bobby reads it."

"When he's not playing with his gun?"

He held out his hand, the last gentleman on earth. "Let's go up to the house. Few things I want to show you."

"You're not going to believe this." Eve threw herself on Annie's office couch and swung her legs up.

"Eve, I'm up to my ears in this will. I won't be able to have dinner."

"Don't you want to know where I've been?"

Annie glanced at Eve's dress. "An orgy?"

Eve laughed. "I've got to find my goddamn suitcases. Maybe if I go to the airport. Can I borrow your car?"

"Yes. Goodbye."

"Five minutes, Annie. *Two* minutes."

Annie sat back abruptly, took her glasses off and tossed them on her desk.

"I was out to Fletch's."

"You went *riding* with him anyway?"

"Drinking. He abducted me, practically. His chauffeur carries a gun."

"He also shoots it. He killed a man last year. An alleged burglar."

"Meaning he wasn't?"

Annie shrugged. "When you work for the founder, the rules of evidence aren't as strictly applied. . . . It's kind of early to have already gotten drunk."

"The world belongs to those who get up early."

Annie looked up at the ceiling. " 'All memorable events transpire in morning time and in a morning atmosphere.' Thoreau."

"Sam reads *him*, too?"

Annie nodded. "Damn him."

"I don't want to talk about you and Sam. I want to talk about me and Fletch."

"Stop calling him *Fletch*. You just got off the plane."

"Jealous?"

Annie put her glasses back on. "The car's out back. The keys're in my bag."

Eve got up and came around the desk. "Annie, Annie, Annie." She put her arms around Annie's neck from behind and rested her cheek on top of her head. "Do you think we'll both wind up bag women?"

"It's not a bag woman I'm afraid of becoming. It's a woman who drinks by herself at the bar in a Chinese restaurant."

Eve sat on the edge of the desk. "Let me guess: Moneda Investing, the mutual funds division of Kallistos Enterprises, has experienced withdrawals of nearly fifty million dollars in the past three months—all of them by clients who turned out to have not names but numbered Swiss bank accounts. To keep the whole thing from going under, Felix had to doctor the rest of the statements to report transactions he never made. . . . Not bad, hey, for someone who just got off the plane?"

Annie just rubbed at her lower lip with a thumbnail.

11

By design, Rancho Maria de la Luz had no cemetery. Esmé Hubbell Hawkes (who, it befell, would have been among the first tenants) had blue-penciled the landscape architect's proposal that one be placed in the community's northwest salient. His idea struck her as morbid and the area as ideal for housing for what she referred to as the Backbone (the name by which the neighborhood came to be informally called)—that is, people whose professions supported the rancho: pharmacists, florists, opticians, haberdashers, grocers, butchers, bakers and so on, but who were not—to continue the anatomical metaphor—its Flesh and Blood.

Not that Felix had wanted to be interred in anything so anonymous as a cemetery—even an exclusive one. Perhaps aware that his circulatory system was like a clogged drainpipe, just an eggshell away from backing up altogether, he had stipulated in a recent codicil to his will that he was to be buried at his vineyard, beneath the yellow rose bush planted at the head of the foremost row of trellised vines. (The bushes, which decorated every row according to a custom originating in the great vineyards of France, were useful as well as beautiful: genus *Rosa* and genus *Vita* are susceptible to the same diseases; a sorry-looking sentinel was a signal that some fungus might be lunching on the vines.)

So it was that midmorning Sunday, a caravan of somber automobiles made its stately way along a dirt road leading from the vineyard's visitors' center to the fields them-selves, stirring up plumes of dust and setting the flock of goats in a pen behind the vinekeeper's house to bleating. Following the lead chauffeur, pistol-packing, porn-perusing Bobby, the drivers peeled off one by one, killed their engines, hopped from behind the wheels, opened the left rear doors and stood at attention.

The vinekeeper and his family, though dazzled by the asynchronous perfection of it all, shifted uneasily in their uncustomary dress clothes. They had hardly known Felix, who was making only his second visit to the vineyard (on the first he had learned the significance of the rose bushes and fallen for a farmer's oldest joke—about the dangers of tractor rot), but they were bereaved for Portia, who had spent a thousand afternoons working alongside them, a bandanna around her forehead and on her back a bush shirt with its sleeves hacked off. It was a wonder that she got neither sunburned nor tanned, but stayed as white as the lily she now clutched in her gloved hand as she disem-barked from her father's Cadillac, wearing a simple black silk suit, a broad-brimmed black hat and sunglasses over eyes bruised by sleeplessness.

"Ought to wait a tad longer 'fore you go ashore, Porsh," Admiral Hawkes said from the back seat. "No sense playing the geek for this mob." There were twice as many mourners as there had been witnesses to the circumstance that necessitated mourning, Felix's death—like Bobby Thom-son's home run, or Woodstock—being an event that more people were claiming to have attended than had gone through the turnstiles.

But Portia was on her way to greet the vinekeeper and

his family and to let them cry on her behalf. She had yet to shed a tear, for her mother had taught her that to cry—or sleep—during crises was to make oneself vulnerable to every kind of opportunist. There was plenty of time for both when matters were once again under control. It had been weeks since she'd been out this way and she followed the two-year-old to the pen to see the kid that had been born.

"De goat was born in de morgening," the little girl said.

Portia remembered Sam's quoting someone: *All memorable events transpire in morning time and in a morning atmosphere.* "Of course he was."

"Mrs. Beaufils?"

Portia turned, to look right at the knot of Warren Cable's necktie. She hadn't realized how tall he was, having usually faced him seated across conference tables or seen him standing behind lecterns at meetings—meetings about water. "Warren. I guess it's right that you be here. But no dancing on the grave, please."

Cable's skin was as dry as parchment, as if he demonstrated his probity by denying his body any moisture that might otherwise have gone into the public reservoirs. "My condolences, Portia. Felix was a credit to his community, whatever differences we may have had." He shaded his eyes to look out over the arbors. "Fine-looking crop of grapes. No one thought you folks'd be able to pull this off, but you've done it with style."

Portia aimed the little girl at her mother and got her going with a pat on the bottom. "I'm no good at double-talk, Warren. Why don't you just say what you came to say?"

Cable bowed his head slightly. "Everyone around here thinks *Felix* was the dam committee"—he smiled—"I guess I don't have to tell you I usually think of it as the *damn* committee. . . . But I know you're the power behind it, just the way you're the one who made all this happen. I want the committee to shut down, Portia. At the same time, I don't want to lose its input and its influence. There's a place for you on the board at Southland. Call it tokenism, call it a sop—people will call it both—it's where the future of this entire region is being shaped. You won't be entirely among antagonists; there're several board members who have good things to say about private ventures like the committee's. The board's the place to try all these different ideas on for size. If we can hang together''—he laughed—''well, then there's a chance we won't die of thirst separately.''

Portia took off her sunglasses and looked him in the eyes. ''I find your proposal vulgar, Mr. Cable. Did you ever offer Felix a seat on the board—for his *in*put and his *in*fluence? Would you ever have, if he were still alive? I ought to accept, and use *my* input and influence to royally fuck things up. I take back what I said about your being here. If you're not gone in five minutes, I'll have my father's driver throw you out. And no working the crowd as you leave.''

Annie leaned down to the limousine's window. ''Admiral Hawkes?''

''Why, Miss Buck. Say, you didn't drag your friend all the way out here on a crackerjack day like this, did you?''

''Eve took my children to the beach, if that's whom you mean.''

Hawkes cocked his head appreciatively. ''Hell of a nice girl, Evie.''

''Please don't do anything to hurt her.''

He squinted. ''Hell do you mean?''

Annie shook her head. ''It just came out. . . . Sir, I know it's not really the time, but I need to talk to you about Moneda Investing.''

Hawkes studied the limousine's roof. ''You know, I've

been leasing this car for nine months and I never knew there was that hatch up there. Hell's it for? Case you get submerged or something?''

Annie would have let it go had Eve not briefed her on the form the Admiral's grief had taken. She opened the door, pulled up the jump seat and sat down. "You can do a mad scene for the benefit of the others if you want to, Admiral Hawkes. But I know how much you know. You told *Evie* all about it. My advice is that a board meeting tomorrow morning wouldn't be at all too soon."

Hawkes tried unsuccessfully to open the skylight. "Shouldn't be too hard to round up a quorum. Hell, there's a flotilla of board members here right now. Bill Scott, Tully Johnstone, John Benoit, Pat Wade. I'll have a word with them soon's Felix is, uh, deployed."

Annie raised up to grip the skylight and slammed it open. She sat back down and brushed her fingertips together. "When Felix started the dam committee I told him he was flying in the face of the logic that led him to buy this vineyard, that he had to think like a farmer or like a water retailer, but he couldn't think like both. I told him any water the committee got its hands on would be water they'd won away from Southland and that it wouldn't've been won without a fight. . . . Admiral Hawkes?"

He had opened the car's bar and was pouring some brandy from a decanter into a highball glass. "Best solution there is to the water shortage—the devil who dwells in the bottle." He cackled. "Funny, when you tote up all the things you forget, the things that stick in your mind. Forty-two years ago, I was an Annapolis plebe taking a course in American military history from a professor I can't for the life of me remember the name of. A Virginian, he was, though, a civilian. Above all things in the world that he hated—and he hated just about everything; he was one mean son-of-a-bitch—he hated Ulysses S. Grant.

He called him—this is the thing I still remember all these years later—'that hulk of a man, Grant, whose only battle was with the devil who dwells in the bottle.' ''

Annie gave in to enervation. She'd heard the story before, after a fashion—heard Sam tell it to her son, who had been writing a report about the Civil War; Sam had made it sound as if it had been a professor of his. How nice, she had thought then, to have a man around the house with such pithy anecdotes in his baggage—nice for the kids and nice for her. Damn him, she thought now— the plagiarist. Doubly so, for he had no doubt appropriated the story from the Admiral by way of Portia.

It had taken Eve only a while to start thinking of Caliente Beach as her own, and she tried telepathically to keep the maroon BMW from parking. As usual, it didn't work, but when Branch got out and walked toward her over the dune she blamed her failure on the single-mindedness of a cop on a scent.

She waved and got a flick of a finger in return, then slipped on the Willie Nelson sweatshirt she'd borrowed from Annie's son. The bikini she'd bought at a mall in Esperanza on the way to the beach had more fabric than the other three in her size combined, but there was no sense making her old friend's boyfriend cope with her breasts first thing Sunday morning.

Branch squinted down at the strand, where Annie's kids were building a sand castle, then over at the sawhorses with their crime scene placards. ''It was up to County to close off the beach, and I don't know why they didn't. I won't ask you to leave, but in the future—''

''Jill and Tony know to stay away from there, Lieutenant Branch. Their mother's a lawyer.''

Branch made an arrêt of sand with the side of his foot. ''I saw Annie's car. I guess she's at the funeral.''

"How come you're not—taking pictures of the mourners?"

"Because Felix wasn't murdered."

The kids ran up to say hello, and Eve noted that the affection was mutual and genuine. She felt a little jealous, for Tony was interested in her only for what she knew about baseball (which wasn't much, these days, her generation—Pete Rose, Garvey, Reggie, the Goose, Nettles, Yaz, Seaver, Rusty—having hung it up, or being about to) and Jill, ripe and ready to burst into puberty, was diffident, as if in her search for a hornbook to prepare for the future she found Eve too weighty a volume, too footnoted. "It must be hard on you," she said when they'd gone back to their handiwork, "being so far away from your kids."

Branch just nodded, then lifted his chin at the sweatshirt. "You a fan?"

Eve looked down at the word *Willie*, shaped like Texas, then up at Branch. "Don't tell me you are. You strike me as more the Kenny Rogers type."

Branch heard that it was a serious insult and wondered what he'd done. But then, Eve had had thirty-six hours to listen to Annie's despairing of him. "If you're going to be here awhile, you'll probably meet Rollie Ashburn. The name may not mean anything, but he wrote—"

"He wrote 'Pale Yellow Princess' and 'Arkansas Women' and 'Forever Wild.' I may be an eastern sophisticate, Lieutenant, but I know my country music. I was married to a man from West, Texas. That's the name of the town—West comma Texas. Rollie Ashburn lives *here?*"

Women, in Branch's experience, were deficient in the irony necessary to appreciate country music. Megan thought salacious one of his favorite songs, the Bellamy Brothers' "If I Said You Have a Beautiful Body Would You Hold It Against Me?" To Annie, all country music sounded and all country singers looked alike, though she knew enough to get jealous when Ashburn took him backstage at a Johnny Cash concert in Bakersfield and introduced him to Emmylou Harris. Portia, perversely, developed a crush on Kris Kristofferson, and listened to his music exclusively—when she wasn't listening to Mahler and Pharaoh Sanders. It felt good to drop a song title and know it would be caught. "Mention 'Tequila Mornings.' That's Rollie's personal favorite."

Just like that, it was a brand-new ball game. Eve patted the blanket next to her. "Can you sit a minute?"

Branch shook his head. "I have work to do. Maybe you can help."

"The price of an introduction to Rollie Ashburn?"

"The man who was killed down here was an Israeli. The *Times* has a correspondent there, doesn't it?"

"Tony Astin—the last time I noticed his byline."

"You know him, then?"

Eve laughed. "Know him? I *vent* with him." It was a cult joke—Mel Brooks as the Two Thousand Year Old Man on his relationship with Cleopatra—but she wasn't surprised to see that Branch got it; he *wasn't* just a cop. "It was just after my divorce. Tony was on cityside and I was on sports and I thought that meant I could bend my rule not to date men I work with. I was wrong. Maybe *you* know him; you were in New York in those days."

She looked out to sea affectedly and Branch took a big glance. Had she been a stranger, and he on a nearby blanket, he would have arranged himself so that he could look at her now and then—through dark glasses or over the top of a book—and would have appreciated the length of haunch, the definition of ankle, the expanse of chest; with the wide beach and limitless ocean for scale, he would have made her smaller than she was, not petite, but . . . manageable; the hair—neither curly nor straight, cut short

but not fashionably so, not red enough to make her a
redhead—would have disappointed him: he liked hair whose
length and color were unequivocal. Had he worked with
her, however, breathed her daily, passed her in hallways
or rubbed shoulders in elevators, he would have been
thankful for the imperfection; and yet, he felt something
like jealous of Tony Astin for having gotten in, as it were,
under the deadline, and was glad he could say, "Nope.
Don't know him."

Eve warned herself to let it go, then went ahead anyway. "Maybe if you told Annie about it, and found that
she wasn't scandalized, you could get on with the rest of
your life."

Your conditional tenses tell me to be wary.
Your coulds *and your* mights *are like barbs on a wire.*

"None of my business, right?" Eve said.

Branch shrugged. Beside her on the blanket was a brand
of suntan lotion he'd never seen before: meet a new woman
and you were introduced to a new array of products; even
the ascetic Megan had her special potions. Men bought
the old reliables—Coppertone, Ivory, Colgate, Gillette,
Wheaties, Coke, Bud, Maxwell House, GE, Chevy, Arrow, Haspel, Florsheim; they trusted in the tried and true,
weren't always being seduced by the new. Or was it every
woman's way of saying she needed special handling and
knew how to get it?

"What did you tell your kids," Eve said, ". . . when it
happened?"

". . . They were young—four and eight."

Enough, Eve, "Not too young to know their father's
gotten a raw deal. That *is* what you got? I've got an idea."
Shut up, Eve. "If you ever want to practice talking about

it, practice on me. If I'm horrified, you'll be right not to tell Annie.''

Branch backed away. "Can I mention your name to Astin?''

Eve stood and walked toward the water. "Just say you've read his stuff. Jouranlists're like cops—they don't have a lot of admirers.''

From his car, Branch watched Eve peel her sweatshirt off and run into the surf—to wash him out of her hair? She ran lightly for her heft. Her bikini didn't dare you to stare and at the same time mock you, like those of the girls at La Ermita Beach, a little farther north, where Derry liked to park on his lunch hour.

Eve ran out of necessity, for she was feeling tingly in the wrong places, charging the frigid Pacific until it tackled her at the knees. She flipped over and swam a strong backstroke, making slits of her eyes against the still lowly sun, putting some distance between her and Branch. She was sure every shark east of Hawaii had gotten her scent, but the danger was relative.

"Hell do you mean, Bobby, you can't find him?''

"I can't *find* him.''

"Well, look again, 'cause he's here.''

" 'S'what I'm saying, sir. He *ain't* here.''

"Pat Wade ain't here.''

"No, sir.''

"*Doc*tor Pat Wade?''

"*No*, sir.'' Bobby went on in the same even voice with which the Admiral had heard him deny that he'd known the man he shot to death in his room off the garage, a room a blind burglar could have smelled contained nothing of value: He'd noticed that Wade wasn't at the funeral home; he'd've mentioned it had Mrs. Beaufils not been a passenger; he'd been about to say something when Miss Buck appeared. "And then there was the burying. I called his house, sir, but there was no answer, so I left a message with his service that he should ought to call you. They said he hadn't checked in all day, had a pile of messages.''

From women who needed Wade's speculum, the Admiral wondered, or the other instrument with which he was accomplished.

12

The Zurich bank did list its phone number, but its gnomes took Sunday off. Litvak's Paris numbers rang unanswered. While waiting for the calls to go through, Branch played with Litvak's bumper sticker, rolling it up, then flattening it, trying to decide whether to put it on his own car or the BMW or give it to Ricky—or send it to Leah Marston; it occurred to him eventually that it was a clue, something he couldn't really call anything else he had.

He dug in his desk drawer for his New York phone book, a twenty-year accumulation of numbers of people who didn't list theirs. Sometimes they didn't answer them, either, but Branch's roll hadn't lost its momentum overnight.

" 'Lo."

"Is this Fred Flakes, the nation's most popular morning disk jockey?"

"Make that the world's, bro."

"This is Branch. Sam Branch."

". . . Holy shit."

"How are you, Fred?"

"Starting when, babe? It's been long time no *habla*."

"Yes, it has."

"You miss me, Sam—is that why you're calling?"

"Now that I think about it, every morning."

"That's bullshit, Sam. I bet you listened to Gambling."

"I'm calling about Joseph Litvak, Fred."

". . . Son-of-a-bitch."

"You do know him, then. You had him on your show."

"I'd ask you how you know that, Sam, but you always were a hell of a cop, regardless of what the limp-wristed brass tried to pin on you."

"Litvak's dead, Fred. He was murdered—Thursday night or Friday morning. The check was still in his pocket."

"You know about the check, hunh?"

"I don't know much. What do you know?"

Flakes took a moment to shape it into an anecdote. "Week before last—a Thursday—I'm in the limo on my way to play tennis, when we ground to a halt due to a water main break or some urban disaster and sat in traffic for about an hour. I'd've got out and walked but I was wearing my shorts and I don't like to run around in midtown like that. Not that the bod's in bad shape, Sam; I've stopped smoking since I saw you last; got off that cocaine express; broke off my long partnership with Jim Beam. I'm just shy, I guess. Anyway, sitting there in the clutches of gridlock, I decided to do some work on the phone, called my secretary, found out that along with the usual geeks and publicity hounds trying to get on the show there was a guy named Joseph Litvak who had a million dollars he wanted to give away— Who killed him, Sambo? Or don't you know that?"

"Not yet."

"Anyway, Litvak was a gofer for a real estate outfit that's building some kind of commercial and residential complex—stores and offices and condos and such—a sort of horizontal Trump Tower, or have you been away so long you don't know what that is, Sam?"

"I've read about it. Building it in Paris?"

"Some suburb. Litvak pronounced it Ni-yee, but don't ask me how to spell it."

Branch wrote *Neuilly* on a pad.

Flakes went on: "Anyhow, various parties own the land and except for this one parcel, they've all been located, made offers to, paid money, generally bought out. But not this one parcel, 'cause they can't find the dude who holds the title, Schatz."

"Schatz."

"Something Schatz. I forget what. It may not matter. The point being, Schatz's family bought the property years ago, before the war. When Hitler came along, they changed their name—to what, Litvak didn't know. For some reason, he thinks Schatz a/k/a whatever it is now lives in the U.S."

Branch tore off the slip with *Neuilly* on it and tucked it in a corner of the blotter holder. He wrote *Schatz* on the next slip, tore it off the pad and stared at it.

"By the way, Sam," Flakes said. "Guess who I saw when I finally made it to the club that afternoon. Coming out of the sauna."

Branch shook his head, as if they were face-to-face.

"Cullen. I didn't recognize him at first with his clothes off. And he's lost a lot of weight. . . . You got a rotten deal, Sam. You know I always felt that and always will."

"And I'll always appreciate your saying so publicly."

"Hell, what's a fifty-thousand-watt radio station for? . . . Anything else I can do you for, babe?"

"Do you know if Litvak did any other interviews while he was in New York?"

"Everything but *The Garden Hotline*, babe. He was good at getting his message across."

"And it's likely he did the same thing anywhere else he stopped along the way."

"More'n likely."

"So if he were in Los Angeles, say—which he was—and if I haven't heard from any deejay there who had him on his show, then read about his murder—which was in the papers out here and which I haven't—then there's a chance he wasn't *on* any shows in Los Angeles, right?"

"You're cooking, old buddy. I can feel it."

"Which could mean he'd either given up his quest or by the time he got to L.A. he'd located he for whom he was questing."

"Eloquently put—although I read William Safire the other day saying if you have to say *whom* you should think of another way to say it."

"This real estate outfit—do you remember the name?"

"I don't, Sam, but it's funny you should ask, 'cause when I asked Litvak the name, he kind of stumbled before he came up with one, like he hadn't expected to be asked, and when I *did* ask, well, I got the feeling he just, you know, ad-libbed it, made up a name."

"Meaning there might not be a real estate outfit—or a horizontal Trump Tower in the works in Ni-yee?"

"And I wouldn't know one way or the other, would I, since Ni-yee's a long way from the Avenue of the Americas. I've been suckered before, babe—it's the chance you take doing live radio."

"And Schatz, before he became an American—was he French or German or what?"

"I got the feeling he was a little bit of everything, Sam."

Like Litvak's business. "Thanks, Fred."

"*De nada*, babe. It was the bumper sticker, wasn't it? You tracked me down through the bumper sticker I autographed for Litvak."

"What bumper sticker?"

Flakes laughed. "If I see Cullen again, you want me to say hello? Or maybe you'd like me to dedicate a song to him."

How about Janie Fricke's "I Can't Take Your Body if Your Heart's Not in It"?

The call to Jerusalem went through in a flash, as if God handled those circuits Himself. A roll was a roll was a roll.

"My name's Branch, Mr. Astin. I've seen your byline. I used to be a New York cop. I'm now a lieutenant in a town in southern California. Rancho Maria de la Luz."

"Half a dozen adobe huts and half a hundred hounds?" Astin said.

Another songwriter? ". . . Sorry?"

"It's a cautionary tale every foreign correspondent gets told before he goes out into the cold, though it's certainly apocryphal. A chap covering the Mexican Revolution or something of the sort filed a dispatch from a town he said was nothing more than 'half a dozen 'dobe huts and half a hundred hounds.' His editors changed it to 'six mud houses and fifty dogs.' "

Branch laughed, but felt off balance. *Cautionary tale, into the cold, chap,* Astin's mid-Atlantic accent. At least he hadn't mentioned Cullen. "The per capita income here is in the high six figures." It wasn't a salvo he'd ever fired before and he got a kick out of the sound it made.

Astin cleared his throat. "I've never been south of San Francisco."

If that was a riposte, Branch thought it an excellent one. Or maybe Astin was the sort who declared his alibi reflexively whenever confronted by a cop, the way some people take their hands out of their pockets when passing one, to show they're empty.

"An Israeli citizen named Joseph Litvak was murdered here last week. I have some idea what he was doing in the United States, but I need to know more. I have some phone numbers from his address book but I'm having a hard time penetrating the switchboards. I'd appreciate any

help you can give me, and there's a story in it, if that's the
kind of story that interests you. This is only a hunch, and
it's off the record at the moment, but Litvak was looking
for someone and it won't surprise me if the murderer turns
out to be the man or woman he was looking for.''

A pause. ''People don't usually say 'or woman' unless
they have reason to believe that it *is* a woman.''

Branch wrote *woman?* on the pad, then crossed it out.

''Who's Schatz?'' Derry said.

Branch turned away from the window. ''You get hold of
the Del Rey night manager?''

Derry tucked the slip back into the blotter holder, sat on
Branch's desk and put his feet on the chair. ''Litvak had
dinner alone in the dining room about six-thirty Thursday.
Cornish game hen for his main course, but we already
knew that, thanks to the autopsy—''

''Just tell me what we didn't know, Jeff.''

''. . . He finished about seven, smoked part of a cigar
in the lobby, started to take the elevator up, then remembered the no-smoking regs, didn't want to put the cigar out
and walked up to his room, which means he was either
close with a buck or just a considerate guy, or both.
Anyway, he was only on the third floor. This is all from
the elevator operator, by the way, not the manager. Name's
Santana. The elevator operator, I mean. The manager's
name's—''

''It doesn't matter, Jeff.''

Derry looked out from under his cap brim, then tugged
it lower over his eyes. ''Litvak came back down around
nine, said no thanks when the bell captain asked if he
wanted his car or a taxi, said he was going to take a little
walk—''

''Is that exactly what he said?''

Derry pushed up the brim. ''I don't get you, Sam.
Litvak's dead, so I can't ask him *exactly* what he said.

Whatever he said, he didn't say it to me, he said it to the bell captain, who said it to the night manager, who said it to me, who's saying it to you.''

"What the hell's the matter with you, Jeff?"

Derry took the cap off and threw it, like an irate manager. "What the hell's the matter with *you*, Sam? There's nothing the matter with *me* except you're on my fucking back.''

After a while, Branch retrieved the cap, dusted it off and held it out to Derry, who wouldn't look at him. Branch hung it on the back of the chair. "You're pissed off because when you asked who Schatz was I asked you about the night manager, and when you told me we already knew Litvak had Cornish game hen I told you to tell me what we don't know, and when you tried to get the names straight for me I said it didn't matter, and when you said Litvak said he was going to take a little walk I asked if that was exactly what he said.''

Derry picked up the cap and felt the brim's curl.

"And because I've been generally . . . bad-tempered.''

Derry put the cap on and tipped it back on his head. "You want to talk about it?''

Branch smiled weakly. " 'It'?''

"Ever been to a therapist, Sam? A shrink, I used to call mine, till he pointed out to me that maybe by calling him that I was saying he wasn't that important to me—that I was putting him in the same category as a flick. Or a fuck.''

This was new ground, and Branch stood very still, regarding the pitfalls.

"I didn't really have to ask," Derry said. "Most men haven't. It isn't manly. When I told my dad I was seeing a therapist he assumed I was gay. He didn't say it, but I could see it in his eyes. I was living with Rita at the time, but I could see in his eyes he thought we were *both* gay, and the living together was a front. A third-generation marine, his eyes said, and he winds up a faggot. My mom thought I was straight, but pussy-whipped, that I was only doing it to keep Rita happy. That told me something, my parents' reaction—something about the quality of the love I'd gotten when I was a kid. A parent has to love a child unconditionally: that doesn't mean they say, 'You're a troublemaker and a noisemaker and're costing me an arm and a leg to feed and clothe and put through school and get your teeth fixed, *but* I love you.' It means they say, 'I love you *and* you're all of those things.' There's a difference. D'you see the difference?''

Branch knit his brow and tried.

Derry pulled his cap forward. "Okay, so Litvak said he was going for a little walk, which could mean he was going to walk some*where* to meet some*one*.''

Branch was glad to have gotten so easily back on the track. "Go on.''

Derry shrugged. "That's it. That was the last anybody saw of him. Anybody at the Del Rey, I mean. Anybody but whoever killed him, probably.'' He held up a finger. "Not quite it. His phone calls, three local: one to American Airlines to make a reservation on a Friday morning flight to New York, connecting with El Al to Jerusalem the next night—meaning he wasn't planning on being dead or even around here anymore; one to Avis, to say he'd be leaving the car he rented in L.A. at the airport; one to Kallistos Enterprises—''

Branch winced. "Now, I'm really sorry about the way I've been acting, Jeff, but I wish you wouldn't do that— treat the bombshells as afterthoughts.''

Derry blushed. "I don't know if it means anything, Sam. I haven't been able to find out who he talked to—or about what—what with them having their own problems. It's a hell of a coincidence, though, isn't it? Litvak calling Kallistos Thursday afternoon, getting murdered that night or the next morning, Felix Beaufils the next night.''

"Felix wasn't murdered," Branch said. "And the coincidence is, Litvak and Felix were both in New York Wednesday, Thursday and Friday of the week before last."

Derry did a take. "Talk about sitting on bombshells."

Branch shrugged. "I got it from Maddox. But so what? They stayed at hotels that're a mile apart and worlds away from each other. Litvak, big spender or not, had a subway token in his pocket; Felix wasn't the subway type. It's not likely they ran into each other. . . . What else?"

"That *is* it," Derry said. "Three local calls, no long-distance, no incoming."

Branch turned back to the window and tried what he'd been trying when Derry came in—to spot something he'd never seen out that window before. He did it whenever he got tired of looking at the office: its Danish modern furniture worn and torn by more than a decade of use by men who weren't by nature inconsiderate slobs, but who'd been contaminated in the line of duty; its wastebaskets brimful of Styrofoam coffee containers and cigarette butts; its pitiful decorations—a primitive landscape by Bobby Nolan's daughter, a poster of Jamie Lee Curtis, Derry's latest crush, a year-old Padres schedule, a calendar whose year was current but that hadn't been turned since February, an illustration of the Heimlich Maneuver, a pair of black lace Frederick's of Hollywood panties that had been found in the men's room, a plastic wreath, unremarked at clement Christmastime and unremarked now.

"Can I ask you a question, Sam?"

"If it's about—"

"No, it's something else. Annie's friend? Eve Zabriskie—"

"Jeff, does it ever occur to you to just take a pass?"

". . . What the fuck is that supposed to mean?"

"Nothing. I'm sorry."

"No. Come on. Let me hear it. What? You think I'm—"

"I don't think anything, Jeff. I don't think anything at all." Branch went to the coffee pot, which was cold, then to the water cooler, which was empty. He ought to have told Astin the RMLP's budget was out of line with the per capita income. He went back to the window and watched the traffic on the Beltway, light even for a Sunday. The fact was, all he did was think; all he did was wonder. He wondered where everyone was; why Maddox had told him about Felix's trip to New York; who killed Joseph Litvak. It was nice that a few things were beyond wondering: that Megan and the kids had gone to church that morning; that it wouldn't rain . . . Was that it?

He wondered if Eve was still at the beach; if he should tell Derry to take an hour off and drive over there; why he didn't. He wondered if Eve was a devotee of unconditional love or if she made do with the conditional kind. He wondered—

His phone rang and Derry answered it. "Yeah? . . . Yeah . . . Jesus . . . Je*sus* . . . We're on our way."

Branch got his blazer off the coatrack and put it on.

Derry was staring at the receiver, like a bad actor in a bad movie.

"What, Jeff?"

"Holy shit, Sam."

Branch waited.

"Another murder, Sam. Jesus. Three murders."

Branch put his hands on Derry's shoulders. "Felix . . . wasn't . . . murdered. Try and— Oh, fuck it, never mind. Who?"

"Tied up with chains and strangled. Wearing women's underwear. His houseboy found him. That was Cooper. Jesus, Sam."

"Who, Jeff?"

"Dr. Wade. Pat Wade."

13

"*Course* we didn't make a deal. We were just talking methodology, terms, like that. You were going to get back to your *people*. No money changed hands, no agreements made, nothing said other than that you'd be in touch. When I didn't hear from you, I figured you—your *people*— had a change of heart. Or got cold feet. It happens.

"Then I read the paper. Good thing I read the paper. Sometimes I go for days without reading the paper, watching the news, hearing it on the radio. I mean, I listen to the radio a lot, but sometimes I get in a certain kind of mood, I don't even hear the news when it comes on. I don't know why. Compared to some of the guys I meet, I'm an unusually well-informed guy. I met a guy last month on my way to— Well, never mind that. But I met this guy, he didn't know—"

"Get to the p-point."

The man brought his face close. "The p-point, m-mother-fucker, is from what I read in the paper you and your *people* no longer require the services of the individual I represent. The guy you wanted eighty-sixed has *been* eighty-sixed. Everybody else lives happily ever after. But for me,

the situation is that another opportunity has presented itself. On the one hand, you—your *people*—no longer
require the services of the individual I represent. On the
other hand, you did—"

He paused as a jet racketed overhead, inundating them
with noise. "First one to take off this way since we been
sitting here. Wind must've shifted or something."

"How much're you asking?"

The man shrugged. "You were seriously considering
paying fifty large for the services of the individual I represent. It seems reasonable to me that you should pay at least
five times that much so people shouldn't find out that's
what you were considering. It sounds like a lot at first, I
know—two hundred fifty thousand dollars. It takes a long
time to say, even if you say a quarter of a million, which
is another way of saying it. But keep in mind, there're no
expenses involved in this kind of arrangement—"

"It's called blackmail. Call it blackmail."

". . . How is it sometimes you, you know, stutter, and
sometimes you don't? Is it 'cause sometimes you're more
nervous than other times? You'd think you'd be nervous
now, but you don't seem to be. I mean, you just said
'blackmail' *twice* without stuttering; that's the kind of
word you sometimes stutter over. . . .

"So call it blackmail. Big fucking deal. What am I,
going to break down and cry you called me a blackmailer?
So I'm a blackmailer, and you're the blackmail*ee*—you
and your *people*. As I was saying before you interrupted,
calling me a blackmailer, it's not such a bad deal, two
hundred fifty large, 'cause there're no expenses involved.
The kind of arrangement you were seriously considering
could've been very expensive, above and beyond the ini-
tial investment. Why? 'Cause when *people* get together and
seriously consider such an arrangement, it can lead to
complications. Such as sometimes one of the people de-
cides he can't take it any longer, he's got to get it off his

conscience that he was party to such an arrangement. This can result in difficulties for the rest of the people, whose consciences may not be bothering them—or not all that much. What do they do? They kill him, too—or have him killed, using the services of the individual I represent or someone like him. It costs you more, in particular on account of a guy with a guilty conscience tends to sleep very light, maybe hires somebody to sit outside his door, doesn't get in his car without first tying a mirror to a broomstick, having a look underneath for any optional extras that weren't there before, generally covers his ass—in short, is very hard to kill. And I'm not talking just one guy, either, 'cause guilty consciences have a way of being contagious, like the flu. The vaccine can get very expensive.

"Now, in *this* kind of arrangement—call it blackmail you want to call it blackmail—you don't have to worry about expenses, about guys with guilty consciences. Why no expenses? It's obvious—there aren't any. Oh, sure, maybe a phone call now and then, but big deal. Why no guilty consciences? 'Cause when *people* pay two hundred fifty large that somebody should keep his mouth shut, they just don't get guilty consciences. I don't know why that is; maybe it's they'd rather live with their guilty conscience than be embarrassed in a public manner, which is what would happen if it got found out that you were seriously considering—"

"I'll be in t-touch."

"Un unh. That's not the way it works from now on. From now on when I say hop, you hop. When I say pay, you pay. I say when and where and in what denominations and what kind of suitcase or whatever the fuck, you're there on time, with the money, in the suitcase or whatever the fuck. You're not there, it costs me a quarter to call the DA and say guess what I heard on the street.

"And in case you're thinking—which you probably are; you're not a stupid guy, you're trying to scope this out, see if there're any angles you can play, anything that'll give you an edge—in case you're thinking what if you—your *people*—what if they take the heat? What if they don't pay? So what if I call the DA, he takes it to a grand jury—how's he going to prove it? It's your word against his, basically, 'cause *I* can't testify, can I? Well, you'd be surprised how many guys're sitting around one joint or another—I can think of three in Soledad alone and two in Te*hach*api, meaning there's broads looking for this kind of opportunity, too—the opportunity, I mean, to tell the DA whatever he'd like to hear in exchange for certain considerations, like knocking a couple of months off here, getting maybe lighter duty there.

"I know it's shocking—corruption of justice and all—but the simple fact is the DA is an elected official and an elected official has got to have a record to run for *re*election on and in the case of the DA the record is convictions. You see what I'm saying? The DA doesn't have to find the individual I represent who was going to pull the trigger, he doesn't have to find any money that might've changed hands, he doesn't have to find a contract—because who would write such a thing down on paper? All he has to find is a couple of guys—or women—who'll say they heard you—your *people*—say they were interested in blowing away Felix Beaufils. It doesn't matter if they heard it in the joint; they heard it."

He tapped Maddox on the shoulder with his forefinger. "So *I'll* be in touch, Mr. Maddox, and you be ready to hop. Don't look so surprised I know your name. I know more than that, I know the names of some of your *people*, too. Now get out—and keep your head down, 'cause here comes another plane."

14

Events had bleached the tan from Jeff Derry's face and put in his eyes a mote of longing for a time when he had been an Olympic volleyball candidate and life's biggest mystery was where those La Ermita girls in bikinis and nothing more carried their car keys and their money.

"There're the maids to talk to, Jeff," Branch said. "And Wade's nurses and secretary and the staffs at his hospitals. Who saw him recently and when and where. Coop and I can finish up."

Derry didn't dare shake his head, so he wagged his finger. "How else am I going to get used to this?"

Branch put an arm around his shoulder and eased him toward the door. "Nobody gets used to it, Jeff. You ever feel used to it, it's time to consider another line of work, otherwise you'll wind up a suspect in someone else's investigation." *The Selected Apothegms of Old Sam Branch*.

Derry turned in the doorway but avoided looking back into the room. "This isn't a murder, either, is it, Sam? I mean, it's a suicide, right?"

"Or an accident. Suicides, even when there's no note, have a way of looking like . . . a cry for help." A sequel to

The Complete Clichés. ''This looks pretty solitary. I think he just miscalculated.''

The nature and extent of the miscalculation finally got to Derry, who gagged and lurched out the door, a hand cupped in front of his mouth.

Glad to be quiet, for there was less risk of being trite, Branch leaned against the doorpost and regarded the secret *garçonnière* of Dr. Patrick Wade:

They had opened the curtains and blinds on arriving, and the habitual sunshine tinted the room ridiculous. It was on the northwest corner of the fifth and top floor of Wade's house, a hyper-modern tower in the section of Rancho Maria de la Luz known from the shallow creek that wound through it as the Burn, and was not so much furnished as equipped: a Bang & Olufsen turntable, receiver and tape deck were on one wall, housed in a lacquered cabinet with folding doors and sliding shelves whose hinges and casters were expensively soundless. Giant JBL Titanium speakers stood at either corner, high-tech menhirs. A catholic collection of albums and cassettes surrounded the hardware. Smetana's *Moldau* was on the turntable, which shut off automatically, so that there was no way to know if it had been played for the occasion; *The Best of Django Reinhardt* was in the tape deck, ditto.

Opposite was the video wall: an Advent screen and a smaller—though hardly small—Toshiba Blackstripe color television; a General Electric VCR tuner and deck joined umbilically to a Mitsubishi video camera, mounted on a bracket near the ceiling and the only, albeit incontrovertible, witness to the death of its owner. The BASF videocassette the deck coughed up when its eject button was depressed was only the latest in a series featuring Patrick Wade, although it differed markedly from the others in being a solo performance.

Wade's co-stars were from all walks of life: a waitress from the Nineteenth Hole Lounge at Holly Hills; another from the International House of Pancakes on Route 6; a hot walker from the Meadowmere; a stringer from the Racquet Club; a shuttle dinghy driver from the Yacht Club; saleswomen from half a dozen shops on El Centro; obstetrics nurses from Blaine-Lewis, pediatrics nurses from St. Francis and Hillside, two emergency room nurses from Downtown—at the same time; an intensive care nurse and a nurse's aide from Episcopalian; nearly every one of the call girls who serviced the Del Rey, the Sutton, Cavendish House and La Playa. Those were the working women.

The women with time on their hands were the wives of just about everybody who was anybody in Rancho Maria de la Luz and environs (everybody, Branch noted with relief and yet without surprise, but Felix Beaufils), and not a few of their daughters: Abbott, Bailey, Conway, de Bree, Elmsford, Fallon, Gannett, Halliburton, Idle, Jordan, Korlear, Lindesman, Morgan, Niles, Ovett, Pugh, Rowayton, Scott, Towd, Vliet, Warner, Youngblood; only a Q, U, X and Z had eluded Wade, and there had been numerous duplications. They hadn't had to play all the tapes to identify the actresses; each was clearly labeled as to its participant, as well as to the date and time; the alphabetical order was by Wade.

The photographers from County Forensics struck their equipment and moved away from the stainless-steel island bed at the center of the room, giving Branch his first unobstructed look in a while at the circumstances of Wade's ultimate orgasm: Wade lay on his back on the black silk fitted sheet that was the only bedclothing, wearing a strapless rose poly-satin merry widow with a ribbon between the cups, hooks down the back and a lacy ruffle at the hip; a rose poly-satin G-string; black stockings with a hand-painted floral design held up by the merry widow's garters; black patent leather spiked heels. Around his neck was a two-inch-wide black leather collar, studded with brass; one end of the collar was notched in such a way that when pulled through a slit in the other end it could be tightened but not loosened; a thin-linked steel chain joined the collar to a pair of black leather manacles locked around Wade's wrists by a sturdy padlock.

The G-string had been pulled down over Wade's hips to expose his genitals, and clots of semen decorated his pubic hair, groin and stomach; his hands, though, had had a more urgent mission at the end; they had grappled at the collar, trying unsuccessfully to loosen its clutch. Wade's face was purple and his eyes bulged with consternation and with longing, for his neck was turned so that they looked at the key to the lock, which was placed where he could see it on a lacquered side table—see it but not reach it, for a hobble lashed to the end of the bed bound his ankles and a wide leather strap with a complicated buckle pinned his chest.

"Madre mía." Escobar said it softly at Branch's shoulder and Branch startled. Escobar touched his arm apologetically and slipped by him to circle the bed. Cooper looked up from dusting the bedstead, sniffing with the contempt of a token black for a token Hispanic, but gave way when Branch nodded to him.

"Why don't you get some coffee, Coop? The houseboy made a pot, and this is a good time."

Cooper's hesitation said he wondered what Branch was holding out on him, but he went out the door, ducking to get under the lintel.

Escobar hovered awhile longer, then stood straight and spread his hands. "I have only read about this, Sam."

Branch nodded. "I have, too. But I forget what it's called."

"It is called autoerotic asphyxia. Masturbatory pleasure is enhanced by self-strangulation, usually with some sort of device such as this around the neck. Often the practitioner loses consciousness, and occasionally is asphyxiated before he can restore his oxygen supply. Its devotees are nearly always males, usually teenaged boys. You have read, as well, I'm sure, about so-called epidemics of teen-aged suicides; in many instances, they are cases such as this—not suicides at all, but accidents.'' He tapped the strap across Wade's chest with a knuckle. ''Unless, of course . . .''

''He could've fastened the strap—and the whatever it's called around his ankles—himself,'' Branch said. ''He must've locked the lock before doing up the straps and put the key on the table. The camera runs on a timer. It has a microphone, but it was switched off. There's no indication that there was anyone else in the room.''

Escobar smiled, for Branch had stopped in mid-crescendo. *''But,* Sam?''

''But it doesn't add up. These tapes show Wade with women—and you should know this, Ray, not just any women; a lot of important ladies in this town're going to be very worried when they hear Pat Wade bought it. The transvestitism, the sadomasochism—it wasn't his bag. The clothes, the paraphernalia—there's nothing else like it any-where in the house; it looks rigged up for the occasion. We haven't looked at all the tapes, of course, but I'll be surprised if we find anything like this. . . .''

Branch took a breath and then went on. This was what he'd been talking about when he made his overture to Escobar at the morgue—thinking out loud to someone like-minded. As close as he was to Derry, he wasn't that close, and hadn't been to anyone since . . . since Cullen.

''Wade's houseboy found him at about noon. This room is off-limits ordinarily, but Wade's answering service called saying he hadn't picked up some important messages—including one from Fletcher Hawkes's chauffeur wonder-ing why Wade wasn't at Felix's funeral, which is where the houseboy thought he was. The staff had Saturday afternoon and night off; as far as the houseboy knows,

Wade was planning to spend the evening alone—he'd prepared a cold dinner for him, sushi; Wade gets—got—his own breakfast.

"The bed in Wade's bedroom hadn't been slept in and the houseboy thought he might've spent the night up here; he sometimes did—watching highlights of his great performances, probably. The houseboy knocked and got no answer, then tried the door even though he was sure it would be locked—he doesn't have a key; it was open, which is understandable because the only way to lock it from the outside is with that key"—Branch pointed to an evidence bag on the lacquered table—"which Cooper found up there"—he pointed to the door's lintel—"which is the advantage of having a very tall cop or two, even if they are uncomfortable in the Hondas. Understandable, though, only if someone was in here, and left after Wade died or while he was dying—someone who didn't know where the key was hidden. If Wade were alone, why wouldn't he lock himself in, unless he just forgot, or didn't care, since the help was off. Fuck it. I don't know. I just don't know."

Escobar smiled. "I've been thinking about what you said the other day, Sam." He shook his head. "So many deaths in so short a time; it is odd, is it not? I've been thinking that you were right: we haven't gotten along, and it is for the reasons you stated; we believe to be true about each other what in fact we know only as hearsay. We ought to work more closely together; we can work well, I believe. We are . . . *simpático*. I am glad you are telling me all this. It makes my job easier. I will do what I can to make yours easier, as well. There are forensic pathologists who specialize"—he rolled his eyes toward Wade—"in this sort of thing. I'll have a look at the literature and speak to some contacts. Perhaps we can find someone who can provide more insight."

More insight than none? Branch took Escobar by the arm and led him to a window that looked out over the rolling lawn and its centerpiece, a bay laurel topiary hedge. "Does that look like anything to you, Ray?"

Escobar blew out a soft puff of air, that oral shrug that is part of the vocabulary of Romance languages. "A football? A primitive mask?"

"It's supposed to be—the houseboy told me this—the female genitals. That stone bench there, just at the clitoris, is where Wade liked to have a cocktail alone after work every day. So he was a *little* sick, but not"—he wagged a thumb over his shoulder—"*this* sick. I wonder if he was *on* anything. Could he've died from an overdose—of something he took by injection, say?"

Escobar turned toward the corpse. "At first glance, it's quite clear he died of strangulation. The pinpoint red spots around the eyes—petechial hemorrhages—result when the flow of blood from the head is cut off. The blood backs up, causing vessels in the eyes to burst. If he had been injected—" He looked back at Branch. "But why are you asking this, Sam?"

Branch shook his head. "I should let you cut him up before I start speculating."

Escobar touched his arm. "Hey, *amigo. No me vaciles.*"

Branch took a handkerchief from an inside blazer pocket and laid it on the windowsill, unwrapping it to reveal its contents—a needle of needles, a needle the size of the pump he used to inflate Ricky's football and basketball.

"*Madre mía.*"

"Umm."

"You know what this is?"

"I think so."

"You found it here?"

"Under the bed—as though it had fallen there."

Escobar bent to peer at the barrel. "It is empty."

"So it seems."

"But why haven't you tagged this? And why did you send away your colleague?"

Branch wrapped the needle and returned it to his pocket.
Escbar drew back. "Sam, you don't think I—"

"No. But the only place I've ever seen a needle like
this— What's it called?"

"A trocar."

"The only place I've ever seen a trocar is in the morgue.
But it isn't used only by pathologists, is it? It's used by
morticians. It's an embalming needle."

"A Bud?" Ashburn said.

"Coffee," Branch said. "I'm working."

Conway Twitty sang "The Rose."

"Lot of people dying these days. You think it's
catching?"

"If anyone ever asks you, Rollie, I didn't ask you what
I'm about to ask you."

"You sound like one of them cops on TV."

"I'm serious."

"I can see that. Your forehead's all twisted up."

"I mean it, Rol. I don't want to hear this on the
grapevine."

"Who the hell'm I going to tell, Sam? My cats? The
goddamn ice plant? The Playmates I got hung up in the
head? I'm just a lonely old bartender, Lieutenant Branch,
and I don't spill my guts to the customers; I listen—like it
says in the manual."

". . . What I mean is, don't tell Jeff."

"Well, now, that's a horse of a different feather, ain't
it? Don't tell Jeff what?"

"Or Cooper."

"Coop don't come in here much. Ceiling's too low and,
well, it's not my doing that Charley Pride's just about the
only black country singer, but I can understand Coop's
thinking maybe there's still some evening up to be done on
Sixteenth Avenue—"

"How do you know about Strock's collection of undertaking equipment?"

". . . Why?"

"Why did I think you wouldn't ask me why?"

"Can't say, hoss. It's not a question that's way out of line."

Shelly West sang "José Cuervo, You Are a Friend of Mine."

"I want to know, that's why."

"Simple as that, hunh? . . . 'Fore you moved out this way, Strock—I called him Tom in those days—used to stop in now and then. To the old place, I mean. All that memory-billy I got out to the house? I used to have it up on the walls—one of Vassar's old fiddles, a guitar of Chet's, a vest of Waylon's, a big old black hat of John's, lots of autographed lead sheets and pictures and shit. I didn't have it up and I can't tell you how I got it and don't *you* tell anyone I'm telling you this, but I also got a certain unmentionable that was worn at least once by Dolly herself. . . . Figured I might be making a comeback, I guess, thought all them trinkets might inspire me. Anyway, me and Tom got to talking one night about the stuff's material—as opposed to spiritual—worth and he allowed as how it might could bring a pretty penny at some kind of auction—up to Bakersfield, say, or L.A.

"That led to a discussion of the field of collecting in general and he mentioned he had a bunch of stuff undertakers use. I said, Oh? He said, Yup, he got interested in it when he was in the army in Korea. He wasn't in Graves Registration, I think it's called, but a buddy of his was and he found out—the buddy, that is—that some of the shit was worth something to collectors. The short of it is we drove out to his place. Had a whole basement full of it—embalming tables and I don't remember what all else anymore. One thing I do remember is this thing they used in the old days to fill up a corpse with embalming fluid, before they had high-pressure hoses or whatever, I guess. A stand, like—a big wooden thing, twelve, fifteen feet high, with a funnel on top and a long hose. The undertaker'd climb up on a ladder or a scaffold, is the way Tom explained it, and pour the fluid into the funnel. It'd run down through the hose and into the body. The point, I seem to recall, was you had to fill up all the veins and arteries after the blood'd been drained out, and you couldn't get enough pressure just doing it at ground level, with a regular needle. I thought it'd be a catchy way to serve a martini. This is a hell of a thing to be talking about on a pretty afternoon like this. Why?''

Terri Gibbs sang ''Somebody's Knocking.''

''And as far as you know, Strock still collects the stuff.''

''Which ain't all that far, seeing as how we kind of went our separate ways when I started hanging around with one of his less respectable subordinates. Why?''

''I'll have a coffee to go, too, Rol. I'm sorry, I only have a twenty.''

''Keep your goddamn money. It'd make me feel like a stool pigeon to take it, and the coffee's from last night, anyway. People ain't exactly breaking down the door to get in, what with this place turning into Dodge City.''

Or New York. ''Come on, Sam, this isn't back east. People just don't get killed left and right.'' Strock had the door cracked open on a chain—like a New Yorker.

He hadn't said anything about killing. ''Can I come in, Chief?''

Strock's eyes flicked into the house. ''. . . Why the trip out here, Sam? I always have the radio on.''

''I didn't want to put it on the radio. And your phone's off the hook.''

The chief turned bright red. ''Oh, yeah, I was, uh,

working out. Uh, just a minute.'' Strock slammed the door.

Branch sat on the stoop. As chief of the RMLP Strock was entitled to a house, a two-story colonial, outside the Backbone in a nameless neighborhood inhabited by retired airline pilots, Navy, Marine and Air Force officers, or their widows; flags flew from poles on many of the lawns— browner than most in the rancho, for here water conservation was a duty, not a deprivation—and there were more signs warning of guard dogs and burglar alarm systems than in other neighborhoods, where such caveats were considered unsporting or undignified. The cars in the drives were American-made—Cadillacs, Lincolns, Oldsmobiles, the odd Corvette or Trans Am—and Strock kept his Mercedes in the garage lest it trigger bitter memories of the Luftwaffe and U-boat wolf packs.

One of the dogs had defecated on Strock's bluegrass and a batch of flies buzzed over the feces, maculating the Sunday serenity. For the hell of it, Branch looked around his feet for a pebble to toss at them, and found instead a small rectangular packet, about an inch by half an inch, of brown transparent paper crimped at the ends and closed by a seam, enclosing something shredded that smelled faintly of mint; it was hard and dry, but that didn't feel like its original state. He put it in his pocket, where he put everything that interested him lately.

Strock threw the door open as if greeting a well-wisher and stood aside for Branch to enter. He wore a gold nylon jumpsuit with its zipper open to his navel, and yellow and blue Nikes; a gold chain was around his neck and a large plain gold cross rested on his admirably flat stomach. ''Now what the hell is this about Pat Wade?'' he bellowed as he led Branch down the hall to the living room.

Branch told Strock almost everything, standing in the center of the room and turning this way and that to take in the decor—vintage *Playboy* with a touch of *Field & Stream*.

Nothing in the way of necrobilia, if that was the word, but there was surely a sanctum for that. Branch couldn't ask to see it, and he found himself being shown the door sooner than he'd've liked.

"I'll be right out to Wade's," Strock said, eyeing Branch's foot on the sill. "You were right not to radio, Sam. Damn. Woman's underwear? Damn. And a hundred tapes, you figure? Damn. At least it was an accident, not another murder. My ass'd be in a sling if there was another murder." He laughed. "Hell'm I saying? *Felix* wasn't murdered."

15

After three margaritas, Eve switched to tequila from the bottle, the better to tell Derry and Ashburn her life story:

"I've done just about everything, or pretty near. Would you believe it, Jeffrey, if I told you I was even in your line of work for a while? No, not a cop; I've always had this thing about uniforms: I wouldn't even join the Girl Scouts unless they let me come in mufti—or is it out of mufti? I *do* like the threads you guys wear. Anyway, I was a P.I."

Derry turned his Dodger cap around by way of saying he wanted to hear the whole thing. Ashburn signaled to a waitress to take over the bartending chores and came out from behind the bar to sit on a stool.

Gary Morris sang "Wind Beneath My Wings."

"My first client hired me to find out if his wife was having an affair, since she took a bus into Manhattan from Leonia, New Jersey, every weekday afternoon. I picked her up at the Port Authority and followed her around, hitting, or so it seemed, every Frusen Glädjé outlet in town—she liked Swiss Chocolate Candy Almond, Harriet did—until I noticed late on the third afternoon that Harriet's husband was following *me*.

"I went out the back door of a Madison Avenue bus I'd followed Harriet on, hauled him out of a taxi he was trying to climb in, and said I couldn't work for anyone who didn't trust me to do my job right, and anyway he was paranoid, his wife had a sweet tooth, that's all. Imagine my surprise—did you already guess this, Jeffrey?—when he confessed that that's why he'd hired me. He said he found spying on a woman spying on a woman 'deliciously thrilling'—the creep.

"My second client won the lottery—eight million bucks with a two-dollar bet on the numbers 5, 14, 23, 32, 41 and— No. You tell *me* what the last number was. Write your answer on the back of a napkin while I go to the ladies' room and the winner'll get a real collector's item, a Zabriskie Detective Agency T-shirt. Be sure to indicate your size—extra small, small, med— Oh, hell, you both got it—fifty. The last number's 50 since the numbers increase by nine, but what's really interesting is all the numbers in the series add up to the first number. See?"

$$1+4=5 \quad 2+3=5 \quad 3+2=5 \quad 4+1=5 \quad 5+0=5$$

"What's even *more* interesting—Abe, my client, showed me this; I never would've figured it out myself—is this: Take *any* number from 2 to 10, add 9, and you've got a number that adds up to the original number. For example, take 7: add 9 and you've got 16. One plus 6 is 7. Add 9 again and you've got 25; 2 plus 5 is 7.

"Look at this . . ."

2	11	20					
3	12	21	30				
4	13	22	31	40			
5	14	23	32	41	50		
6	15	24	33	42	51	60	
7	16	25	34	43	52	61	70

8	17	26	35	44	53	62	71	80	
9	18	27	36	45	54	63	72	81	90
10	19	28	37	46	55	64	73	82	91	100

"If you're hooked, to 11 don't add 9, add 18; to 12 add 27, to 13 add 36. I've gone as high as 30 and it just keeps on keeping on. . . . Anyway, Abe wanted protection from his neighbors, who he thought were conspiring to murder him for his millions. I protected him for two weeks, which consisted mostly of watching soap operas with Abe and Ethel, his wife, then told him that if he wanted to blow his money, why didn't he throw a party for his neighbors, who were pissed off at him, all right, but only because he was barricaded in his apartment with a private detective standing guard. It was a nice party, and Abe gave me a nice bonus, which was a good thing because it was another month before I got another client. Which brings me, Rollie, to Charlie Fox.''

"*The* Charlie Fox?" Derry said.

"Ol' Charlie?" Ashburn said.

"Jeff?" Branch said. "Hello, Rol. Miss Zabriskie."

"Pull up a stool, Sambo," Ashburn said. "You know Eve here was a gumshoe, once upon a time?"

"I've got some business to discuss with Jeff."

"Course you do. Just listen a spell."

Lee Greenwood sang "You Turn Me Inside Out."

Eve sucked some salt and took a swig. "Before I tell you about Charlie Fox, I should tell you about me and Goose Gossage—"

Derry giggled. "Goddamn, Sam. Can you believe it? Eve here knows the Goose—"

"The little lady, Officer Derry, has the goddamn floor." Ashburn wiped the tequila bottle with the palm of his hand, offered it to Branch, who looked past it at Derry, then drank from it himself.

Eve swiveled on her chair to include Branch. She was

wearing her surplice top again and took a reef in it lest
Derry ignite. "I did a piece once on the musical tastes of
New York baseball players and in particular on how much
the Goose loved Charlie's music, playing cassettes all the
time on his portable radio and cassette player. No Walkman
for the Goose; he had a ghetto blaster. Charlie and Goose
got to know each other because of the piece and when
Charlie mentioned to the Goose that he wanted to hire a
detective, the Goose told him the reporter who wrote that
piece, me, was one. Charlie couldn't think of anything
better than a detective who knew her country music, and
he called me up."

Ashburn chuckled. "Charlie need to find the right key?"

"I'll be in the car—Officer Derry," Branch said.

Tanya Tucker sang "Texas When I Die."

It was Eve who joined him, holding a container of
coffee carefully in both hands. "I'm sorry. It's my fault."

"Where's Jeff?"

"Being sick. He should stick to milk."

"He's on duty."

"Oh, hell, Branch. Even Sherlock Holmes took a break.
Did a little blow." She put the coffee on the roof to open
the passenger door, reached out for it when she was seated
and put it on the dashboard. She hugged herself. "Nights're
mighty cold in these parts."

"I'll only be a minute with Jeff."

Eve laughed. "Speaking of keeping the chilly wind off,
how come you haven't called Annie lately?"

"I've been busy."

"Men."

Branch turned his head toward her.

"Go ahead. Say it."

He looked back out the windshield. "I was just trying to
picture you going down to locker rooms for interviews

after ball games. It must've been like giving a kid the run of an ice cream factory."

Eve sat sideways, tucking her legs under her. "Johnny Carson said that to me once. I'm not name-dropping, just letting you know that what I'm about to say isn't an ad lib, although it was at the time. Johnny had me on his show in recognition of a certain celebrity I had as a result of being one of the first femme writers to crash the male bastion of the old locker room. He said just that: wasn't it like being a kid given the run of an ice cream factory—only I think he said chocolate factory. I said that in fact what it most reminded me of was a trip I took to England with my parents when I was twelve. We went to Stonehenge, which I was wildly excited about because I'd read a bunch of books, and I was disappointed to find it was so *small*."

Branch laughed.

"What happened to you in New York? I can find out, you know, with a phone call. I have alumni privileges at the *Times*. And my father's—" She faced frontward.

"Your father's what?"

"Did you get hold of Tony Astin?"

"I'll tell you at dinner tomorrow night. You and Annie."

"You *did* call her."

"You don't know everything, do you?"

Eve put her head out the window. "Hey, Jeffrey. Over here."

Derry sidled up to the car, looking pathetic in his baseball cap. "Sorry, Sam."

"Are you free for dinner tomorrow night?" Branch said. "I'm having Annie and Eve over for spaghetti. My spaghetti's world-famous," he said to Eve.

Derry bent to see inside the car. "Uh, sure. I guess. I mean, if it's okay with—"

"I can't wait, Jeff," Eve said.

"Good night, Eve," Branch said.

"I didn't finish telling you about Charlie Fox. Rollie

tells me you're writing a country song. I can get it to Charlie.''

"Good night, Eve."

"Cops." She got out and slammed the door.

Branch got on the Beltway, just to be moving. Derry sipped Eve's coffee, which she'd left behind.

After a while, Branch said, "Well?"

Derry shook his head. "I'm having a hell of a time tracking down Wade's movements. But look at this, Sam." He put the coffee on the dashboard and reached inside his blazer. "I caught up on some paperwork while I was waiting for people to return my calls, and went through Felix's possessions. The hospital sent them over 'cause nobody picked them up. Look what I found."

Branch held up the ticket stub Derry handed him, to catch the light.

"Hell's a jitney, anyway, Sam? I mean, it's a *bus*, right?"

"It's a bus, only people who go to the Hamptons wouldn't ride it if they called it a— Goddamnit, Jeff, why didn't you tell me about this sooner? It's been hours, right?"

"I couldn't find you, Sam. Where the hell've you been? I called you on the radio. I called your house. I went *by* your house. I figured you must be at the Crash, so I went there. Eve was there, and, well . . . I called the bus company, Sam, the Hampton Jitney. Felix took the bus— the Jitney—to Southampton the Friday before last. The *same* bus Litvak took. Litvak came back Sunday night on a seven o'clock bus. Felix must've driven or . . . Is there a plane?"

"And a train," Branch said absently.

"I'd've told you sooner, Sam, but I didn't know where the hell you were. Where the hell were you?"

". . . I went for a drive. I had the radio off."

The radio and his conscience.

Branch had passed the shank of the evening reviewing Wade's video collection. He started out using the Fast Forward button on the deck, but that had somehow made it worse, trivializing a dead man's obsession by making it look like a silent comedy. The sound heads didn't engage during Fast Forward and at normal speed Branch understood why Wade hadn't used his camera's microphone to record the sounds of passion; after the fact, he had added music tracks to the tapes, selecting pieces that echoed the action. To a rather athletic session with one of the call girls, for example, Wade had laid in "Jump (For My Love)" by the Pointer Sisters; a somber, almost ritualistic encounter with the wife of the rancho's Episcopal minister was accompanied by the Albinoni Adagio; over the gambol with the two nurses, Cyndi Lauper sang "Girls Just Want to Have Fun," and over Wade watching the House of Pancakes waitress masturbate, "She Bop."

Branch hadn't been turned on by any of it; rather, as by all solipsism, he'd been alienated. He'd thought about going home, but went instead to headquarters, where he spent some time staring out the window at the Beltway, as usual, wondering. Still high among the things he wondered was why Maddox had told him about Felix's trip to New York. Rather than wonder longer, he called Kallistos Enterprises. The operator reminded him that it was Sunday night. There was no answer at Maddox's home number.

Branch went back to the window and stared awhile longer. He could ask Portia about Felix's trip, but he couldn't, he convinced himself, ask her over the phone. So he took a drive, and turned the radio off.

"Sam? Is anything wrong?"

"I was out this way. I just wondered if you were okay."

"Come in. Would you like a drink? The staff has the night off. We'll have to serve ourselves. Oh, Sam. Will you hold me?"

Would a starving man eat?

After forever, without another word, Portia took his hand and led him upstairs to a guest bedroom (even lust has its etiquette), undressing him and then herself before kissing him coolly and kneeling to take him in her mouth. They'd ended up standing before a full-length mirror on the back of a closet door, she bent forward with her hands braced against the doorposts, but with her head up, her eyes on the reflection of his, daring him to keep them open all the way.

"Is this sick, Sam? Felix is barely in the ground."

Branch eased out of her and rolled on his back on the bed, where they'd staggered locked together, like clowns inside the same costume.

"Or is it something the living must do to prove they're alive?"

Wasn't coition a metaphor for death? *We're tapers too, and at our own cost die:* John Donne.

"Talk to me, Sam. So I don't think I'm dreaming."

Branch turned on his side and propped his head on his hand. "What was Felix doing in New York the week before last?"

She hit at his chest. "Don't! Don't be businesslike. . . . Why?"

"Howard Maddox says he was trying to get restaurants there interested in the champagne."

"Yes."

"That he hired a public relations firm to do a publicity campaign."

"If you know this, why're you asking?"

"What I'm asking is why did Maddox tell me?"

"I don't know what you mean."

"I mean . . ." Branch shook his head. "I don't know what I mean."

Portia massaged his shoulder. "You're tired, Sam. All these deaths. Patrick Wade—God." She pulled at his arm to get him to lie closer to her. "I'm going to Ixtapa for a few days, for a rest. Come with me, Sam. You need a rest, too."

Why not? He could bring the kids. Megan would approve. "Did Felix know Joseph Litvak? Did you?"

"Who? Oh—the man at Caliente Beach. Of course not."

"Felix and Litvak were in New York at the same time."

Portia raised her eyebrows. "Oh?"

"A call to Kallistos was made from Litvak's room at the Del Rey." Why the passive voice, the possibility that someone other than Litvak might have made it?

"To whom at Kallistos?"

"We're working on it. Do you know anyone named Schatz?"

She shook her head without reflecting at all. "Do you know that it wasn't till I went to Berkeley that I met a Jew? My father always said—still does, no doubt—that he wasn't concerned that Jews would try and move in to the rancho—he *was* concerned about blacks and Mexicans— because Jews know their place. He did wish he could have Jewish servants, for the same reason."

Had he said Schatz was Jewish? Or was she talking about Litvak? "What about Felix? Did he know a Schatz?"

"It's a ridiculous question, Sam. Felix knew thousands of people."

Maddox's triple chains. "Where was Felix on Thursday night?"

". . . At the Del Rey."

"The Del *Rey?*"

"For the Governors' meeting, Sam. The first Thursday of every month." Portia rolled away from him. "Don't talk anymore about Felix, Sam. You're making me feel dirty."

Branch switched on the radio. Rosanne Cash sang "Seven Year Ache."

"Where're we going?" Derry said.

"I thought I'd take you home."

"My car's at the Crash."

"I'll pick you up in the morning and take you by there."

Derry laughed. "Hey, Sam, you don't have to ride herd on me. I'm puked out."

Branch kept going toward Costa Chica, where Derry had a bungalow.

"You're pissed at me, aren't you—for saying you ought to see a shrink?"

"I thought you didn't call them that."

"Fuck you, Sam."

". . . Can I sleep on your couch?"

"What're you, Sam, my baby-sitter?"

"I'm crashing. If I don't stop soon, I will crash."

"Suit yourself. You'll have to share it with the dog."

Better that than drive home, which would mean taking the Beltway back to Rancho Maria de la Luz Boulevard, the boulevard to El Centro, El Centro to Sequoia, Sequoia to Calle Verde, staying on Calle Verde past Mesquite, past Durango, past Twin Forks and Switchback and Circle to El Segundo, to number nine, to home, to bed. He would sleep better with Derry's dog than with the knowledge that he'd turned off Calle Verde at Mesquite, which led to Gila which led to El Paso which led to Portia. When she came back from Mexico, when the smell of her was gone from his fingers, he would ask her why Felix had gone to Southampton, on a bus, with a Jew.

16

"Mr. *Branch.*"

"Morning, Mrs. Puckett."

With just her eyes, nose and hands over the fence, Branch's backyard neighbor looked like Kilroy—in a Padres cap. "You gone plain crazy, wasting water like that?"

"This is runoff from the washing machine, Mrs. Puckett."

"I can see that. I can see that plain's I can see you. I can also see you're fixing to fill that wading pool. For your children, I expect; I've never seen *you* wading. Don't tell me you're going to use runoff from the washing machine when *they* get here." A retired secondary school teacher, she had quashed countless conspiracies in her time.

"No, ma'am. I thought what I'd do is fill the pool with clean water—"

"You see? You're in league with those high-and-mighty San Fran*cis*cans. They can't wait for us to dry up and blow away."

"—fill the pool with clean water, then bail a little bit out every day, boil it and use it for washing. There'll be some evaporation, but the weeping willow'll keep the

121

direct sun off. The kids'll be here for only two weeks.
Right now, I'm just testing the pool for leaks."

She sniffed at his story for leaks, then attacked her
weeds with a spray, pushing up the sleeves of her Padres
jacket as the morning warmed. She hadn't been a baseball
fan until it became current that three San Diego pitchers
were members of the John Birch Society. What would she
think if she knew that he was running water in the wading
pool only as cover for the burial of the trocar and the dried
packet of whatever it was in a waterproof pouch in a
Carr's Table Water Crackers tin in a hole at the base of the
weeping willow?

And what would Derry think if he knew that the inter-
ment was the reason Branch had slipped out of his house at
six in the morning, shaky from three hours' sleep on the
floor, having lost the scuffle for the couch to the Labrador?

Strock shaved most mornings, lately, in the men's room,
with the hot water running. "I figure I'm saving water this
way, Sam. Home, it takes twice as long to get hot. . . .
You're in early."

Should he tell Strock to put a plug in the sink and boil
his shaving water in the kitchen? Or bring Mrs. Puckett
around the next morning? Or move? Or just let it slide?
He'd be on Maui before the water ran out, bathing in
coconut milk. "I'm hoping for a phone call from Israel—
about Litvak."

Strock had shaved his upper lip first and was working
on his chin. Branch shaved his left cheek first, then his
chin, then his right cheek, *then* his upper lip. "I'll tell
you, Sam, I had this picture of you out getting your hands
dirty this morning finding Litvak's killer—not making long-
distance phone calls. Where's Derry?"

"It's his day off."

"With all these homicides, Sam, do you think officers
should be getting days off?"

Would it help to take an ad in the paper? Or rent a billboard on the Beltway? FELIX WASN'T MURDERED!

Strock wiped the mirror with the heel of his hand and looked at Branch's reflection. "I know what you're thinking, Sam—that there's only been one homicide. But tell me the truth, could you face your maker this very minute and say Pat Wade's death was an accident?"

The mirror steamed up before Branch could read Strock's expression; the back of his head told him nothing. "Escobar's report's in. It's on your desk. He called it—"

"I know, I know. Autoerotic whatever it is. What do you think of Escobar, Sam?" Strock shaved his right cheek.

". . . He's competent."

"You know the story about what he did in Miami, don't you?"

". . . I've heard talk, yes."

Strock chuckled. "You hear it once, you have to love it always: This guy, the manager of the nightclub in a big hotel on the beach, gets killed in his office. The shit beaten out of him with a blunt instrument, skull fractured, jaw fractured, teeth all over the place. The office is a wreck, the victim has abrasions on his knuckles, like maybe he got in a couple of licks before he bought the ranch. The cops question the assistant manager, who happens to have a black eye, which he says he got trying to keep someone from stealing the radio out of his Cadillac. The cops don't buy that and they charge him with murder. The motive—that he was skimming money from the till and the manager found out about it. Escobar does the autopsy." Strock had stopped shaving, though he let the water run, and leaned on his hands on the sink, looking into the mirror not at Branch or at himself but at some middle distance of stored anecdotes and memories.

"SOP, if you find teeth lying around a DOA, is to make

sure they're all *his* teeth. If they're not all his teeth, if some of them are somebody else's teeth—the perpetrator's, say, knocked out in a struggle—and if you've got a suspect who *has* all his teeth, or isn't missing the ones you've got, then the suspect's not the perpetrator. It's that simple. To find out whose teeth they were, you either fit them in the empty sockets in the victim's mouth or you make X-rays of the teeth and the victim's jaw. Escobar said he fit the teeth in the sockets at the scene, that they all fit, and were therefore the victim's, that X-rays weren't necessary. . . .

"However, the assistant manager's missing two teeth, which he says he lost fighting for his radio, which, by the way, the guy got. His attorneys are smart enough to ask the DA if their client lost his teeth killing his boss, where are they? And why didn't Escobar notice that there were two more empty sockets than there were teeth? And how come, if he did notice, didn't he look for two teeth? And how come, if he did look for them, didn't he find them inside the victim's mouth, under his tongue—which is where the forensics dentist the defense hired found them? . . .

"Then there was the time of death. The police forensics report put it, based on body temperature and decomposition, at—I don't remember exactly, but Wednesday morning, say. Wednesday morning, the suspect has a very good alibi—he was on a plane to New York to visit his sick mother. But Escobar says *no es verdad*, the victim died Tuesday night, which happens to be the night the suspect showed up at a hospital with the black eye and two teeth knocked out. The assistant manager's indicted, tried, convicted. . . .

"A year later almost, another nightclub manager's arrested on a weapons charge. He tells the DA he's got a song to sing, the DA says let's hear it, the song is he knows of a vice detective who was shaking down night-club managers, the victim included, for a cut of the action in exchange for overlooking the serving of liquor to minors and other code violations. The victim, this manager says, objected to a proposed increase in the pad, threatened to do some singing himself, the vice detective threatened to beat the shit out of him with a baseball bat he carried around with him for, uh, emphasis. The DA sets up a sting, the vice detective tumbles for it, gets arrested. He's got all his teeth, but he's also got a girlfriend who says she took a drive with him once out to the Everglades, where he threw something looking very much like a baseball bat into the swamp. She's got a good memory, they find the spot, the alligators haven't eaten it, there's the bat with the manager's bloodstains on it. The vice detective goes away for the duration, the assistant manager goes free—or he would have if he weren't dead, stabbed by another inmate in a prison riot—'' Strock suddenly stood straight and attacked his left cheek.

The steam was making Branch groggy; he noticed that it brought out a message, written with a fingertip, on the mirror over the sink to Strock's right: *Strock is a asshole*.

Strock turned on Branch. "Another year goes by, the department puts on a big anticorruption effort, comes up with an armload of cops—street cops, desk cops, brass—who knew about the vice detective's, uh, overreaction. A major cover-up was in place, and had been from the word go. One of the participants, it was pretty obvious, but nobody was ever able to prove it, was Escobar, who got cute with the teeth and the time of death so the case against the assistant manager would stand up. He was offered the opportunity to resign, and took it. . . . Kind of like your situation, Sam."

"Not at all like my situation, Strock, and it's goddamn cheap of you to say so."

A pause.

Strock turned back to the sink, finished shaving, turned off the hot, turned on the cold, rinsed his face, his razor, his brush, and dried off with the blue and yellow striped towel he'd had around his neck—a Racquet Club towel, distinctive as a deterrent to thieves. "I don't want anybody thinking they know what I want to hear, Sam, that's all I'm saying. You saw those tapes. Whether those women knew Wade was making them or not, every one of them's at a disadvantage. People at a disadvantage are potential killers, I've always found."

A disadvantage was what Branch was at, for he'd expected Strock to buy Escobar's verdict and retail it enthusiastically, lauding both the designer and the tailor. "That gives us a lot of suspects."

Strock turned off the water and smiled into the clearing mirror. "That's better than none . . . . I apologize, Sam, for the slander. You're right. It was cheap."

"And it's cheap to flog a story like that, from this distance, without any perspective. You don't know what it's like working in a big city. You don't know about the politics and the pressures. DAs, City Hall, the feds—their eyes're bigger than their stomachs; they want everything and they want it yesterday. The cops—and the MEs—are in the middle. And they don't even get the scraps; they get the shit." Branch headed for the door.

"Sam."

"Later. Tomorrow. Some other time."

"I'm taking some shit these days myself, Sam, so I know a little bit about what you're talking about. Not on the same scale, no, but . . . a little bit."

Branch turned on him. "You don't know a fucking thing about what I'm talking about, Tom. Shit from whom? The Governors? The City Council? Aura? Tom, this place is cloud-cuckoo-land. We're not cops, we're doormen, bodyguards, chauffeurs, parking lot attendants. Family, you called us; but we're not family, we're slaves, performing animals."

Strock picked some lint from his towel. "I feel that way myself a lot of the time, Sam. Maybe it's the price we pay for not getting shot at a lot, having garbage thrown at us off the tops of buildings. . . . What I was talking about was—maybe you've read about it—this thing up in Manhattan Beach, where I used to work. Some important folks got themselves mixed up in a little, uh, hanky-panky involving a madam who ran a—"

"I read about it."

"Well, then, maybe you read that there's a DA up there who's trying to improve his image by suggesting that maybe the cops knew about it—and have for a long time— and were getting paid to look the other way." He patted his hip pocket. "I got myself a subpoena asking me to take a drive up there and talk to a grand jury."

". . . If you didn't know anything, Tom, you didn't—"

"You know that's not how it works, Sam. That's what we've been talking about. I guess I told that story on Ray Escobar 'cause I wanted to remind myself that there're worse things than looking the other way—which isn't what I did, Sam. That's the God's honest truth." He laughed. "Hell, why'm I saying that to you? It's the grand jury I got to convince."

Branch looked down at his shoes. "You want Wade's case kept open awhile longer?"

"For the record, we'll go with Escobar's verdict. But let's just keep an open mind, Sam. That's all. Maybe something'll fall our way. Shake?"

Branch looked up to take Strock's hand, and when Strock had gone out the door looked back at his shoes, which had a fringe of mud around the soles from his morning outing. Maybe he wasn't awake yet; maybe he was still at Derry's, grappling with the Labrador. Otherwise, it made no sense that he was being told to keep his mind open to the possibility that Wade had been murdered—told it by the man who collected embalming needles. And it made even less sense that if Wade had been murdered, and if the embalming needle was part of the murderer's MO, the murderer would have been so careless as to leave it behind. Did less sense have greater weight than no sense? Branch went to get some coffee, stopping at his desk on the way to drop into his blazer pocket Strock's keys, which he'd lifted from the sink while Strock shaved. He'd go down to the shop in a while and have the boys make a copy of Strock's house key. If Strock missed them in the meantime, he'd be the one to find them; Strock was forever misplacing his keys, and mounting massive searches for them, enlisting the help of everyone in sight.

"Lieutenant Branch."

"Mr. Astin."

"It's Sam, isn't it?"

"Yeah."

"Call me Tony."

"Okay."

"Naturally, after getting your call, Sam, I cabled New York to ask the lads on Metro to verify that you *had* been a member of the NYPD."

"Naturally."

"I'm a little sorry, Sam. I didn't mean to stir up old memories."

"Eve Zabriskie says hello."

There was a pause.

"Eve Zabriskie. She went out with you before she made a rule not to date colleagues."

Another pause, then a big laugh. *"Touché,* Sam. That's vintage Eve. She's out there, I take it."

"In one of the 'dobe huts."

"I'm sorry, Sam, if I was a little arch. Eve can tell you

it comes from taking literally that famous *New Yorker* cartoon: 'The reporters are here, Madam—and the gentleman from the *Times.*' Surely Eve hasn't moved to California.''

''She's doing a piece on some colorful locals, and visiting an expatriate New York friend.''

''Meaning you.''

''Uh, no. Eve and I just met. I needed some expert help and she suggested you.''

''So you *hadn't* seen my byline.''

''No.''

''Ah, well. Ask Eve to tell you the story about the Royal Worcester china.''

''Okay.''

''Well, Sam—what do you know about crime in Israel?''

''Nothing.''

''That's partly because there isn't any—not to speak of. Crimes of violence are rare here. One could go on endlessly—and does—about that being the case in a nation of soldiers, while in the United States, a nation of civilians, violence is commonplace.''

''Umm.''

''There is an increasing amount of white-collar crime— embezzlement, forgery, fraud, tax evasion. As in the States, there is a certain cachet to such crimes and their perpetrators; they are called, proudly, *Jewish* crimes.''

''What did you find out about Litvak, Tony?''

Astin laughed. ''The government periodically denies that organized crime exists in Israel. That in itself should tell you it's a problem—nowhere near the problem it is in the States, or Europe, but a problem. It's similarly organized around a loose coalition of so-called families, whose members aren't necessarily blood relatives; it's involved in the same enterprises—drugs, liquor, loan-sharking, construction. . . .

''Litvak was what's known as a *parnossah geben*. As

with most Hebrew or Yiddish words, there's no simple translation. My Israeli, uh, girlfriend, pressed for one, said it's someone who exists that the police might have something to do. He was arrested several times as a young man, mostly for youthful offenses—car theft, armed robbery, narcotics possession; there were no convictions. Litvak's uncle—his parents appear to be deceased—is an army colonel, only moderately important but with enough influence to keep his nephew out of the, uh—does one still say slammer, Sam?''

He had never said slammer: detention, lockup, downtown, Rikers, upstate. Nor heard a felon say it either: they talked of *doing points*. "Sure."

"Litvak had no visible means of support, Sam, yet he lived very well, both here and in Paris. I happen to know the latter because I was posted there for a time and I recognize the address you gave me as being what we journalists call posh; his apartment here is equally so. He drives—drove—a Citroën, and had a string—we journalists would call them a bevy—of beautiful girlfriends—"

"Tony?"

"I know I'm rambling on, Sam—"

"It's not that. Where'd you get it all?"

Astin laughed. "I should've mentioned it earlier, Sam—my, uh, girlfriend's a police intelligence officer."

Hence the uncertainty about the extent of her commitment? "Go on."

"I can't—*we* can't—go so far as to say Litvak was a gang *member*. He appears to have worked at one time or another for several different organizations—as a free-lance gofer and courier, mostly. Most recently— This is interesting, Sam; you mentioned that some people out there were producing champagne?"

"Yes."

"Well, most recently Litvak appears to have been involved with a gang called Baruch—the word means good luck—that operates behind the front of a legitimate liquor exporting business: Rafelson Sons. According to my, uh, friend, Rafelson is about to undertake a rather expensive effort to market in the States a new Israeli . . . champagne.''

"Hunh.''

"Indeed. Oh, and there's this one last thing. As I said, I worked in Paris for a time and I've made a few calls to old friends: There's no construction project in Neuilly of the kind you described, and none is in the offing.''

"Hunh.''

"If I find out anything more, Sam, I'll call you. I may write about this, I may not; I'm not sure yet. And say hello to Eve for me, will you?''

"Thanks, Tony. Thanks a lot. Uh, *mazel tov*.''

"You mean *Todah rabah*, Sam. But *Bavakasha*.''

"You must be exhausted, Lieutenant Branch.''

Was Mayor Aura Quivers offering to carry his grocery bags?

"It seems ages since we talked at the Beaufilses' party. So much has happened since then.''

That tobacco smell again. Was it a cologne, or was a politician's life really just so many smoke-filled rooms? "If you'll excuse me, Miss Quivers, I'm having guests for dinner and I still have some shopping to do.''

She took a bag from him and set it on the fender of a Rolls parked in the no-standing zone outside the supermarket, then patted it to say he should put his other bag down with it. "You have a chip on your shoulder, Lieutenant, the size of a sequoia. I just wanted you to know I'm delighted the Wade investigation's closed.''

"Is it?''

She made a wet, disapproving noise. "Sam, really. Doesn't it make sense to you that I'd know what's going on in the department in a case like this? It's not collusion, it's cooperation. The fabric of this community has been seriously strained; it can't withstand too much more pressure; our collective goal must be salving, healing, repairing. Now we can get on with it.''

"While we're at it, there's a pothole on La Brea."

"Fuck you, Branch." Aura Quivers was dressed in cowboy boots, wheat jeans, a pale blue western-style shirt with imitation pearl buttons and arrowhead trim around the pockets; the clothes didn't suit her mature figure at all, but she looked good in them, looked as though she could ride and rope, as well as cuss. "I'm sorry, Sam. You're right to be cynical. Why am I talking to you about something like this in a supermarket parking lot? I saw you driving away from headquarters and I followed you, that's why. What I really want to say to you is difficult. And very confidential . . ."

Branch took a step back, but made himself listen.

"I need someone in your department whom I can trust. For some"—she raised her eyebrows—"call it undercover work. Your . . . difficulty in New York, Sam—there're two sides to it. What you were, above all, was loyal. It's loyalty I'm looking for—a loyalty that surpasses camaraderie. . . . There's a possibility that Chief Strock may be implicated—"

"He told me about the subpoena."

The eyebrows again. "Really? The best defense is a good offense, I suppose."

"The best defense is a good defense. If I saw or heard anything that made me think the chief wasn't doing his job properly—"

Aura Quivers got close again. "You'd tell me, wouldn't you, Sam?"

Branch looked down past her breasts at his shoes. There was less mud, but there was still mud.

She touched a button of Branch's blazer. "Of course you would. . . . How's Annie?"

". . . Fine."

"There's something else I want to say to you, Sam. If you'd ever care to have a drink . . ." She put a finger to his lips. "Don't say I'm your boss and that you don't think bosses should date the help. Don't say anything at all. Just . . . keep it in mind."

If she hadn't used his name Branch would've wondered if she thought he was someone else. He hefted his bags and walked toward his car. Putting the groceries in the trunk, he saw Aura Quivers backing up the Rolls, which he hadn't known was hers. He didn't know anything about her. He noticed her vanity plate: HER HONOR.

17

Eve lifted the lid of the casserole and sniffed at the sauce. "One thing about divorced men—they all can cook."

Branch put pasta in a pot of boiling water. "How long were you married?"

"A year. And I was so optimistic. I even had the paper run an item about it. *'Times* Reporter Has Nuptials.' It sounded like a disease. In a way, it was."

Branch stirred the pasta until the water boiled again, took the pot off the stove and covered it with a blue and white checked towel and the towel with the lid. He switched on the stopwatch hanging from a magnetic hook on the refrigerator.

"And a secret method of cooking pasta?"

"You let it sit like this for eleven minutes. It cooks perfectly, and you don't have to scald yourself in the process." He was proud of his kitchenmanship and liked to share his secrets; why did he resent Megan's doing it?

Eve fingered the stopwatch. "Do you do everything to the split second?"

Branch turned his back on the innuendo. "I used to use

it to time my runs, but I gave up running. It's too hot here most of the year.''

"So what do you do for exercise?"

Branch laughed. "Lately, the Jane Fonda workout."

Eve nodded. "I saw the book in the living room. I can understand its popularity; even people who hate her would like to fuck her. Guys who hate her . . . Did you catch any murderers today, Lieutenant Branch?"

Branch got the colander down from its hook and put it in the sink. "On television they catch them; in real life, we stumble over them."

"Eve knows that," Annie said from the doorway. "Her . . ." She swallowed the rest of it and held out an empty pilsner glass. "Jeff would like another beer."

"There's wine with dinner," Branch said.

Eve looked at the stopwatch. "Nine minutes." She took a Bud from the refrigerator and handed it to Annie. "Jeff can drink a beer in nine minutes, easy."

Annie went back to the living room.

"Her what?" Branch said.

Eve shrugged. "I can't imagine. . . . Patrick Wade asked me for a date the other night. It sounds like I missed something."

Missed being his missing Z.

"To the chef." Derry raised his wineglass.

"To no more murders for a while," Annie said.

Derry wagged a finger. "*Felix* wasn't murdered."

"But Wade *was?*" Eve said.

"There's been one murder and two accidents." Branch didn't look at Derry; before the women arrived he'd left out more than he'd told him about what kind of day he'd had.

"One murderer shouldn't be hard to stumble over," Eve said.

Branch twirled some pasta around his fork. "Can we talk about something else?"

"Nothing's more interesting than murder," Eve said. "Nothing. I can understand people's motives for murder, but never their motivation."

"When I lived in New York," Annie said, "I'd've killed for a bigger apartment."

"Killed, yes, but not murdered. Murder's—"

"Please pass the cheese, Jeff," Branch said. "And what did you all do today?"

"Ran," Derry said. "Played racquet ball. Pumped some iron. Took a nap."

"I should think so," Eve said. "I went to the airport and got my luggage back. Hysteria always works."

". . . Annie?"

"The usual."

"Oh, tell him, Annie. He's going to find out anyway."

Branch passed Annie the basket of garlic bread, but didn't let go when she took it. "Yes?"

"I can't, Sam. It's privileged."

"You guys're in the same fix as Frank and Joyce on *Hill Street Blues*." Eve hunched her shoulders defensively. "I know, I know—it's just television; in real life, the handsome cop and the beautiful lawyer tell each other everything."

Branch let go of the basket. "She doesn't have to tell me everything. But it'd be nice if she'd tell me what I'm going to find out anyway."

"Don't talk about me as if I weren't here." Annie passed the bread to Derry without taking any and sat with her hands in her lap. She wore a baggy gray sweatshirt, jeans and English riding boots, a turquoise necklace, cloisonné earrings. Her long brown hair was up in a French roll. She looked terrific and she looked like Derry's date—young, casual but with style, ready for anything. In his navy Alan Paine V-neck sweater, his uniform shirt, slacks and shoes, Branch felt like a father having a look at his daughter's new boyfriend. Who, then, was Eve? She was in jeans, too—Levi's, like Annie's, but a touch less worn—a maroon silk blouse with short puffed sleeves over a black cotton camisole with lace at the bodice (another gift from the Allman Brothers), black suede high-heeled boots; she didn't look maternal, just . . . womanly.

"So let's hear about Pat Wade's tapes, guys," Eve said.

"What am I going to find out, Annie?"

Annie tried to rend her napkin.

"She's giving you a little of your own medicine," Eve said.

"Don't talk about me as if I weren't *here*."

"She thinks it's time you told her why you left New York."

"Shut up, Eve. Please."

"I think so, too." Eve leaned toward Derry. "Do you know?"

Branch took advantage of Derry's full mouth. "I've told Jeff about it."

Derry swallowed and put his fork down. "Come on now, Sam—that's not true. You told me what you thought I needed to know to be your partner. That was how you put it. What *you* thought *I* needed." He picked up the fork, gripping it like a mace that gave him the floor. "All you told me was that you got in trouble because you played by the rules, because you wouldn't rock the boat. That was supposed to make me feel I could always trust you when the going got tough; you'd never sell out your partner. . . . Ever hear of a character disorder?"

Branch pushed his food around purposelessly. "Maybe we could talk about this tomorrow, Jeff."

"It's the flip side of neurosis. A neurotic takes responsibility for everything; a person with a character disorder takes responsibility for nothing. Things're going bad in a relationship, he doesn't try and work it out, he splits, finds someone else, says, See? It wasn't my fault. I'm lovable. Too bad the last one didn't see that. Things're going bad at work—''

"Okay, Jeff. I get the point."

". . . Reagan has a bad one; he can't take responsibility for not going to church; he has to say the Secret Service won't let him."

Branch would have liked to pick that up and run with it; he could inveigh against Reagan for hours—days. But Derry plucked it away.

"You got in trouble in New York because you had a run-in with the system. Your reaction was—and is—that it was the system's fault. I'm sure it was, partly; systems do that—screw people who're only trying to work within them. But you did *some*thing to bring about the conflict; you have *some* responsibility. If you could face up to that—and talking about it would be a beginning—you'd put it in a context that would remove the necessity of pinning the blame, which is the compulsion that makes both the neurotic and the character disorder sick people. I'm not saying you didn't suffer, Sam. Neuroses and character disorders are substitutes for legitimate suffering. But the substitution is a sickness. . . .

"You're sick, Sam. And you should see someone who can help you get well, because it's only with help that you're *going* to get well. . . . I have an appointment tomorrow morning with my therapist. I told him I'd give the time over to you and he said if you showed up he'd see you. I offered to pay for it, but he said payment is part of the process, that showing up isn't enough, that the patient can't think of himself as a charity case. Eight o'clock. He's in the city, charges fifty-five an hour; our insurance covers fifteen of it."

Branch pursed his lips, as if giving the offer genuine consideration. "I have to call the Paris police. There's an eight-hour time difference."

Derry shook his head. "It's always something, Sam. My mom can't drive a stick. My dad complains that he has to take her everywhere. She complains that she never has time to herself, and so does he. She won't learn to drive a stick and he won't teach her—or buy an automatic. They're locked in to their mutual irresponsibility. And you're locked in to yours. *I'll* call the Paris police."

Branch sipped his wine.

Annie breathed in and out through her nose.

Eve balled up her napkin and put it beside her plate. "I'd say I'm half-and-half. I always take responsibility, but it always turns out to be someone else's."

"Shut up, Eve," Annie said.

"I'm uncomfortable, for Christ's sake."

"Then go home. Take the car. I'll take a taxi."

Branch reached for Annie's arm, but she pressed it to her side. "I don't know how this got started—"

"It didn't *get* started. It's the way things are—the way you are. You and your deep, dark secret—"

"Can we back up about ten steps? Eve said you have something to tell me—"

"*Eve* said."

Eve scraped her chair back and got up, but there was nowhere to go.

"Something I'm going to find out anyway—"

"You might, you might not."

"Something to do with Felix, I infer, since you're involved with his will. You know this, but I'll say it anyway—"

"Don't bother."

"As an officer of the court—"

"I *said* don't bother. Felix wasn't murdered. His will does not fall under your jurisdiction—"

"I'll see it when it's probated."

"*When* it's probated. *Until* it's probated, it's none of your goddamn business." Annie whirled on Eve. "Or yours. I don't care what anybody told you; it's only hear-say. If you speak one word—"

"Hold on, counselor." Eve stood with knees slightly bent, feet firmly planted, as *her* therapist taught her to have run-ins with the system. "What I was told has nothing to do with Felix's will; it has to do with the commission of a crime—"

"What crime?" Branch said.

Annie got up, hurling her napkin on the table. "God damn you, Eve." She went into the living room for her bag. "*You* call a taxi. I'm taking the car." She left the front door open.

"What crime?" Branch said.

"Sam," Derry said.

"Shut up, Jeff. . . . What crime?"

Eve went to the front door and watched Annie drive away. She went outside and sat on the steps.

"You're a crazy man, Sam," Derry said. "Can't you hear what we're saying to you?"

"I hear what *you're* saying to me. Or did Annie put you up to it?"

Derry put his head back and closed his eyes. After a moment, he opened them and leaned toward Branch. "Sam, whatever's going on inside you, it's affecting your work. I didn't want to say anything in front of Annie, but I ran into Howard Maddox at the bank this afternoon. I thought you were going to ask him what he knew about Felix's bus ride."

"Back off, Jeff. You've watched too much television. People aren't always in when you call them. They don't always call you back. . . ." His retort ended on a dying fall, for he hadn't tried to reach Maddox at all, for he didn't want to hear what Portia ought to have told him, or consider why she hadn't.

Derry didn't back off; he pushed it. "Since I thought you'd asked him what he knew, *I* asked him what he'd told you. He didn't know what I was talking about. He said whatever it was you wanted to know, maybe you got the answer last night, from Portia. Oh? When was that? 'Bout nine o'clock. Nine o'clock? Yes. He left about ten-thirty. You came by the Crash at eleven, Sam. You didn't tell me you'd seen Portia. You drank my fucking Bushmill's, you slept on my fucking couch, and you didn't—''

"Good night, Jeff." Branch stood and scraped his plate into the serving dish. He scraped Annie's plate and Derry's and Eve's, stacking them on his, with the silverware in the center. He took the stack to the kitchen. He put the dishes in the sink and filled it with water. He'd taken two showers since Portia (one at Derry's, who lived in a different water district), but he knew he still smelled of her; he hoped the dishes would be easier to clean. He got a bottle of Johnnie Red from under the counter, a glass from the cupboard, some ice from the refrigerator. He filled half the glass with Scotch and went out the back door and sat on the steps.

Derry's Cobra peeled out of the driveway, leaving some rubber.

"*Is* there a taxi?" Eve said through the screen.

18

New York.

August.

"*Sam, Sam, Sam. It's good to see you. Have a seat. No, not that chair; it's right under the light, for hard guys I want to sweat a little.*" *Cullen laughed and motioned to a chair alongside his desk.* "*What brings you downtown, Sam? Lord, I miss the streets. I never thought I'd hear myself say it. This*"—*he waved at a stack of paper in the center of his blotter*—"*this is a hundred times more deadly than the streets. A thousand times.*"

"*I guess you heard about the ten-nine on West Street, Inspector*—"

"*Harry, Sam. Harry. Inspector sounds—I don't know—stuck up. Yeah, I heard about it. A fag, wasn't it?*"

"*The victim was gay, yes. The weapon*—"

"*Gay. We live in strange times, Sam, when euphemisms like that gain currency. Time was—and it was within my time, Sam, not that long ago—you called a man a fag or a spic or a spade because it made it very clear to both of you where each of you stood. Gay? I can't say gay.*"

"*. . . The weapon was a twenty-five-caliber automatic*—

*the same twenty-five-caliber automatic that's killed five
other men in the last six months.''*

"Five other, Sam?"

"Each of the first five was handled by a different
detective—and that's five cases out of thirty-five hundred a
year in Downtown West, Harry. Nobody saw the pattern
till now. Jacky LaRusso had the sixth one and also the first
one. He remembered the twenty-five-caliber automatic, he
checked the ballistics, it was the same gun. We checked all
the other homicides in the precinct and came up with four
more committed with the same weapon. We've got a serial
murderer on our hands.''

"These, uh, men, Sam—they were all''—he waggled his
hand—''you know?"

"We're still working on that, but it looks that way.''

"So this is a, uh, vendetta?"

"It looks like it's somebody who doesn't like gay men,
yes.''

Cullen laughed. "Well, then, it shouldn't take you too
long to zero in on the perpetrator, should it, Sam? There're
probably only four or five million people who fit the
description, right?"

". . . Right.''

"Who knows about this, Sam? Besides Jacky and the
others in Downtown West, I mean?"

"Not all of them know. Jacky, Don Miller—Jacky's
partner—and Tom Allen, of course.''

"Of course. I didn't suppose you'd come to me without
first informing your boss.'' Cullen smiled. "Why did you
come to me, Sam?"

"I need more men, Harry. Captain Allen gave me six
uniformed officers on a short-term basis, to stake out the
neighborhood where the shootings all occurred. But I need
men in clothes, and for a longer time.''

"Things're very tight, Sam. When aren't they? There're
other unsolved homicides in Downtown West, as you well

know. There's the Crandall homicide, for one, which people down here would like to see wrapped up because Mr. Crandall had a considerable number of friends in high places who are acting in concert to make of themselves a considerable pain in the ass. There's the antirobbery program, which the commissioner thinks so highly of, although —this is off the record, Sam—his enthusiasm is not as great as that of the mayor, who, after all, appointed the commissioner. But you know all this, Sam. Tom Allen has offered you what is his to offer. You'll just have to make the best of it.''

''I told Tom I was coming to see you, and he said it was okay with him because he'd like to give me more men. Without them, it could take a year, Harry. Remember Berkowitz.''

''Of course I remember Berkowitz, Sam. The only thing is, Berkowitz was killing women, young girls, girls many of the men on the case came to think of as their daughters. I have a daughter, Sam—she's much older than the girls Berkowitz was preying on, and was never the sort to go around necking in the back seats of automobiles—or at least I hope not, but one never knows everything, does one, about one's daughter? You have one, too, don't you, Sam?''

''She'll be four on Monday.''

''Wish her many happy returns for me, will you, Sam? The point I'm making— Well, you know the point I'm making. The point I'm making is Berkowitz was killing girls; this fellow— I assume the perpetrator is a man, but perhaps I shouldn't. Just last Thanksgiving, or maybe it was Christmas, my daughter was complaining about the plethora of attractive, uh, homosexuals, and the simultaneous dearth of good-looking straight men. Maybe some woman's out taking potshots at these guys, not that I suspect my daughter.'' Cullen laughed.

''Five men, Harry.''

Cullen swiveled to look out his window, which had a fine view of the Tombs. "I might be able to give you three, Sam. From Borough Command."

"I don't want them."

Cullen swiveled back, holding out a hand at once helpless and intractable. "You're in no position, Lieutenant Branch, to bargain with someone you've come begging to."

"Three guys from Borough Command means three guys in silk suits, smoking big cigars, sitting around all day with their feet up on a desk, talking on the phone to their girlfriends, their bookies—to reporters telling them what hot shit they are. I want guys to work on the street in clothes they don't mind getting dirty."

Cullen fingered the cigar in his breast pocket; his suit was tropical wool. "Maybe you're right, Sam. For an absolute certainty we don't want the press on this. They'll want to know why it took us so long to see the pattern. They watch too much television, reporters; they see too many movies; they think the department is all one big happy family, a bunch of guys sitting around telling war stories. One of them says he worked on a ten-nine with a twenty-five-caliber automatic, another guy says wait a minute, I worked on one of those last month, a faggot, right? Right. And they go out and nail the son-of-a-bitch. But why am I telling you this, Sam? You know it already and your instinct not to let the press in on this is the right instinct. . . . I'll see what I can do to get you some more men, Sam. I can't promise anything, but I'll see what I can do."

September.

"Seven, Sam?"

"You can't write the number. Just say . . . several. No. Just say we're investigating a possible connection between this Jane Street murder and other . . . incidents of violence directed against members of the gay community."

"I write better than that, Sam. . . . You giving this to anyone else?"

"No. And when the other papers try to match it I won't comment. But I don't have any manpower; I need some publicity. I need to scare the guy and I need to put gays on their guard."

"You have any leads?"

"I just told you, I don't have any men. I asked for some men in August, when the last murder occurred—this part is all off the record—and I got two guys from Clerical whose idea of working in clothes was wearing nylon windbreakers and white socks. We thought we had something when a guy from Narcotics told us about a dealer who was bragging that he'd killed a homosexual in the Village. Trouble was, he'd been in Rahway when the first three gays got killed. We thought we had something when we found out a security guard at a trucking company warehouse near the scene of one of the murders carried a twenty-five-caliber automatic—"

"Which is the murder weapon?"

"This is a good story. Too bad you can't use it. We found out he carried a twenty-five-caliber automatic, Jacky LaRusso got to know him, pretended he was a gun freak, convinced the guy he should go with him to that shooting range on West Twentieth—you know the place? Jacky hung around after he left, swept up his cartridges. Wrong gun, but it was good police work. So, no, I don't have any leads. Why the hell else would I be buying you dinner in a place like this?"

"If I can write 'seven,' Sam, I'll get the front page. If I write 'incidents of violence' I'm a candidate for Metropolitan Briefs."

"How about . . . a series of murders?"

"How about seven?"

"Forget it. I'll call the Times.*"*

"You want page one in the Times, *Sam, you want the*

split *page, you'll have to say seven. Otherwise, it's back
with the shipping news.''*

"How about several?"

*"Several's awfully close to seven. My fingers could slip
on the keyboard."*

"That's your problem."

"What the hell, Branch?"

"Hello, Harry."

"Inspector Cullen, you rat fuck."

". . . I don't understand, Inspector."

"In a pig's ass you don't understand, Branch. You seen
the fucking Herald?"

"Today's Herald?"

*"I'm due upstairs in five minutes, Branch. To the ques-
tion, did I know anything about this, my answer is going to
be no. What's your answer going to be when they ask you
the same question?"*

". . . Did you *know* anything about it?"

"You got it."

". . . I got it."

"At least you're not a stupid rat fuck, Branch."

October.

*"Lieutenant Branch, this is Commissioner Montgomery.
I'm Chief Martin, Inspectional Services. Lieutenant, we
read in the paper today—and heard it on the radio, those
of us who were up at six and happened to be listening to
the Fred Flakes show; my wife's a fan; I like a little quiet
first thing in the morning—we read and heard about an
unidentified source saying you informed your superior officers in Borough Command on August second and shortly
thereafter that in your capacity as commander of the Downtown West squad you were investigating a series of murders of, uh, homosexual men, all committed with the same
twenty-five-caliber automatic pistol. Is that what you did,
Lieutenant?"*

". . . One of my men, Detective Sergeant LaRusso, came to me on the morning of the second and said he'd handled a murder late the night before that bore similarities to one he'd investigated six months earlier. Ballistics showed that, in fact, the two victims had been killed with the same gun. I ordered a computer check of other homicides in the precinct—and later, citywide—and came up with four other murders involving the same twenty-five-caliber automatic. That took most of the next three days, and the evening of August fourth I informed Captain Allen of my findings. Captain Allen authorized overtime for several uniformed officers to participate in a stakeout of the area from West Fourteenth Street south to Canal Street and from the Hudson River to—"

"Okay, Lieutenant, I think we're getting a little sidetracked here. We've all read the reports, we understand what the setup was, we know the procedures you followed. As far as I know, there're no complaints about the quality of your investigation—even though there's now been a seventh homicide and even though you haven't come up with a perpetrator. These things take time; we all understand that. The problem we have, Lieutenant, and it's a major problem, is that every newspaper and radio and television station in town has a reporter waiting downstairs wanting to know how seven citizens of this city— forget about their sexual preferences; they were citizens —how seven citizens could get murdered by the same perpetrator without said fact coming to the attention of the borough commander, Inspector Cullen; the borough commander's executive officer, Inspector Maclanahan; and the borough's detective operations chief, Inspector Applebaum— not to mention the chief of detectives, the chief of police, and the commissioner. You just said you informed Captain Allen, who oversees three squads, including Downtown West, which was SOP. But what we've read in the paper and heard on the radio, those of us who were up at six, is

the assertion that you informed not only Captain Allen but superiors at Borough Command, with the intent that the information be passed through the usual channels to head-quarters. Can you, uh, elaborate on that assertion, Lieu-tenant Branch?''

"In September, after the seventh murder, there was a report in the Herald giving some details of our investiga-tion. I was the source of that report. I acted . . . out of pique. I'd asked Captain Allen for more manpower; he'd given me what he could; he couldn't give me any more without taking manpower away from investigations that had higher priorities. I was unable to look at the bigger picture; I took it personally; I acted unprofessionally. I regret that, and I'm making this apology and'll follow it up with a formal letter to the chief and to you, Mr. Commissioner. As for the reports in today's paper, and the radio broadcast, I was not their source, and have no information as to who was.''

The commissioner cleared his throat and Martin re-ceded. "It's well known that you're an unusually popular commander, Lieutenant Branch.''

"I hope that's so, sir.''

"So it's not unlikely that if you were not the source of these latest reports, one of your men might be, with an eye to taking the . . . heat off you.''

"With all respect, sir, I don't want to speculate on that. I'm sure Chief Martin—''

"Indeed, Inspectional Services will look into the matter, Lieutenant. The point, however, is that there remains the assertion—whatever its source—that you informed not only Captain Allen of the nature of your investigation, but also other superiors in Borough Command. Is that so, Lieu-tenant?''

". . . No, sir.''

"You told only Captain Allen, your immediate superior?''

". . . Yes, sir.''

"And expected that he would pass the information up the chain of command?"

"Sir, again with all respect, I don't think—"

"Of course not, Lieutenant. You're a loyal soldier; you've made that patently clear. . . . There have been intolerable lapses of judgment in this case. Branch—injudicious behavior unsuitable for men with posts in the Detective Bureau. Captain Allen, I'm sure you know, has been transferred to uniformed duty in Morningside Heights. Inspector Applebaum retired last month, obviating a similar transfer. Inspector Maclanahan has taken medical leave because of a recurring heart condition. Inspector Cullen, it would seem, was only the victim of these derelictions of duty, and his head and heads above his will not roll, although letters of reprimand will be put into a number of records.

"Which brings me to you, Lieutenant. You're the protégé of some important men at headquarters; they anticipated the answers you've just given us and prevailed on me to modify the punishment I was prepared to mete out to you. I don't like being put in such a position, since the answers you've given were lies, lies intended to cover up for your superiors; at the same time, there are exigencies that as an appointed official who works every day with career civil servants I must pay heed to. . . .

"Nineteen years in the Department, Lieutenant. An exemplary record, in particular as commander of the Downtown West Squad, which was the Department's most corrupt and inefficient squad before you took over. It grieves me to have to tell you that you will report in full uniform one week from today at eight A.M. to the Jamaica West Precinct in Queens. Unless . . . unless you decide you would prefer to retire with full benefits. You have a week to decide. That's all, Lieutenant. Chief, I'll see you in my office."

19

"Quelle histoire." Supine on the grass of Branch's backyard, Eve tried to balance her glass on her forehead.

"You see why I haven't told Annie."

"Not exactly." Eve sat up, drank off her Scotch, set the glass on the grass and grasped her knees in her arms. "I owe you a story, the rest of the story about how I met Charlie Fox. It's not that I can't go without talking about myself for any length of time; it's relevant."

"You want another drink?"

"I'll come with you. I'm getting cold."

Branch gave her a hand up, and thought about putting it on the small of her back as she went up the steps. Her back was half again the breadth of Annie's yet her spine was an elegant ridge beneath her silk blouse, damp from the grass. He made a fist instead. *Between the motion/And the act/Falls the Shadow:* T. S. Eliot.

Eve sat with her elbows on the kitchen table, talking into her glass. "I'll never forget the day Charlie walked into my office—I had a cubicle in 1501 Broadway, which you know if you've ever been in it is a perfect building to play at being a private detective; I even thought about having my name painted on the window so it'd show up on the wall when the sun shone through it, just like in the movies; it was way too expensive, and who was going to see it on the seventeenth floor, so I settled for it on the frosted glass door—the way he walked in and sat down in the leather client's chair and stretched out his legs and tipped his straw hat back on his head and said in that incredible voice of his, which since you're writing a country song you must know *does* sound like bourbon over nails, just like Julie Beth Whitelaw said in the song she wrote about him—said he had a business proposition if I was a'tall innerestid. I slipped into my drawl, the way I do around Southerners—I told you I was married to one, from West comma Texas, and I talked like Dolly Parton—and said is a pig innerestid in slops?

"Charlie said he wanted me to find his granddaughter, Bright. Bright's the daughter of Ben Fox, Charlie's son by his first marriage, to Bobbie Baird, who since you're writing a country song you must know is the daughter of Buck Baird, and who's now married to Skeeter Carpenter of the Yazoo River Band, which since you're writing a country song you must know means Bobbie went from Beethoven to Mantovani as far as musical balls're concerned—or, if you prefer a pop metaphor, from Bruce Springsteen to Christopher Cross.

"Ben Fox and his wife, Texas—Texas Kitridge, the daughter of Amarillo Bob Kitridge, since you must love the byzantine relationships of country musicians as much as I do—Ben and Texas split up and custody of Bright went to Texas, with the stipulation that Texas was supposed to live within fifty miles of Nashville, where Ben's a top session picker and sometime producer, but she ran off with a man everybody called Just John because when he told you his name was John and you said John what? he said Just John. Just John worked for a contractor who built a house next door to where Texas lived with Bright. Texas let the workmen drink from a hose in her yard and I guess one kind of hosing led to another.

"Ben Fox didn't seem to care at all what happened to Bright, and certainly not to Texas, since no sooner was she out of his house than in moved Peach Blackwood, whose latest album Ben'd produced, hoping she'd be the next Reba McEntire but who you must know is just another Barbara Mandrell. But Charlie cared. Charlie's so kind he brakes for armadillos, as Julie Beth Whitelaw said in her song, and he cared enough to hire me to do the finding.

"Before he did, though, he said tell me a thang or two about yersef, and I said you mean how'd a nice girl like me wind up in a racket like this? He said in pertikilar and I said he'd said it hissef in a song: 'I did it 'cause my daddy said don'tcha dare.' . . ."

Branch waited, then laughed. "That's the end of the story?"

"No. I'm trying to get up the courage to tell you the end."

"Because you didn't find Bright?"

"Oh, I found Bright. I was good at that job, in my own half-assed way, but that's another story. This story isn't really about Charlie Fox or Ben or Texas or Just John or Bright. It's a story about me, who, as I've said a number of times, was once upon a time married."

"To a fellow from West comma Texas."

"Right."

Branch waited.

"You don't see, do you?"

"See what?"

"The connection."

" . . . No, I guess I don't."

"Shit. That means I have to explain it. You see, on the one hand, there's this fellow from West comma Texas to whom I was married. On the other hand . . . there're these fingers."

"Terrible."

"Not so terrible for half a bottle of Johnnie Red."

"Only about a third. The bottle was two-thirds full, or one-third empty, if you look at things that way. So you drank half of two-thirds—"

"Which is half a bottle, just like I said."

"You were talking about the fingers on your other hand."

"I know what I was talking about. I've only drunk a third of a bottle."

"Shall I open another?"

"Hell, yes. This one was only two-thirds full. . . . Anyway, on the one hand, there's the fellow from West comma Texas, to whom I was married— You see? I'm not drunk; I've said whom twice—the objective pronoun in the relative case."

"You mean the relative pronoun in the objective case."

"That's what I said. . . . Anyway, on the—"

"Why not go straight to the other hand?"

"That's what I was *go*ing to do. On the *oth*er hand, there's my father. . . ."

Branch waited.

Eve looked up at him. "That's where the story ended the last time, didn't it?"

"Pretty damned abruptly."

"You'd know why if I told you the rest of it."

"Take your time. We've got this whole bottle, three-thirds full."

"My father . . ." Eve looked to Branch for prompting.

"Told you not to be a private detective."

"With good reason."

"He was one?"

"Close."

". . . Ah. *Now* I get it. Just a few hours ago, before all the screaming started, when I said there's a difference between television cops and real-life cops, Annie said, 'Eve knows that. Her father's . . .' And then she stopped.''

"Pretty damned abruptly."

"And furthermore, *last* night, in the parking lot outside the Crash, *you* said if you wanted to find out about my past you could call the *New York Times, or* you could call your father. And then *you* stopped—pretty damned abruptly. . . . Now, why would two women, on two consecutive nights, stop themselves from talking to me about the father of one of them? Unless . . .''

"Tick tock. Tick tock."

"Unless her father was a cop."

"Da dum."

"A cop on the NYPD."

"One of New York's finest."

"A cop I know and who knows me."

"Door number one, door number two, or door number three?''

Branch shook his head. "I don't know any cops named Zabriskie."

"That's the point."

". . . I lost you."

"You were *so* close."

Branch snapped his fingers. "Zabriskie's the name of the fellow from West comma Texas."

"You wouldn't think it, would you? You'd think someone from West comma Texas would be named . . . Branch. Where're you from, Branch?''

"Brooklyn comma New York."

"So's my father."

"Whose name is . . . ?"

"I can't say it, Branch. You're going to have to."

". . . Harry Cullen."

"Bingo."

* * *

The only place, really, that could accommodate the coincidence was the bed.

"You're a big girl," Branch said.

Eve made a muscle. "Like Christine Lahti, Sigourney Weaver, Joanna Cassidy, Kathleen Turner, Vanessa Redgrave. Pauline Kael called them—us—'heroically feminine, the marvellous new towering Venuses changing our image of women.' I have it on the bulletin board in my kitchen."

"Never heard of a couple of them. And Vanessa Redgrave's not new."

"She's the prototype."

After they'd wrestled some more, Branch said, "I get the feeling you're trying to keep this from happening."

"I hardly know you."

"And you think a few more minutes'll make a difference?"

"Minutes? Are you one of the sprinters? Anyway, you're Annie's boyfriend."

"So you weren't intending to ever take your clothes off."

"I like being touched and touching with clothes on. This is an Anne Klein blouse; I wouldn't let just anybody muss it up."

Branch got off the bed, keeping his back to her as he left the room to hide the protrusion in his pants. "I'll make some coffee."

When he came back with the pot and two mugs, Eve was sitting up in bed, looking at a *Playboy* she'd found in the drawer of the end table. "I was snooping to see if you had condoms."

"In the bathroom."

"Not very handy, for a guy who runs his life by a stopwatch. Do you masturbate much?"

"Not as much as I once did."

"Bursitis?"

"Astigmatism. I just can't do it with my glasses on."

Eve laughed. "Do you know that Waylon Jennings song 'Maybe I'm Used (But Baby I Ain't Used Up)'? . . . Can I hear your song?"

Branch sat on the bed, filled the mugs and passed her one.

She closed the magazine and used it as a tray. "Rollie says your song's too complicated."

Maybe Rollie was right; he should write something like the first and only song he'd ever written, a song sung to induce a nap in Ricky, aged two:

Life's a bucking bronco. Life's a rolling stone.
Life is too many heartaches, too many miles from home.
Life's behind the eight ball, up a creek without a paddle.
A car without any gasoline, a horse without a saddle.
Life's a pretty married lady, a handsome married man.
No corkscrew for your bottle, no opener for your can.
But I'm really glad to be alive.
I hope I live to a hundred and five.
My reason for that is not at all tricky.
I love life 'cause my name is Ricky.

"Are you going to tell me what I'm going to find out?" Branch said. "Since we're not going to get physical."

Eve shrieked. "I haven't heard anyone say that in *years*. Do you have MTV in these parts?"

"I lost custody of my television."

"One of the most extraordinary cultural documents of our time is the video of Olivia Newton-John's 'Physical.' It starts with her—in her headband—dancing around a bunch of fat guys doing exercises. Cut to her with what we're supposed to think are the same guys, less and less fat, finally to her with bodybuilder types. At the end of the song, the *guys* go off together, hand in hand, arm in arm, leaving her dancing by herself. I just don't get it. What're they saying—that the best women can hope for is to be masturbated over?" Eve took her mug off the magazine and opened it to the centerfold—a young woman in an approximation of a leotard working out on a weight machine. "You know how people talk about where they were when Jack Kennedy was killed? This girl wasn't even *born* when Jack Kennedy was killed. She was two when Bobby was killed. . . . Would you like to meet a girl like this someday?"

"Do you do this a lot?" Branch said. "Pet first and make demands later?"

"I haven't made any demands."

"Whatever."

Eve closed the magazine and rested her chin on her knees. "That stuff Jeff was talking about—he got it from a book. Not that there's anything wrong with that; it's just that I've read it, too. It changed my life. It made me understand the difference between falling in love and being in love. Do you know the difference?"

"Eve, don't make me your straight man."

"Falling in love is a regression to an infantile state, to a time when there's no limits to your ego, when you and the world are one thing. Like infancy, it doesn't last forever; sooner or later, ego boundaries're established, reality intrudes. He wants to do it, she doesn't; she wants to watch *Dynasty,* he wants to play Boggle—You're not even listening."

"Oh. Sorry. I didn't know that was required—or even desirable."

Eve shook her head. "I don't envy men these days. There're more of us than you, but you're not scoring right and left, not by a long shot. Every woman I know is weary of it, weary of putting on a nightie and doing all of his favorite things. A lot of them can't even remember what they are. Even the ones who want to get pregnant are hoping it'll take right away; the prospect of six months or a year of purposeful fucking isn't a pleasant one.''

''And what is it you all want instead?''

''Instead? I'd say it's what we want as well as. Honesty, commitment, sharing.''

''Have you tried Boy Scouts?''

Eve laughed. ''You're a decent man. I can see that, and Annie doesn't only bad-mouth you. I bet you're a good father; it's too bad your kids can't have more of you.''

''. . . But?''

''But you're fucked up. You don't have to be a professional analysand to see it. Jeff can see it and, as sweet as he is, and as well-meaning, Jeff is only a little more than a dumb jock. He's right, though, that you need help. You know the clichés about having a fool for a client if you're your own lawyer— Sorry. I shouldn't've mentioned lawyers. Look—would you fix your own car? I don't mean changing the oil and cleaning the points. I mean a major tune-up.''

''Speaking of lawyers . . .''

''Yes?''

''What crime?''

Eve laughed. ''Okay. You deserve to change the subject. . . . I suppose I can tell you.''

''Since I'm going to find out anyway.''

''. . . Actually, more interesting than what crime is why Wade mentioned it to me.''

''Wade?''

''The night Felix died. He'd heard I was writing a piece about Felix, and said I should ask him about Moneda Investing. I did ask Maddox, who was remarkably cool given that the shit was about to hit the fan.''

''Eve, please don't make me ask you what shit, what fan, what about Moneda.''

''I was pausing for effect. . . . Moneda's a terribly successful mutual fund. It's had profits of more than forty percent for each of the last five years. Its investors are the *crème de la* of southern California: Hollywood actors, directors, moguls. Lots of doctors. Some of its accounts are for as much as ten million dollars. Over the past three months almost fifty million dollars has been withdrawn from Moneda, enough to put it out of business if Felix hadn't hit on the resourceful idea of making it look as though it hadn't happened by altering the other customers' statements to show transactions never made and profits never earned. The withdrawals were all by customers who don't have names, just Swiss bank accounts. Annie thinks the withdrawals were orchestrated; the timing and the manner were such that it's pretty clearly a plot.''

"A plot by whom?"

"It's just speculation."

"Speculate."

"It's not even my speculation. It's Annie's. For all I know, she's revised it."

Branch sighed.

". . . Southland Hydro."

". . . Hunh."

"It has a nice logic to it, doesn't it? No money from Felix, no dam; no dam, no competition for Southland."

"Did Wade have an account with Moneda?"

"Indeed. And he was on the board."

"Finally, a motive. He knew too much."

"Motive? I thought his death was an accident."

Branch ticked off fingers to enumerate his points. "Southland makes big investments in Moneda, then pulls its money out and the rug from under Felix. . . . Wade finds out and makes allusions about it to you and maybe to others. . . . Someone kills Wade—"

"I thought his death was an *ac*cident."

"—making it *look* like an accident."

"Oh ho . . . Maybe Felix killed him. No. Felix couldn't kill him; Felix was dead."

Branch's phone rang, and he let it—seven times.

"Annie," Eve said. "Her ears're burning 'cause I'm telling you what she told me not to—not to mention that I'm lying in your bed."

Branch studied his hand, but he'd almost forgotten everything he'd just said. "Where does Litvak fit in? Your friend Astin told me Litvak works for mobsters who're exporting champagne—"

"You talked to Tony?"

"Felix is making champagne. . . . Litvak and Felix are in New York at the same time, they take a bus ride together. . . . Litvak calls Kallistos when he gets out here. . . . Felix is at a meeting at Litvak's hotel the night Litvak's killed. . . ." He feared to add one more thing, lest it disturb the angle of repose and everything slide away. "And who's Schatz?"

"Schatz?"

"The check Litvak was carrying—which was from a Swiss bank, by the way, speaking of Swiss banks—was supposedly intended to buy out the owner, named Schatz, of a piece of land in a suburb of Paris that was in the way of a commercial development. Astin has friends in Paris who told him there's no such development. So maybe Litvak isn't looking to buy *out* Schatz, he's just looking *for* Schatz, who's changed his name; the million dollars is just . . . bait, to make Schatz come out from behind his alias, or . . . Or what?"

"I can't follow this. . . . What if that phone call was business? Murder business."

"I have a beeper."

Eve looked up at the ceiling. "Paris. When Tony was posted to Paris he asked me to come with him. Another bridge I burned without even crossing it. . . . As long as we're talking coincidences, Felix and Portia met in Paris. Annie told me."

Branch had managed to forget that. Now he remembered: She had gone to an oenology convention—and "to breathe some history," she had told him, implying that the present—and he—were deficient in oxygen. She had sent him one postcard: *Having a wonderful time*—but no wish that he were there. Her one-week trip became a six-month sojourn, and when she returned it was with a portly millionaire in her baggage.

"Did Schatz kill Litvak—whoever Schatz is? What the hell is that?"

Branch found the beeper in the pocket of his blazer and turned it off.

Eve sighed. "You guys're all so wired up. Your beepers, your car phones, your computers. Or else you're out running."

Branch dialed headquarters. While it rang, he checked his slacks for stains, something he hadn't had to do since his senior year in college. There'd been plenty then; Megan bore her virtue to the altar, and for two nights thereafter. "This is Branch."

"We got a call from Mrs. Beaufils, Lieutenant," the dispatcher said. "She asked if you could come out to her house. She said it's an emergency."

"Then why're you calling me? Send a patrol."

"She asked for you, sir."

". . . Call her back and— No, never mind. I'll go."

"Should I send a patrol as backup, Lieutenant?"

". . . I'll call you."

Branch went into the bathroom. It took forever for the urine to come, so fouled up was his system, and when it did it sprayed crazily, wetting the toilet seat, the floor, the bath rug. He tore off a yard of toilet paper and crouched to mop up. *Always clean your quarters before responding to an emergency:* Sam Branch's *The Joy of Police Work.*

"Ever think of sitting down?" Eve said from the door. "Men're amazing. Because they can pee standing up they wouldn't *think* of peeing sitting down. Believe it or not, that's the reason I finally got divorced from old Zabriskie. We had a tiny little apartment on St. Mark's Place with the bathroom in the living room, which was also the bedroom and the kitchen. Whenever he got up at night to pee he'd turn on the light and it'd shine in my eyes and wake me up. I asked him, please, motherfucker, don't turn on the light, but he said he *had* to turn it on so he could see where he was *pee*ing. I said— Well, you can figure out what I said, but he just wouldn't do it, wouldn't even *try* it.'' She strutted in place. ''He was from West comma Texas, where they piss all over the landscape.'' She hugged herself and poked at the bath rug with a toe. ''The city never sleeps, I guess. Even this dump.''

Branch edged past her into the bedroom, giving her an ell having failed to gain an inch. His footwork impressed him; he was altogether sober. ''You can stay here if you like. Otherwise, there *is* a cab.''

''You asshole. You think I don't know you're going to see Portia?''

Branch unlocked the top drawer of the dresser and took out his shoulder holster. ''It's an emergency.''

Eve gave him the finger, listlessly.

20

El Segundo to Calle Verde. Past Circle, past Switch-back, past Twin Forks and Durango to Mesquite, which led to Gila which led to El Paso, which led, for the third time in four nights, to Portia.

The night before (was this only the morning after the night after?), Branch had departed from headquarters, tak-ing the Beltway to Rancho Maria de la Luz Boulevard, the boulevard to El Centro, El Centro to Sequoia, Sequoia to Calle Verde, Calle Verde to Mesquite, to Gila, to El Paso, to ask Portia the question he'd convinced himself couldn't be asked on the phone. What was the question? Oh: What had Maddox meant?

Three nights before (was this only three nights and a morning after?), having taken a break from the matter of Joseph Litvak to cruise near Holly Hills, keeping an eye out for the vandals who the previous Friday had stolen a golf cart from the caddy shack and gone joy-riding over the ninth and tenth fairways, answering the call that came through County (who had notified County? and what did it matter?), he had gone by way of Country Club Drive to de la Borda, de la Borda to Chula Vista, Chula Vista to

Sequoia to Calle Verde to Mesquite to Gila to El Paso, not knowing what to expect, having been told only that there was need of an ambulance, reminding himself that it was better, sometimes, not to know what to expect, for expectation was inimical to improvisation.

Both times he had driven with the economy of instinct honed by practice, taking the corners outside, inside, outside, downshifting and braking at the same time (even on the second trip, when haste was hardly called for, for he was going only to ask a question he'd convinced himself couldn't be asked on the phone), seeing little but the pathmarks that signified nothing to the layman but were vivid to the professional who knows his territory—all but the last short stretch—and how to traverse it.

All but the last short stretch because the first trip had been *the* first trip, the virgin venture, the maiden voyage to Portia's marriage abode—the first trip because El Paso, with a guardhouse at one end, a cul-de-sac at the other, and Dobermans at three of the five estates along it, wasn't a street that needed regular patrolling; because duty had never called him there before, and above all because he wasn't one to rub his own nose in the traces of his failures. (He hadn't stayed in New York, had he?)

When Branch was courting Portia (besieging her, she would have said) she lived alone (with not even a servant) in the penthouse apartment of Hacienda el Refugio, at twenty stories the rancho's tallest building, a glass tower whose most attractive feature—to Portia, at any rate—was its basement garage from which a gentleman caller could ascend directly to the penthouse, an arrangement far preferable to his parking in a driveway so that neighbors (try though she had, Esmé Hubbell Hawkes hadn't been able to prevent even the most secluded estates in the community from having neighbors) could know, if they cared to, how often—and how many different—dinner guests stayed for breakfast.

Portia said once she thought it might be possible never to leave the penthouse—said it standing nude before the floor-to-ceiling window, an English Oval in one hand and a bottle of Stolichnaya in the other, taking drags and sips by turns. "There's the terrace, for fresh air. I have everything delivered anyway—food, prepared or to be prepared, whichever I feel like, liquor, cigarettes. My books are here, my records, the television, the radio. Oh, I suppose I'd want to go downstairs to use the gym and sauna and pool, but I could live without so many things I pretend are important to me. I wouldn't care if I never played another set of tennis. Everyone cheats—do you know that? Everyone. Or another round of golf—God, they play badly here, the women *and* the men. Parties—bah, humbug. Clothes—who needs them?"

"You'd miss driving your car."

The set of Portia's shoulders said that she smiled, for they had met because of her driving—driving her Porsche (her previous Porsche, a 911 Carrera) at speed on Country Club Drive at two o'clock in the afternoon, her left hand on the wheel, her right, she told him later, after they made love for the first time, in her crotch, though she was sure that one day she could come from the speed alone. He had pursued her (unnecessarily; he knew, as did everyone, who she was and where she was going) along Country Club to de la Borda, de la Borda to Chula Vista, Chula Vista to Sequoia to El Centro to Rancho Maria de la Luz Boulevard to the front entrance of Hacienda el Refugio, where she hopped out of the car, held the keys out to the valet and a hundred-dollar bill to Branch—not as a bribe, but because she thought it would "cover everything." It covered far from it, for Branch charged her with leaving the scene of an accident (she'd winged a Daimler doubled-parked outside Elizabeth Arden on El Centro), resisting arrest and reckless endangerment, along with the gamut of moving violations; not even her status as daughter of the founder kept her from losing her license for sixty days, on the morning of the first of which she phoned Branch at home and demanded that he drive her to Holly Hills for her golf game, since it was all his fault. He heard the call for what it was and went around to the H el R, as it was known locally, for what the Admiral's daughter called their shake-down cruise.

"And flying," Portia said. "I'd miss flying. I could go out for drives at night—you wouldn't arrest me again, Sam, would you? I'd stay on the back roads or drive down by the beach—in county jurisdiction. I could fly at night, too. I love flying then most of all." She put her cigarette out in a big stone ashtray, came away from the window and knelt beside the bed. "Let's do it, Sam. Let's just stay here, fuck our brains out, gorge ourselves on caviar and pâté from Dino's, on pasta from the Ticino, on steaks from the Baron, on Scotch and vodka, watch ball games, eat popcorn, drink beer, read books, fuck our brains out again. Don't say you have to work. You'd quit your job—or better yet, just never show up again. That's the point—we'd disappear. No one would know where we'd gone. Oh, they'd hear the Porsche some nights—and maybe we'd buzz them in the Falcon, scare the shit out of them—and they'd wonder if it was us—the Flying Dutchpersons." She laughed and took a belt of vodka and laid her head on his chest.

Let's. Our. Ourselves. We. Us. Jussives, subjunctives, forms of the first person plural—they weren't frequent in Portia's diction; she used the singular, the indicative, the imperative, for that was how her mind worked—solipsistically, objectively, commandingly. Lying there, his fingertips feeling the pulse just beneath the skin of her temple, Branch reflected on the difference long enough that she took it as a rejection—her mind worked like that, as well: he who hesitated was lost and not worth finding—and got to her feet with a snort and went into the bathroom to shower. She was a long time at it, and in the dressing room, and when she returned to the bedroom, wearing a white sweater of knitted silk, black silk slacks, black boots—hunting clothes; she could go to a cocktail party or a truck stop—it was to get her bag and car keys. She left without a word and never again mentioned a longing that they be a couple of recluses—or that she ever had; never again suggested that they do anything together except fuck their brains out.

Until the night before, the night before the night before this morning, when she had said—what was it?—*I'm going to Ixtapa for a few days, for a rest. Come with me, Sam.* Had it been an order, and was this the follow-up, delivered through the dispatcher so that he would hop to it? She hadn't told the dispatcher to tell Lieutenant Branch to pack a bag, to bring a bathing suit and a snorkel; but there were shops at the airport, shops in Ixtapa; she would outfit him in resort wear and pick up the tab; it would be only fair, given the shortness of the notice.

This morning—it was quarter to three by the clock on the dashboard of his dilapidated Chevrolet Townsman station wagon (and therefore could have been any time at all, any day, any week, any year—could have been the day and the week and the year the Branches rolled in this same car at just about this hour into Rancho Maria de la Luz, weary and bruised and quarrelsome from their cross-country flight from ignominy)—this morning Branch drove like a novice, sitting forward with his forearms, practically, on the steering wheel, peering through the streaked and bird-fouled windshield at every traffic sign and street post, braking late, accelerating tentatively, cornering on the verge of a shunt or a stall, thinking every light was his destination, expectations overflowing his mind.

But not the expectation that he would have to stop at the guardhouse. He'd been waved through in the BMW, but off-duty as he was, and driving the Townsman, whose headlights worked only on high beam, he was confronted with the upraised palm of a guard in powder-blue khaki. He rolled the window down halfway—as far as it would go—and held out his shield.

The guard had seen that one before—or been trained to look out for it—and he came around to the door, one hand on the butt of his revolver. "Help you?" He was short, and walked compensatorily on the balls of his feet.

"Police business." Branch hadn't shifted out of drive, only braked, and he rolled a little as he pocketed the shield.

The guard put his hand on the fender. "Let's see that again, friend."

Branch put it in park. "Lieutenant Branch. Rancho Police."

The guard held his left hand out and his face said he had forever. When Branch gave him the shield, he did everything but bite it before handing it back. "Haven't seen you before, Branch."

"Haven't seen you, Mr. . . . ?"

"Wiggins. *Cap*tain Wiggins." He squinted now, and shaded his eyes from the guardhouse light. "Wait—didn't you drive through here last—"

"Captain of a bunch of glorified night watchmen, Wiggins. And it's Lieutenant Branch and it's your job to know that. You know—and you know I know—that all private security personnel're required to attend orientation sessions at Rancho police headquarters—sessions that include meeting personally every member of the force. Maybe you thought being a *cap*tain you were exempt; but you're not exempt, *Cap*tain, and the reason isn't that we want to make small talk with you: we don't want to get shot by you if we happen to drive past your checkpoint in a civilian car on the way to an emergency." What the hell—might as well alienate everyone.

Wiggins rubbed his fingertips together as if the shield had been covered with something unpleasant. "Trouble somewhere on El Paso, Lieutenant? We monitor you. Haven't heard anything."

Branch pocketed the shield. "Officer Cooper handles liaison with private security personnel, Wiggins. I want to hear from him this afternoon that you were in touch with him this morning." He gunned the engine. "Who's been through here tonight?"

Wiggins reached into the guardhouse for a clipboard, but made a point of not looking at it. "A Mr. Milo to see Mrs. Beaufils. He was expected. Eighty-two Celica, light blue, state plates, county sticker, parking permits for Esperanza Beach, the Muni Golf Course, tourist decals from Disneyland, Sea World, Point Reyes, bumper sticker saying *I brake for yard sales*. Early fifties, five eight, five ten, one sixty, one seventy-five, a thing on his left cheek, like a birthmark. Blue suit, blue shirt, red tie. Balding, but doesn't try to hide it; brown hair, what's left of it. . . . Someone you're looking for—Lieu*ten*ant?"

Branch stepped on the accelerator, popped into drive and lurched away from the guardhouse. *Silence is the best repartee:* Oscar Wilde

Branch paused with a finger on the doorbell. The Celica was in the gravel driveway, the lights were on in two-thirds of the windows; sprinklers cha-chaed on the lawn, squandering the last of the Colorado River water—unless it was Perrier. Not a picture anything was wrong with—except, perhaps, for the Townsman, with its filigree of rust. But an emergency was an emergency, and if he'd moved with something less than haste until now, well . . . now was the time for emergency measures. He tried the doorknob, felt it turn, opened the door and went in.

Mozart was on the stereo in the living room; not emergency Mozart, something early, just this side of precious.

The music had no audience, although a book splayed face down on the sofa said that it had had: *The Jewel in the Crown,* notwithstanding her carelessness with its binding, Portia's favorite book—a quarter of it, actually; it was the first of a tetralogy—one she reread every couple of years. She had been reading it at the H el R, four and a half years earlier (was this only four and a half years later?); had she read it once in the interval, or twice, or . . .

Move, Branch!

He did—at the sound of a voice, Portia's, upraised, somewhere down one of the hallways that radiated from the entry foyer.

Door Number One, Door Number Two or Door Number Three? Who had said that to him only recently?

Oh, yeah: Eve.

Branch chose Two, moved along its wall for what seemed like a mile and came to a door that was open wide for anyone to walk in; he stayed outside, and in the shadows, hoping to see but not be seen. Not orthodox emergency procedure, but then . . .

"Mrs. B, Mrs. B, Mrs. B, I wish you wouldn't do this to me, I'm losing my patience, I'm wasting valuable time. I got a long drive ahead of me, all the way back to— Well, never mind that. I don't have time to, pardon my French, fuck around with you. You've had plenty of time to talk to your *p-people*—"

"I don't know what you're talking about." Portia: cool, a little weary, like someone who could use a few days in Ixtapa.

"Ah, come on now, Mrs. B—"

"Don't address me like that."

A laugh, with nothing but derision in it. "Lady, you're in no fucking position to tell me what to say or how to say it. I want to call you Mrs. B, I call you Mrs. B. I want to call you cunt-bitch-douchebag, I call you cunt-bitch-douchebag. I want, in fact, you should suck my cock, you better start limbering up your—''

Flesh against flesh, and Branch moved through the door. ''Portia.''

''Sam?''

''Who the fuck . . . ?''

''Put it away, motherfucker.'' Branch pointed at the Ruger .38 that had materialized in the man's hand; his pistol was in his shoulder holster—not emergency procedure at all, downright dumb.

The room was an interior decorator's idea of a library— shelves of leather-bound sets but not a single book you'd want to read, dark leather chairs, a heavy wooden captain's desk, Empire lamps that spilled pools of light around their feet and left their faces in shadow.

But there was enough light that Branch saw the trace of a smile on the man's face as the Ruger disappeared into his suit coat. ''I get it. This is the, uh, other guy, the guy's going get in your pants regular now that—''

Portia struck at the smile. The man caught her wrist and whirled her around to use as a shield against Branch's gun, which was finally in evidence.

''What do you say *you* put it away, pretty boy, seeing as how—''

Portia drove an elbow into his midriff and broke free as he bent over gasping, as if he had spat her out.

Still downright dumb, Branch relaxed and was altogether unprepared when the man came out of his crouch like a pulling guard and slammed into him hip-high, knocking the wind out of Branch and the gun from his hand.

Portia picked the gun up and shot the man twice in the back.

He turned and stared at her and his hand went inside his coat but no farther.

She shot him in the chest.

He flopped into one of the leather chairs, his elbows on

the arms, his chin in his chest, looking like a snoozing clubman but for the blood and the shattered fingers of the hand that had reached for the gun.

Branch got his breath back and moved his mouth, but nothing came out. He went to the man and felt for a pulse in his wrist, his neck. He turned toward Portia.

She was gone. The gun was on the big captain's desk, neatly centered on the blotter. Branch slipped it in his holster, where it felt twice as heavy with three chambers empty as it had when full.

Suddenly clever as clever, Branch took the Celica, having looked for the key and found it on a ring in the man's right coat pocket. He took El Paso to Gila, breaking asunder Wiggins's shout to stop, throwing him a left-handed salute, Gila to Mesquite to Calle Verde to Sequoia to El Centro to Rancho Maria de la Luz Boulevard. A hundred yards from the guardhouse at the entrance to the rancho, he stopped and backed the Celica into a parking space outside Tourneau. All the watches in the window said something different. He left the key in the ignition and walked to an alley that led to the parking lot behind the shops. The only cars in the lot were the heaps belonging to the cleaning people who worked nights in the bigger stores. He walked across the lot, through a scrim of Lombardy poplars and into the darkness.

21

So it was that the rancho became notorious, an adjective few of the newspapers and magazines that splashed the community's misadventures, the radio and television networks that trumpeted them, had the imagination to forgo—although a glance at *Roget's*, say, would have told their editors and writers that the synonym for disreputable, discreditable, dishonorable, unrespectable, ignoble, ignominious, infamous and inglorious wasn't apposite.

Nor was LOVE TRIANGLE SLAYING—the battle cry on the lips of the first wave of reporters to descend on Rancho Maria de la Luz from as far away as London, Tokyo and Sydney, lured by the scent of a Sodom-by-the-Sea—an emotionally or geometrically accurate metaphor. The man Lieutenant Sam Branch was alleged to have killed with his Smith & Wesson model 13 .357 magnum in the library of his ex-lover's palatial (always palatial) mansion was a total stranger, not his ex-lover's husband—who was already dead. (The killing of a lover's—ex or current—husband is, curiously, an act *Roget's* does not synonymize, listing *mariticide*—and *uxoricide*—among its "words in *-cide* referring to both doer or agent and deed," but not—to coin

174

a word badly in need of minting—*emulocide,* from the Latin *aemulator,* a rival.)

Uninhibited and unembarrassed about attempting to characterize a place with which they were thoroughly unfamiliar, the reporters bivouacked at the Del Rey, Las Brisas, the Holiday Inn; fanned out each morning in search of fresh dirt; regrouped for lunch at the Crash to pool what was commonplace, while each ferreted away something to keep his dispatch exclusive and his editors happy; returned there after filing their stories to drink and smoke and reminisce of other *crimes passionnels* they had covered, talking of Jean and Candace and Klaus and Doctors Sam and Carl with fraternal affection. Eventually, they got it straight, with particular help from Lyle Wiggins—*Cap*tain Lyle Wiggins—of the Argus Protection Agency, and Howard Maddox, guy Friday to the late founder, president and chief executive officer of Kallistos Enterprises.

Wiggins's refrain that Lieutenant Sam Branch of the Rancho Maria de la Luz Police had behaved curiously and disrespectfully to a fellow keeper of the peace was doggerel to the reporters, who had quickly anathematized the rent-a-cops who kept them from roaming willy-nilly during their search-and-destroy missions; his revelation that Branch had been making his second visit to the palatial Beaufils mansion in less than thirty-six hours, however, coupled with Officer Jeff Derry's testimony (before a county grand jury whose minutes were leaked by an assistant prosecutor to the press) that his partner hadn't mentioned the first visit at their rendezvous just after he had paid it, was a ditty they asked Wiggins to sing again and again.

Maddox needed no backup vocals: He had been in the palatial mansion, working late, and had taken a break from his labors in the office wing, whose bathrooms were being painted—a cosmetic job ordered long before Felix's death—to use one whose ventilating system made it an ideal if unintentional blind from which to eavesdrop on

conversations in the library. (Maddox took pains to point
out that in all his years with Kallistos, he had never known
Mrs. Beaufils to entertain a visitor there, for it was Felix's
retreat and reeked of his cigars—and, now, of their ghosts.)
He had overheard Mrs. Beaufils and the imminent victim
in heated discourse. Having missed the opening salvos, he
was unable to say just what was in dispute, but he *had*
heard both parties, at least once each, use the word
blackmail—Mrs. Beaufils in refusing to pay it, her adver-
sary in impressing on her the consequences of her failure
to. An attack of contrition sent Maddox scurrying back to
the office wing before Branch arrived, so he was not aware
of the argument's escalation and did not even hear the
shots—that soundproof office door.

The identification of Portia's antagonist as one Milo
Mularky (more than one reporter had to swear to his
editors that he hadn't made up the name), a/k/a Harry
Milo, Miles Harris and Harry Mills, age fifty-six, of Ojai,
and the determination of his métiers—loan shark, confidence man, weapons smuggler and agent for a professional
killer known only as El Bozo (for his youth, from the
Spanish for the down on adolescent chins)—put an end to
the need to conjecture:

Portia Beaufils and Sam Branch had negotiated with
Mularky to have Felix Beaufils murdered; when Felix died
in his singular fashion, Mularky saw an opportunity to turn
the apparent loss of a one-shot fee into a regular income;
Branch (whose blemished record was introduced into evidence) and Portia lured the would-be blackmailer into a
trap, and sprung it; Portia panicked and fled, leaving her
paramour to face the discordant music. Her canary-yellow
928S left a noisy trail that the Highway Patrol followed to
an airfield outside La Cienega, where she hangared her
Falcon; she was airborne within an hour of the gunplay,
cleared for a flight to San Francisco; she hadn't turned up
there, and might have gone anywhere at all on the Falcon's

two thousand miles' worth of fuel. Where Branch had gone (apparently on foot—at the start, at any rate, after taking, then abandoning, Mularky's car) was also anybody's guess.

To vary the menu, the reporters also wrote about the death during perverse rapture of another prominent citizen (Portia's doctor) and the murder of a foreigner who had a check for a million dollars in his pocket. But what they always came back to was not the death of Joseph Litvak or Patrick Wade or Milo Mularky, but of Felix Beaufils—came back to this delicious irony: Portia Beaufils had accidentally killed the husband she had plotted to have murdered.

"If Sam's got the cloud, I reckon I ended up with the silver lining." Rollie Ashburn brought Eve a hamburger and sat down across the aisle of the Crash's first-class cabin. "Business ain't ever been this good—all on account of his misfortune. I'm crying all the way to the bank."

"Sam's misfortune is his own doing," Eve said. "*Some-body should make a buck off it.*"

"If what you mean is him carrying a torch for Portia all these years—"

"What I mean, Rollie, is Sam didn't kill Mularky, and if he wants to take the rap for it, that's his goddamn business."

Ashburn looked up and down the aisle, but with the reporters skipping lunch in their scramble to keep the story from dying a natural death, Eve was his only customer. "Want to run that by me again?"

"Sam Branch did not kill Mularky."

Ashburn reached for one of her french fries. "Suppose you're going to say Portia did."

"Portia did."

Ashburn stopped the fry short of its destination. "Sam

handed her his piece, let her do his dirty work? Not
likely.''

"Sam dropped his piece in the struggle.''

"First I've heard of a struggle.''

"That's because you know only what you've read in the
papers and what you've read in the papers has been a lot of
unconscionable free association.''

"And you got the inside poop?''

"Nope. I just made it up.''

Ashburn snorted.

"Look, Rol, in my long experience as a journalist and a
homo sapien, I've arrived at one truth: things are usually
what they seem to be.''

"You want to try saying that another way?''

"Blackmailers don't kill their victims, they keep on
blackmailing them. So even if Mularky was packing heat,
he was no threat to Branch and Portia. Branch wouldn't
shoot to kill unless his life was in danger. Ergo: he didn't
kill Mularky, someone else did. The only someone else
was Portia. Since she did it with Branch's gun, he either
handed it to her, which as you said isn't likely, or he
dropped it and she picked it up. Branch doesn't have
butterfingers, so there must've been a struggle.''

". . . Well, how come Sam split?''

"I told you, Rol—he's taking the rap for her.''

Ashburn ate the fry, wiped his hands on a paper napkin,
then tore the napkin in two along the fold. "You told this
to anybody else?''

"Nope.''

"Any reason in particular?''

"People believe what they want, Rol. I'm no iconoclast.''

Ashburn put the halves together and tore them in two.
"Saw Annie Buck at the Crown station this morning.''

"You have any pecan pie?''

"She said you'd moved into Jeff Derry's place.''

"Not *in*to, next to. The hotels're full of reporters and

Jeff's neighbor's gone to Europe for a month. Gave me use of his car, too—a GTO. The radio plays nothing but surfer music. Did you ever notice that about radios, Rol? They play only what the owner wants to hear. Hispanic kids can get only salsa on their radios, black kids hip-hop and Motown, WASP kids MOR; radicals can get only National Public Radio, shut-ins call-in shows, golden agers stations that play Carlton Fredericks. Everyone's his own antenna.''

Ashburn lowered the tray from the back of the seat in front of him and sorted the pieces. ''You know, none of this is worth losing a friend over.''

''Annie needs to be by herself. Whether or not she thinks Sam's guilty, she has to deal with the fact that he *was* at Portia's—and had been the night before, as well.''

''What about you?''

''I'm fine. Oh, maybe I'll have coffee.''

''What I meant, young lady, is how're *you* dealing with the fact Sam was at Portia's?''

''I don't know what you're talking about.''

Ashburn smiled. ''Teddy Weymouth, runs Teddy's Taxi, told me the other morning one of his ole boys picked a woman up at Branch's place right around the time all the shooting was going on over to Portia's.''

''Hunh.''

''Said she was right stacked, the ole boy picked her up.''

''How nice for him.''

Ashburn went for coffee and brought one for himself. ''Being there at the time, I reckon you got an idea whether it's true Portia phoned Sam, like the papers've been saying.''

''Semi-true.''

''Meaning what?''

''Meaning *some*one called the cops and requested Lieutenant Branch's presence at Portia's place. It's on the record; the dispatcher played his tape for the whole world to hear. But admit it, Rollie, it's strange: a personalized call for help? RSVP? Regrets only?''

Ashburn balled up the pieces of napkin. "You going to tell me what happened, or am I going to beat you with a hot chain?"

Eve shrugged. "It's obvious."

"To you, maybe, being from a hotbed of intellectualism. But I'm just a country boy."

"It'll cost you a piece of pecan pie. Not a big piece—a very, very small piece."

"Whipped cream?"

"Hold the whipped cream— Well, maybe just a touch of whipped cream."

Ashburn brought out the whole pie and the container of whipped cream and let Eve cut her own and garnish it.

After she'd eaten some, Eve said, "What happened is, *Port*ia didn't call the cops."

"Portia didn't call the cops."

"*Port*ia didn't call the cops."

"I heard you, goddamn it. Well, who did?"

"That, Rollo, is the question." Eve lowered her head and finished the pie, then wiped her mouth with a napkin. "We do know, having heard the tape on countless newscasts, that the caller was a woman. Some of us felt it didn't necessarily sound like Portia, but others pointed out that she was under stress—and also was trying to talk so Mularky—God, can that be his name?—couldn't hear her, since he was in the house when she called, which we know from comparing the police dispatcher's log with the private guard's, and she'd probably excused herself on some pretext—"

"Voiceprints," Ashburn said. "If it wasn't Portia, they can do voiceprints to tell who it was."

Eve shook her head. "I mean, yes, they can do voiceprints, but voiceprints're like fingerprints: you have to have something to compare them with—*and* you have to be broad-minded enough to think that the guy who appears to be the murderer maybe isn't.''

Ashburn separated the pieces of napkin. "Mularky was expected by Portia. He didn't just drop in—" He stopped as Eve chuckled. "What?"

"Go ahead. You're onto something. . . . Go a*head*. It's free and it's fun."

". . . He didn't just drop in. His name—one of his aliases—was on the private guard's list, like you just said, because Portia called the guard saying he was expected. But if that's so, then why did she wait till after he got there to call Sam? Why, come to think of it, didn't she call Sam soon as she knew he was coming so Sam could lurk in the brush along El Paso or behind them trees up the drive to Portia's spread, could hide there and ambush Mularky before he even got to the house, bushwhack him with a gun he'd get rid of so nobody'd ever find it, so they'd call it a robbery or a nut case or whatever the hell they wanted to call it?" Ashburn laughed—"You're right, it *is* fun"—then tried to retrieve the laugh and maul it out of recognition. " 'Cept, of course, it ain't fun for Sam.''

"There's one more thing," Eve said. "If Portia *wasn't* expecting Branch, then how did he get in the house? She was leaving for Mexico in the morning and'd given the staff a week off. There was no maid or butler on duty."

"The cops said the front door was unlocked when they got there."

"And the papers've been speculating that Portia unlocked it. But if she *wasn't* expecting Branch, why would she, and who did?"

"Sam, maybe. When he left."

"Why would he do that?"

Ashburn shrugged. "Maybe they weren't too careful 'bout locking up out there."

"They were very careful. The butler swears to it."

Ashburn snapped his fingers. "Maybe Maddox unlocked it."

"Why would he do that?"

"Because . . ." Ashburn pinched the bridge of his nose, then shook his head. "Damn. I don't know why."

"It would make sense that Maddox unlocked the door only if he also made the phone calls purporting to be from Portia—or had someone make them."

Ashburn slapped the tray. "The servants. He had one of the maids make the calls."

Eve wrinkled her nose. "I thought of that, but the maids all have accents—and were either in their quarters or with friends or relatives. Their stories check."

Ashburn frowned. "Now how the hell can that be? I mean, if you're right that the cops haven't taken finger-prints or voiceprints because they think it's cut-and-dried that Sam killed Mularky, then why in the hell would they be checking servants' stories?"

Eve smiled. "They haven't. I have. . . . Well, Jeff and I, actually."

22

"P-press kit, Miss Zabriskie?"

"Brochure. Handout. Folder. Whatever you want to call it. You gave it to me the night of the party, remember? Your computer wrote it—anticipated most of my questions and answered them exhaustively."

Maddox touched the knot of his tie, a dowdy Johnny Carson. "Ah, yes. I'm afraid the-the-the-the—"

"I know. It's been chaos. No harm done. But now that things've quieted down, I thought I'd take a look at it. I left it in the office, I'm sure of it."

Maddox's feet, in beige Hush Puppies today, to go with his suit of iridescent brown, began their autonomic dance. "I-I-I—"

Eve gave him a smile of encouragement.

Maddox returned it, warped and listless. "I'm afraid the house is still a c-crime scene, as you can see from the police placards. They've asked me to see that nothing's disturbed."

"Howard, come on. It's a re*port,* not a love letter. It's in the office, not the library. That is where it happened, isn't it—in the library?"

"Y-yes—"

"Then what's the big deal? Look, if you want, I'll call Chief Strock, explain to him that I can't do my piece without it, ask him for a, uh, dispensation. Where's a phone I can use?"

Maddox looked around the entrance foyer of the Beaufils mansion as if he were a stranger there himself.

Eve started for the spiral stairs to the second floor. "Oh, never mind. I'll find one upstairs. I have to go to the bathroom." She got to the third step before Maddox headed her off, one hand on the banister, the other raised prohibitively. "*How*ard. Do you think I'm going to steal the linens?"

"Of c-course not. B-b-but—"

"I'm going to pop if I don't pee, How. *You* call Strock, tell him the situation, ask him *pl*ease can I have the stuff you gave me. I'll just be a sec." She patted the hand on the banister and got around him before he could say there were plenty of bathrooms on the ground floor. She took the stairs two at a time, made a left down the corridor to the master bedroom, found the bathroom door to be the second on the right, not the third as Jeff Derry had estimated, went in, locked the door and turned on the cold water tap. She listened at the door for a moment, heard nothing that sounded like Hush Puppies on marble, and went through the bathroom's other door into the master bedroom.

It was like being in the furniture department at Bloomingdale's, a place that always made Eve feel like a small child: If it could be overstuffed, it was; if it could have a twin, it did; all the colors were coordinated, all the motifs had echoes elsewhere; flounces, valances, drapes, sashes, things she didn't know the names of, abounded; there were more mirrors than in a fun house; everything looked very old and at the same time brand new; the bed, which was the size of some bedrooms Eve had been in, held dominion, yet appeared to have never been slept in, certainly not gamboled over. The only contemporary touches—they were as discordant as a college pennant would have been, or a lava lamp—were a stainless-steel trolley holding a television, a videocassette recorder and a shelf of cassettes, and the telephone, a danMark 2 in pearl gray; the trolley sulked in a corner, audibly silent; the phone had a side table all to itself, looking like an alien chieftain who has taken over the headquarters of a defeated race of aesthetes.

The phone was what she'd come for, and she was taking too long at her pretended emergency, but Eve couldn't resist a look at the books on the shelf of the phone's side table and piled on its distant twin—and at the videotapes. The books across the bed were the latest best-sellers by authors who wrote nothing but: Michener, Ludlum, Bach, Greeley, Jakes, Fast, Robbins, Wallace; they looked uncracked. The books beneath the phone were timeless and respectfully abused: *Green Mansions, Howard's End, A Farewell to Arms, In Patagonia, Winter Brothers, The Year of Decision: 1846.* Each had at least one marker in it, the last a dozen, strips from the pages of a notepad propped against one of a pair of fat lamps whose bases looked like Schmoos. Was it snobbism or feminism or a little of each that made her certain which side had been Felix's and which Portia's?

The store-bought tapes were recent movies that she guessed came, like the current books, from some mail-order club: *Yentl, Arthur, Falling in Love, On Golden Pond, Indiana Jones and the Temple of Doom, Tootsie, The Natural;* the only oddballs were *Purple Rain* and *Repo Man.* Some tapes had been used for bootlegging off television: on one were recorded, according to a tense handwriting that lacked the grace she would have expected of Portia's (again, she knew who had watched what), *The Americanization of Emily, The Jerk* and *I Know Where I'm*

Going; on another, *Three Days of the Condor, Caddy Shack* and *Walkabout;* on another, *Robin and Marian, The Graduate* and *Casablanca;* on another, *Some Like It Hot, The Late Show* and *Pennies from Heaven.*

Eve's stomach felt suddenly hollow and she told herself there was nothing to be afraid of, knowing that it wasn't fear she felt but jealousy. The movies Portia had pirated happened to be among Eve's favorites; they were litmus movies, movies she used to determine if someone had been alive and kicking in the last quarter of the twentieth century, or just going through the motions. That Portia thought enough of them to preserve them made Eve like her and hate her at the same time; she'd have liked to reminisce about them with Portia—about the rainy farewell in *Emily;* about Bernadette Peters saying she'd miss the stuuuuf; about Roger Livesey's incredible voice, "the old spy-fucker," Bill Murray's vendetta against the golf course gopher; about the Dreamtime; about Audrey Hepburn's ageless beauty (why wasn't she *Hepburn?*), Dustin's re- markable debut, the usual suspects, "Nobody's perfect"; about Lily and Art, about whatshername with the rouged nipples. And she'd have liked to kick Portia in the shins— and Branch, too, and warn them to never lay eyes on each other again if they didn't want to be eviscerated.

A mature reaction, and so appropriate to the circum- stances.

Maybe Portia hadn't recorded the movies at all; maybe they were cover for her collection of pornography.

Eve opened the first case and found inside a cassette with a handwritten label that said what the label on the outside of the case said. She opened two other cases, with the same result; the last case she opened was empty. She opened the VCR and found a tape inside—the tape of *Yentl.* Then what was in the *Yentl* case?

A tape with no label.

Eve put the tape in the big canvas shoulder bag she'd

brought for the occasion, feeling like . . . what? A sleuth, or a mistrustful parent?

She returned to the bed, unplugged the modular jack at the base of the phone and slipped the phone in the bag, covering it with a sweater she'd also calculated she would need. She went into the bathroom, shut the bedroom door, flushed the toilet and turned off the water. She took a look in the mirror, poked at her recalcitrant hair, and backed out into the hall—and into Maddox.

She screamed. "Jesus, Howard."

"I was be-c-coming concerned."

"Yeah, well. That doesn't mean you have to sneak up on a person, How." She saw the leather folder in his hand and snatched it away. "Oh, you got it. Thanks. I told you the chief would be understanding."

"I didn't feel it necessary to involve the ch-chief."

Eve ducked her head to tuck the folder in the canvas bag. "Of course it wasn't necessary. You're just such a goody-goody." She looked up and down the hall, like a childish conspirator. "How?"

Maddox looked pained at the nickname. "Y-yes?"

"Can I see the library? I won't touch anything, I promise. I won't even go inside. I just want to peek through the door. Please. *Please*."

"I'm afraid—"

"Oh, I know I can't. It's just that this is all so . . . well, kinky, isn't it?" She bent toward him suddenly and kissed his cheek. "Thanks, How. I've got to be going. No need to see me out." She clattered down the stairs, wishing she'd worn felony shoes instead of high-heeled boots, feeling a pain between her shoulder blades born of turning her back on a man she was sure one shouldn't.

Derry held the danMark 2 like a crippled bird. "I don't get it."

"It has a memory."

"You said that. I don't know what that means. You mean it's like a . . . a keepsake."

Eve laughed. "How quaint, Jeffrey. It means it remembers numbers you've called and can call them again. You call your hairdresser, right—or your broker; the number's busy, naturally; you don't want to have to push all those buttons again; so you just press this button and the phone automatically dials the last number you called; press *this* button and it dials the number before last; press this, *then* this, and it redials all the numbers you've called in sequence, up to ten numbers. Spiffy, no?"

Derry put the phone down on the dining table of his neighbor's bungalow, which Eve had made over into their command post, complete with charts and diagrams and lists of things to do. "Let's just slow down a minute, okay? We think someone pretending to be Portia called Mularky and the cops—called from outside the house. If we're right, what good is this phone, memory or no memory? The calls on it are Portia's calls, and they probably *were* to her hairdresser and her broker. And her dressmaker and her acupuncturist and her astrologer and—"

"Okay, Jeff, I know Portia's not your type."

"Furthermore, since you stole the phone it can't be used as evidence. *If* we'd been able to convince a judge the phone might be evidential, and *if* he'd given us a search warrant, then we might've been able to use it to support our case. Stolen, removed from the premises, well, it's no goddamn use at all. For all anyone knows, *we* might've dialed the numbers."

"We don't have a case, Jeff, and we're not conducting a formal investigation. We're flying blind, in very bad weather, with no radar and no help from the ground. Our only hope is that this'll land us somewhere where we can find somebody who'll tell us something we want to know." Eve tossed her hands. "Listen to me—using flying metaphors. You'd think *I* was Portia."

"Fuck Portia," Derry muttered.

Eve pulled out a chair and sat. "There's something I should tell you."

Derry waited.

"After Sam left, there was another phone call. I'd just called a taxi, so I answered, thinking it might be them saying the cab'd be there sooner than they'd said, or later. Whoever it was hung up. I'm sure it was Portia."

"So?"

"Come on, Jeff, don't play dumb. The gospel according to the newspapers . . . Well, you know what it is. It's ridiculous, but it has a large congregation. Here's what we're saying: *Some*one called Mularky and invited him to Portia's; that same someone called the private guard and the cops; after Mularky got there—this is the new part, Jeffrey, so pay attention—after Mularky got there, but before Sam got there, Portia *did* excuse herself and *did* make a call—to Sam, not to the cops—the call I answered."

"So?"

"So she called on this phone, the phone in her bedroom. Trust my woman's intuition: It's the only place a woman feels truly safe, inviolate. I don't know what excuse she gave and I don't know why Mularky bought it; I don't care if the bedroom's a quarter-mile from the library, and up a flight of stairs the size of a small Alp; I don't care if there're a half-dozen phones on the ground floor she might've used. She used this phone, which is why I want it to tell me whom it's been talking to lately. You must have a contact at the phone company. We need some kind of machine that can listen to the beeps and tell us what the numbers are. . . . Jeff?"

Derry had his back to her and was looking out the bungalow's window at the strip of Costa Chica beach visible between the bungalows across the street.

Eve got up and stepped close to him, but didn't touch him. "There's nothing to be jealous about."

"Well, what the hell were you still doing there at that hour?"

"At Sam's?"

"Yes, at Sam's."

". . . Talking. He'd had a rough night."

"Thanks to me, you mean?"

"You said what you had to, Jeff, and it was important that he hear it. . . . You weren't home yourself, you know."

He turned on her. "What do you mean by that?"

"I went by Annie's on the way to the Holiday Inn. Your car was there. Don't look at me like that; I wasn't spying. I couldn't stay with Annie, but I wanted her to know I was okay." Eve shrugged. "Okay, maybe I wanted her to know I wasn't at Sam's. So I had the taxi take me by her house. I didn't want to call because I knew she'd have the machine on and I didn't want to talk to the machine. I'd written her a note at Sam's and I wanted to leave it in her mailbox. You can skip right over a message on your machine, but it's harder to ignore a note. I don't know why that is: an electronic culture's guilt about having forsaken the written word or something—"

"Fuck you, Eve." Derry moved away from the window.

Eve stepped closer to study the reflection revealed to her by his doing so. "I feel the way Richard Burton did. He said if he had his life to live over again, he'd like to have a better complexion."

"Are you ever serious? Are you ever straight? Or is life for you just a string of one-liners?"

"I'm no better at life than anybody else, Jeff. And I'm no worse." She went to Derry and put her hands on his shoulders and squeezed the back of his neck. "Relax, Jeff. I was interested in Sam for a moment, sure, and you were in Annie. It's understandable: two people have a fight in front of witnesses and the witnesses know one thing for sure—two people're potentially available who weren't just

a few minutes before. It's in all of us to be curious about
what it would be like to be with someone new; it's our
shared character disorder—our national fear of commitment. Whether you and I can get it on remains to be seen;
I'm reluctant—a reasonable reluctance, I think—to sleep
with men I work with; it's not professional. We are working together, after a fashion. Let's get the job done, or do
the best we can, and then we'll see."

"You'll be going back to New York."

Eve heard his contempt for the place—and for her for
not saying that it was so. "I'm not a prisoner, Jeff. I was
when I worked for the paper; the weekly paychecks were
shackles. If I've kept on living there it's because it's what
I know. I'm not easy; I couldn't live just anywhere. But I
could get to like California. Hell, you should see me on
the Beltway: a county cop stopped me yesterday on my
way back from the city; when I said everyone else was
going as fast as I was, he said, 'Yeah, but you were
leading the pack.' "

Derry smiled and his neck felt less like iron. "What
were you doing in the city?"

"Picking someone up at the airport."

"Who?"

"I don't know if I want to tell you."

Derry turned to face her. "What the hell're you talking
about?"

Eve sighed, and from the drawer of a desk took the
magazine Fletch Hawkes showed her the morning of what
she still thought of as their horseback ride. It was her own
copy, actually, purchased at the 7 Eleven on the Beltway.
(She'd told the checkout girl it was for her brother, who
was hospitalized with a terminal disease.) "Page one twelve,
and following. The dark one."

Derry took a peek. *"What?"*

"Jeff, you're *blush*ing."

"Eve, for Christ's sake—"

"Her name—I swear to God and don't ask me to explain it all now—is Maria de la Luz."

Derry laughed.

"I swear to God."

"Maria de la Luz? There *is* a Maria de la Luz? *This* is Maria de—"

"Later, Jeff. First, let's see whom Portia's been calling."

23

Feeling the gun barrel's cold kiss, smelling its unmistakable musk, Escobar composed his own autopsy: *Gunshot wound from a small-caliber handgun fired from extremely close range into the back of the neck, leaving a sharply outlined circular hole surrounded by abraded skin altogether measuring one-third of an inch in diameter, the hole again surrounded by a halo of dense black and dark brown powder tattooing to a radius of one-third of an inch in width; entry wound between the second and third vertebrae, exit wound one-quarter inch above the thyroid notch.*

And the newspaper headline: CORONER KILLED FOR A QUARTER.

"I have no money, *amigo*. I am just now on my way to the bank. Come with me and I will give you money. But please don't kill me."

"Drive up to La Ermita, Ray."

". . . Sam?"

Branch slid back down behind the bucket seat of Escobar's Charger. "I can see you fine from here, Ray, so don't do anything stupid. When we get to the beach, pour some coffee from that Thermos of yours and make like you're

193

communing with the ocean before going to work. The lifeguards'll be on duty, but I don't think they'll be curious about someone talking to himself. They'll think you're a dirty old man waiting for the girls to show up. . . . How've you been?''

"Fine, Sam . . . And you?''

"A little tired. I wasn't sure how long the bus ride'd take, or when you left for work, so I got up real early.''

"A bus from the city? I'm not prying, Sam, It's just nervous chatter. You gave me quite a scare.''

"Is your bank in Rancho Maria, Ray?''

"There's a branch just north of La Ermita, in fact. *Mi dinero es su dinero*, you know that.''

"I don't want you making a big withdrawal. Someday, someone'd ask you about it. You know how that happens.''

". . . Of course I've read what the papers have been saying about your time in New York, Sam. It's not something that . . . civilians can understand.''

"And I heard a story about you in Miami. About you and a lot of teeth.''

". . . I don't understand, *amigo*.''

"Strock told me. Why did he tell me, Ray? It's never so much what people tell you as why. Why did Strock go out of his way to tell me about someone else's old sin? I find an embalming needle under Wade's bed. Strock collects embalming needles. If he killed Wade, he has to know it's missing. He knows it wasn't at Wade's . . . he was there. And he knows I didn't turn it in as evidence. Does he think I didn't find it? Does he think I found it and didn't think it meant anything and threw it away?'' Branch had been going around like this for days—around and down and down.

"I've been thinking a lot about Wade, Sam. He *was* asphyxiated. There's no question about that, and no indication that he was injected—not even with air, which might have produced an embolism. Perhaps the trocar was—this will amuse you, you whom I've accused of speculating too much, while contending that I confine myself to facts—perhaps the trocar was a symbol of some sort, left at the scene as a signature. . . . I've been asking around, too—quietly. There's an LAPD detective who's written a couple of articles in criminology journals about autoerotic asphyxia. I've been trying to contact him, without any luck; he was in Hawaii on vacation, then busy with work that'd piled up."

Branch had had the thought, in his first days of fugitiveness, of going to Hawaii—permanently; he'd grow marijuana and become a fruitarian and never talk to anyone again. Then he'd been reminded of the paradox that folks in out-of-the-way places are always suspicious of people out their way and that it is the city that is good ground for the anonymous, the eccentric, the inverse. No one asked any questions at the cheap hotel, which was disinfected and had a view of the navy yard; the work shirt and chinos for which he'd swapped his blazer, slacks and dress shirt at a pawnshop could be washed by hand in the sink and dried overnight on the fire escape; he could eat heartily for two dollars at the Harborside Diner (four blocks from the harbor) and see three movies for fifty cents at the Luxor Theater. And he liked the way his beard was growing in.

"By the way, Ray, I didn't kill Mularky."

Escobar smiled. "I knew that, Sam. The two wounds in the back had to have been inflicted before the chest wound, given that the victim was found seated in a chair and there was no sign that he'd been moved to it, but rather had fallen backwards into it. Either was fatal: one entered the victim's heart after penetrating the infraspinous fossa of the scapula; the other— Forgive me, Sam; this is irrelevant. The point is, you would never have fired the third shot, and probably not the second. Speculation of a high order, I confess. I didn't make it on the record; it wasn't called for. And I'm afraid it wouldn't stand up in court, if it comes to that, Sam, if your personal investigation doesn't bear fruit—but enough for me. . . . Here we are at La Ermita Beach. And as you said, there's no one here but the lifeguards. . . . What *are* you hoping to find out, Sam?''

Branch slid a little lower, slipping his gun into its shoulder holster and zipping the nylon windbreaker he'd bought for a dollar at a flea market. It was bright yellow and said WIDE WORLD OF SPORTS in royal blue letters on the back and he'd been right in thinking that it would efface its wearer. "I'm looking for a woman.''

Escobar paused in the act of unscrewing the top of his Thermos. "A woman? What woman?''

Lying on his sprung bed, watching the paint buckle on the ceiling, listening to the throb of the navy yard, Branch had run recent events over and over through his memory. One brief scene in the kitchen of the Beaufils mansion had proved unexpectedly popular:

What I'd like to tell the reporters, Sam, Strock had said, *about this Litvak, is who killed the son-of-a-bitch.*

The man he was looking for. Or the woman.

To keep Litvak from forcing the million dollars on him?

Or her. Maybe he doesn't want people to know who he is. Maybe he's not who his friends and neighbors think he is. Maybe he'd rather they didn't find out who he is.

Or she.

Branch spoke deliberately. "Portia was surprised to see me the other night, too surprised for it to have been she who called headquarters and asked for me—which she wouldn't've done, in any case; she'd've called me directly; it wasn't her way to go through channels. But a woman did call, saying she was Portia. Who? I don't know. Why? Because I think she wanted me to find Portia and Mularky together.'' He accelerated a little to keep Escobar from interrupting. "I didn't know Mularky, but he was known by cops—in the city or the county if not in the rancho. So if I'd started asking around—he had that birthmark on his face—it wouldn't've taken long to find out he arranged contract murders and to infer that Portia'd been negotiating for one. Whose? Felix's? Felix was dead, making killing him redundant—and precluding any payment. So they weren't talking murder; they were talking blackmail. . . .

"That's the way it looked. But what if that wasn't the way it was? The woman who called headquarters: What if *she* was the one who'd wanted Felix killed? What if *she* was the one Mularky was blackmailing? What if she was only trying to make it *look* like Portia was the blackmail target, and therefore the murder-for-hire client—make it look like that to me, that is? To make it look like that to me, she had to make it look like that to Mularky, too, who presumably knew whom he'd been dealing with. Therefore, he hadn't been dealing with the woman; he'd been dealing with an intermediary, an intermediary who lured him to Portia's by saying that murder was murder, but blackmail's serious business, he'd better talk directly to the boss, which is who Mularky thought Portia was.

"It's not so farfetched; it's the script the papers've been pitching, with Portia and me in the starring roles. I'm just recasting it to make it a little more credible, if less box-office. The point was that both Mularky and I think Portia was behind the plot to kill Felix. All I had to do to think it was to *see* Portia and Mularky together, not necessarily confront them. That's why the door was unlocked. The front door was unlocked, Ray—because Portia was expecting me, the papers've been saying. But she wasn't expecting me."

Escobar heard that the pause invited catechization. "I'm sorry, Sam. I've lost you. Did this . . . this woman unlock the door? To do that, she'd've had to be in the house."

"Mularky stuttered, Ray. Just once. He told Portia to stop wasting his time. He said he had a long drive ahead of him, and almost said where to. Ojai, we now know. He said"—Branch tipped his head back and shut his eyes, the better to get into the part—" 'I don't have time to, pardon my French, fuck around with you. You've had plenty of time to talk to your *p-people*. . . .' "

"I'm sorry, Sam. I still don't—"

"He said it unnaturally. With emphasis. As though he were imitating someone."

". . . Howard Maddox?"

"He's a born intermediary, don't you think?"

Escobar shook his head. "It doesn't make sense. So you hear Portia arguing with Mularky. Then what?"

"As I just said, I find out who Mularky is, I put two and two together, I nail him and Portia for conspiring to murder Felix."

"Pardon me, Sam, but I thought you were supposed to be Portia's lover."

"Not in this scenario. In this scenario, I'm Portia's *ex*-lover; I'm jealous; I'm looking for revenge. Maddox, the woman, their people—they never imagined anyone would kill Mularky; the killing was an unexpected bonus; when he was handed it, Maddox threw the script away and improvised. From what I read in the papers, he was brilliant—pinning half the allegedly overheard conversation on a dead man and half on a woman who took it on the lam."

"Why would Maddox want Felix killed?"

"Why does anyone want anyone killed? Money. Power. Love. Maybe Maddox was in love with Portia. Maybe he was thirsty. Maybe Felix took away his water cooler to use on his grapes. Anyway, I'm not saying Maddox was acting on his own; maybe there *were* people."

"And they are?"

"I don't know."

"And who's the mysterious woman?"

"I don't know."

"Portia *did* kill Mularky, Sam. You're not denying that?"

"No."

"Why, Sam?"

"I don't know why."

Escobar sipped his coffee, which had grown cold. He tossed it out the window and refilled the cup from the Thermos. "Would you like some of this, *hermano?*"

"No, thanks." Branch had found that one imperative of life on the run was that you not drink too many liquids; there weren't as many toilets available as there were to the unsuspected.

"But you do want something—something from me."

"I want you to go to Strock's house and see if you can tell if he's missing an embalming needle."

Escobar laughed. "Forgive me, Sam. But this is all so . . . so melodramatic. And so without focus. You suspect a *wom*an of some complicity in a plot to murder Felix, but Felix, I needn't point out, wasn't murdered. And now you want me to determine whether Strock is missing the trocar that *wasn't* used to kill Patrick Wade. I'm sorry, but this is speculation of the *high*est order."

And delivered from the floorboards of a car to someone who was pretending he wasn't talking to you. It would merit a separate chapter in his memoirs. "It all fits together, Ray. Not the pieces I have, but I don't have all the pieces. . . . Strock's gone up the coast to answer his subpoena in the S and M investigation. He doesn't have servants, or a dog. You can walk right in—anytime after midnight, I'd say; most of his neighborhood's asleep by then."

Escobar laughed. "Walk right in, Sam? I'm afraid picking locks isn't one of my skills."

Branch took out his keys and slipped one off its ring and handed it over the seat. "I think this is the front door, although it may be the door from the garage. I don't have any idea where in the house he might keep his collection. Don't forget to look in the basement."

Escobar studied the key as if it were the key to more than a door. "If *I'm* right, Sam—if perhaps someone did plant a trocar in Wade's room to make it seem as though Strock, the collector of trocars, dropped it there . . . Well, then, who would that have been?"

"I suppose you're a suspect, Ray, since you're a collector of trocars, too."

Escobar turned to look down at Branch. "You say it with seriousness in your voice, so I must respond seriously, and not be offended. . . . I did not do such a thing."

Branch nodded. "That's good to know, Ray. It's a piece I can throw away; I've got to get rid of all the pieces that don't belong."

Escobar turned forward and dropped the key in the pocket of his suit coat. "To the bank, Sam?"

"And then to someplace where I can get out. Quintana would be good. There's that park down by the harbor. I can catch a Greyhound in town."

"Where to, Sam? Or would you rather not tell me?"

"To L.A., just overnight. I want to talk to that LAPD detective. I don't want you asking questions that might get you in trouble."

"Sam, be reasonable. The risk you're taking now is one thing; to walk into a station house in Los Angeles, posing as—what?—a journalist? Your face is on posters, Sam. The beard makes a difference, but not a great difference."

Branch had seen too many faces that looked nothing like the faces on posters to think it risky to walk into a station house, where faces on posters rarely came under their own power. He also knew the power of a free meal. "I'll call first and invite him out to lunch. With any luck, I shouldn't have to show any ID. So many reporters're slobs these days, I won't even have to apologize for my clothes."

Escobar shrugged. "His name is Kaplowitz."

"Kaplowitz."

"Lieutenant Kaplowitz. I didn't get a given name. The journal articles were signed F. Kaplowitz."

Branch stretched his legs as Escobar backed up the Charger. "I also want to mail a letter to my kids. I want them to know I'm okay and sorry I spoiled their vacation plans, but I don't want a postmark from around here."

"I am sorry, *hermano*, about your children."

"Yeah." Somewhere Branch had heard a story about a wife Escobar had left behind (along with those teeth) on the midden of his past. He didn't know if there were children and he didn't ask—not out of discretion but out of something like pique. No—that wasn't it; he was uneasy about what Escobar wasn't asking him. And about something he'd found under the passenger seat—another small rectangular packet, an inch by half an inch, of brown transparent paper containing something that smelled like mint. Like the one he'd found on Strock's doorstep and had buried, along with the trocar, in a waterproof pouch in a Carr's Table Water Crackers tin in a hole at the base of his weeping willow.

24

Annie Buck drove like hell, lately. The danger kept her mind off her neglect of her children, her housekeeping, her hair. Cops didn't chase her, although she didn't slow down at speed traps on the freeway and ran every yellow light—and a couple of reds—that confronted her in the city; perhaps their computer checks of her license plate came up with the warning that she was a virago with a grudge against policemen and was better left alone.

Warren Cable's secretary didn't try to stop her, either, when she strode through the foyer of Southland Hydro's penthouse suite and shouldered open the big oak door. But then, she was expected—although probably not in jeans and running shoes and a souvenir T-shirt from a conference of feminist executives: 20 YEARS OF WOMEN ON TOP.

"Why, Miss Buck." Cable tossed aside some thick report and pressed his fingertips together under his chin.

Annie sat in one of his Breuer chairs, took a cigarette from her bag and rummaged for a matchbook.

He leaned across the desk and flicked a flame from a lighter shaped like a mermaid. "I didn't know you smoked, Annie."

That was another risk she was taking. "I have ten minutes, Warren." She looked at her watch. "Eight minutes."

Cable read the inscription on the T-shirt while trying to appear not to. "I want you to know, Annie, that I'm sorry about what's happened. It's shocking, just shocking. Lieutenant Branch—"

"Seven minutes."

Cable put his fingertips together again, pressing them hard this time, until he had himself under control. "You're aware that prior to these, uh, unfortunate developments, I had extended an offer to Mrs. Beaufils to sit on Southland's board—"

"In exchange for her disbanding the dam committee, yes. The committee will have its regular meeting a week from tomorrow. At the Renford, if you'd care to attend. It'll be dull stuff—electing a successor to Felix."

Cable slammed his hands on the desk. "Damn it, Annie, why won't you listen to reason? You can meet till hell freezes over. Without a realizable alternative to the existing aqueduct infrastructure there's nothing to be gained from *meetings*. This is a time for action. We don't *have* much longer."

Annie knocked the ash off the cigarette. "Did you know Pat Wade was my client, too?"

Cable's fingertips came together momentarily, then flicked here and there over his watch, his cuff links, his sapphire stickpin—taking inventory of his assets. "Oh?"

"That's hardly the word. Doctors don't have much use for lawyers. But I did do his will."

". . . I see."

"What do you see?"

"I'm not sure. Why're you telling me this?"

"He asked me to."

Cable laughed. "From beyond the pale?"

"So to speak. He named me his executor, in the course

of which duty I've just been to his bank, clearing out his safe-deposit box. One of the items in it is a letter addressed to you.''

"Indeed?" Cable cocked his head reminiscently. "I didn't know Dr. Wade all that well. We played doubles once or twice at the Racquet Club, and had drinks afterwards. I had no need of his specialty myself, of course"—he laughed—"but my wife consulted him, I believe, before our, uh, parting of the ways and her return to—where was it she was from? Ah, yes—Indiana.''

"A brave admission, since I'm sure you've heard the rumors about Dr. Wade's predilection for intimacy with his patients.'' She was catching his diction. "There're three copies of the letter. As instructed, I've read the copy addressed to me; I'm delivering the one addressed to you; and I'm on my way to deliver the third to the *Times-Ledger*, per his instructions. I've taken the liberty of making another copy, which is in a safe place.''

Cable leaned his elbows on the desk, a poker player ready to check and raise. "And may I see *my* copy?''

Annie sprung the latches on her briefcase and took out a stiff business envelope. She hefted it momentarily, then tossed it on the desk. "His handwriting's quite crabbed. I can save you trying to decipher it.'' She knocked the ash off the cigarette into a crystal ashtray and recited from memory. "April ninth, a Wednesday, ninety-five thousand dollars, payable to the Banque Romande, Zurich. April eleventh, a Friday, one hundred eighty thousand dollars, ditto. April fifteenth, a Tuesday, two hundred eleven thousand dollars, again ditto. May seventh, a Wednesday, six hundred thousand dollars; May ninth, a Friday, three hundred fifty thousand dollars; May thirteenth, a Tuesday, two hundred forty thousand. Wednesday, June fourth, five hundred eighty thousand; Friday, June thirteenth, one hundred ninety-five thousand; Tuesday, June seventeenth, two hundred forty-six thousand. Wednesday, Friday, Tuesday—like clockwork. Two million, six hundred ninety-seven thousand dollars. And that's just that one account. The Thursday-Thursday-Friday account totaled two million, four hundred sixty-six thousand, five hundred eighty-five dollars. My son has a Macintosh; it not only did the addition, it has a program—my son wrote it—that tells you the day of the week for any date—past, present or future. What's your birthdate? I can tell you what day of the week it was.''

Cable finished reading the letter, holding it up to catch the light, then folded it and returned it to the envelope. ''I'm afraid I don't see the import of this, uh, document.''

''The *im*port, Warren, is that you wanted the *damn* committee out of your hair, and knew that one way— perhaps the only way—to do it was to ruin Felix. You didn't murder him, but you did the next—''

''Felix wasn't murdered.'' Cable laughed, as if he'd been waiting for *his* chance to say it and had thought it might never come.

Annie ground the cigarette out. ''What you did's no crime. It was your money. But the ethics and morality leave something to be desired. I'm sure the *Times-Ledger* will agree.'' She closed her briefcase and stood up.

''Sit a moment longer, Annie.'' Cable looked at his watch, an Audemars Piguet Royal Oak. ''You owe me thirty more seconds of your time.''

Annie stayed standing, feeling suddenly vulnerable in her smart-ass T-shirt.

Cable centered the envelope on his desk and kept a protective hand near it as he spoke. ''I'm no fool, Miss Buck. Of course I understand what this letter implies—that Southland invested money in Moneda, then withdrew it systematically so as to put the fund in jeopardy of bankruptcy. I can tell you quite simply that it's not so. These sums bear no resemblance to the investment transactions we regularly make. There's no way on earth that we could juggle such enormous quantities of money and not have the sleight-of-hand come under public scrutiny.'' Cable got up and went to the window, which had a view of Japan. ''I'd heard rumors about Moneda's difficulties even before Felix's death. It comes as no surprise to hear it alleged that Southland might have conspired to instigate those difficulties—although I must say the, uh, source was unexpected.'' He turned toward her; backlighted, his face was difficult to read. ''Where *did* Dr. Wade get this information—and who was *his* source?''

Annie's breath was short and her thighs were trembling. She'd expected feigned ignorance or abject denial—not studious indifference; Cable might as well be wondering how a fly had infiltrated his aerie.

Cable turned back to the window. ''No, of course you don't know. You're only his executor, not his . . . confidante. Do you think it's possible, Miss Buck—or rather, don't you think it's entirely likely—that his *source* was someone very close to Felix, either inside Moneda or . . . in his bed? You alluded to Wade's fabled cocksmanship—forgive me, but I think it's time to get crude. Do you think it's possible—or rather, don't you know for a virtual certainty—that Wade was fucking Portia, that she found she liked it more than occasionally, that she entered into negotiations with this underworld character, Mularky—hah!—to have Felix exterminated, and that she contrived to embezzle money from Moneda both for her own gain and to cast suspicion on, say, Southland, in the hope that it—we—*I*—would appear to have been not only the catalyst for the fall of the Beaufils empire but the instigator of his demise?'' He laughed and faced her again. ''Such conjecture is endemic in the media these days. I'm afraid I'm a victim of the contagion.''

''Meaning you know it's not true?'' Annie's voice was thin, girlish.

Cable came at her like a priest, all unction and busyness. ''You did the right thing, Annie, coming to me first.

I fully understand your acting out of anger, and I'm not about to be so petty as to ask for an apology. Let's work together to find out who's behind this. It's the least we can do for Felix.''

Or was it a spider he was? For she felt ensnared by his deft web, like gossamer yet as tough as braided steel. "What . . . ? Who . . . ?"

"Let's meet again in a few hours." Cable had his hand on her back and was moving her toward the door. "At two, say. At your office. I'll bring something I think will shed light on the matter—a rather blinding light, I fear."

And she was in the foyer, and he was backing into his office, whispering reassuringly as the oak door clicked shut that everything would be fine, that time was on their side.

Time? Was it even a factor? Time didn't exist in southern California; with its handmaidens, History and Tradition, and its Daughter, Truth, it had been paved over.

25

Derry's contact at the phone company was a redhead with whom he'd clearly *had* contact. Eve wanted to shove the danMark 2 up her short yellow skirt.

On the other hand, she did the favor Derry asked with alacrity and hovered only a little while before leaving them with the list of numbers and names.

"You see?" Eve said. "Her last call was to Branch. It would've been just after he'd left, just like I said. When I answered, she hung up. I don't want to brag, Jeff, but it was brilliant of me to think of this. And there's no call to the police, just like I said. . . . And the other calls—she didn't talk much, for a jet-setter: All-City Limo: she wanted a car to take her to the airport for her trip to Mexico . . . Elizabeth Arden: she wanted some of her specially brewed suntan lotion . . . Her father: she's a devoted daughter . . . Eugene Marston? Area code five one six? That's Long Island. Who the hell is Eugene Marston on Long Island and what is he to Portia?"

"He's Leah Marston's husband," Derry said.

"Another old girlfriend, Jeff?"

Derry smiled. He'd noted Eve's displeasure with the redhead, and enjoyed it. And he enjoyed knowing something she didn't. "Leah Marston is Joseph Litvak's sister."

". . . Holy shit."

Derry shut his eyes, which was what Branch sometimes did when trying to figure out what things meant. All he saw were swirls of green on black.

"Do you think the phone company has a videocassette player?" Eve said.

Derry opened his eyes. "What?"

"Do you think the phone company has a—"

"I heard you, Eve. Goddamn it. I meant, *why?*"

"I have a tape I want to look at. I found it in Felix and Portia's bedroom."

"The way you found the phone?"

"The phone paid off, didn't it? They had a bunch of cassettes, some prerecorded movies, some movies recorded off the tube. The cassettes're in cases, cardboard cases. One of the movies was *Yentl*. God, *Yentl*. The cassette of *Yentl* was in the VCR, but there was some other tape in the *Yentl* case. A tape with no label. I took it."

"Why?"

Eve shrugged. "Because there was one more tape than there were cases. Because my father's a cop. Because I like playing shamus. I don't know why."

"You have it with you?"

Eve patted her bag.

"Let's see it."

Eve found the cassette and handed it to him.

"Were the other tapes this brand—BASF?"

"Only a man would notice a thing like that, Jeff. Why?"

Derry put the cassette back in her bag. "There's an electronics store across the street. I bought my stereo there. I know a guy. I'll meet you at the elevator; I just want to say goodbye to Torry."

"I hate women with names like that—Torry . . . Casey . . . It turns men on, I know, but—"

"Eve?"

"I know—shut up. Why the sudden interest in video? Shouldn't we be calling Leah Marston?"

"BASF is the brand Pat Wade used."

". . . Holy shit."

A woman, dressed in a long white lab coat, a pair of reading glasses on her nose, a stethoscope around her neck, a rubber hammer threaded through one buttonhole, stood by an empty bed, made up with only a maroon satin sheet, looking at a chart on a metal clipboard. There was the sound of music—Pachelbel's Canon in D. After a beat, a nurse entered. Tall and broad-shouldered, she moved awkwardly in her white heels and short white skirt. She wore a cowled headdress and in her hands carried a tray of surgical instruments, which she held out for the doctor's inspection, kowtowing.

"I've finished sterilizing these, Doctor."

The doctor looked up angrily. "Can't you see I'm busy?"

The nurse backed toward the door. "I'm sorry, Doctor."

The doctor removed her glasses. "Patsy, wait."

The nurse stopped, but kept her eyes downcast. The doctor went to her and put a hand on her shoulder. "I'm sorry I was short, Patsy. It's been a long day."

"The episiotomy was beautiful, Doctor."

The doctor smiled appreciatively and held her more intimately. "It turns you on, doesn't it, Patsy, to see me working . . . down there like that?"

The nurse looked at the doctor adoringly. "I love you so much, Doctor. I ache for you."

The doctor touched the nurse's breasts. "I've always known that, Patsy."

They kissed, letting the tray of instruments, the glasses and the clipboard fall to the floor with a clatter. When they finally broke, the doctor stepped back and unbuttoned her lab coat, revealing that she wore nothing underneath but a gold chain around her waist. "Look at me, Patsy."

Patsy barely dared to lift her eyes. "You're so beautiful, Doctor."

"Patsy?"

"Yes?"

"I want you to hurt me, Patsy. I want you—" Patsy started to protest, but the doctor slapped her across the mouth. "You will do as I say, young lady!"

As Patsy cowered, the doctor slipped off her coat, tossed it aside and lay down on her back on the bed. "Pick up the instruments and put them on the table." The nurse hesitated and the doctor kicked her in the thigh with a spiked heel. "On the table, Patsy!"

The nurse did as she said.

"The scalpel, Patsy. Pick up the scalpel."

"Hey."

Derry leaned forward and shut off the tape. "Let's go."

"Je-e-e-ff."

Derry went out of the video department and across the showroom floor and out into the street. He walked to the curb and inhaled the fumes of a bus that was pulling away. He held his breath as long as he could, hoping to induce some hallucination that would expunge the image of Aura Quivers and Patrick Wade at play. So the doctor had had a *Q* in his alphabet soup.

He startled as Eve touched his arm. "Now what?"

"Now we go to Strock."

"Uh, I don't think so. The night Felix was—the night Felix died, I overheard a conversation. The mayor's also fucking the chief. I thought it might be common knowledge, but your face says otherwise. . . . For him, she wears gloves. Lace gloves."

26

"I know that look on your face, Mr. Samuels. You're thinking, 'Funny, she doesn't *look* Jewish.' "

Mr. Samuels, né Branch, laughed. "The people who suggested I call you managed to avoid pronouns. And I don't think they had a clue about your, uh, ethnicity."

Lieutenant Kaplowitz of the Los Angeles Police Department was the punch line to the joke about the guy who tells his friend he visited Heaven and had a talk with God. Tell me about it, the friend says, and the guy says, "Well, first of all, she's black."

And a fox. Six two, with a figure and face like a fashion model and a voice like Tina Turner's. She turned the heads of the expatriate New Yorkers at Joe Allen's, where she'd suggested they eat when she heard Samuels was a free lance based in New York.

Kaplowitz spread her elbows on the table and laced her fingers together, a born storyteller. "I started life with a good slave name—Martha Washington. I was Muslimized in college and changed my name to Fatima Rashad. Four years ago, I was on a SWAT team at a hostage situation in Anaheim. Two bloods were holding the owner and three

212

customers of a jewelry store they'd fucked up the act of trying to knock over. They demanded a million dollars, a plane to Libya and cheeseburgers and fries from a Burger King across the street. God help the black people of this country. I dressed up in a waitress's uniform, delivered their junk food and smoked 'em. . . . I got to know the jeweler. Lou Kaplowitz.''

That explained, as well, the gold rings on every finger, the ruby necklace and the wristwatch with a sapphire stem.

Kaplowitz sat back and put her hands in her lap, as if suddenly self-conscious about the rings. "So you're writing about the goings on down in Rancho Maria de la Luz, Mr. Samuels. Writing for whom, did you say?'' She eyed his Wide World of Sports jacket.

Branch tried to remember the name of the magazine Eve was writing for, and realized it had never come up, in which case free-lancers must be pretty footloose. "Several magazines're interested. I'm waiting for the best offer.''

"And you said someone down there mentioned my work. Who?''

"All I can say is it's someone who knows your work and thought it might be of interest to me.''

Kaplowitz turned the stem of her wineglass between her fingers. "I've done several articles about serial murders—consecutive killings by a single perpetrator over an extended period of time. They're not to be confused with mass murders—the McDonald's killings, say, or the Texas tower. Interestingly, this cop, Branch, down in Rancho Maria, was involved in a serial murder investigation in New York. But you probably know all about that.''

He filled his mouth with chef's salad, and nodded.

"Since January of eighty-one, at least ten people in California have been killed in circumstances that were arranged to look like incidents of autoerotic asphyxia. From what I've read, one of the deaths in Rancho Maria was such a case.''

Branch swallowed. "The coroner's verdict was that it was an accident. But there may have been a motive for murder."

"It's a clever choice of MO. Every year, between five hundred and a thousand people die of sadomasochistic self-strangulation. Most of them are teenaged boys, typically outwardly well-adjusted kids who discover that some normal teenage pastimes that cause breathlessness—riding on a roller coaster, say—also trigger strong erotic feelings. The easiest way to combine the two sensations is to choke themselves while masturbating.

"Most coroners have never seen a case; most parents have never even heard of it. There may be as many as two or three times the number of known cases that never get reported. Many of those that are are misdiagnosed as suicides—either through ignorance or intentionally; it's easier for some parents to bear the social stigma of having a son who hanged himself than of having one who was trying to have some perverted fun.

"Occasionally, a boy will have a mentor—an older man, usually a sociopath and a student of serious erotica: Sade, Burroughs, that crowd—who teaches him the, uh, pardon the expression, ropes. A couple of times, a mentor has been charged with homicide, but in only one case that I know of has it been made to stick; the guy was in the room at the time and didn't intervene.

"I said it was a clever MO and all of this is why: autoerotic asphyxia's arcane; it's stigmatized; it's hushed up. The few pathologists and criminologists who're familiar with it see it—when they see it—for what they know it to be. They don't think murder. The ten cases I mentioned have one characteristic in common that makes them different from the stereotype: none of the victims was a teenager. They were all men in their thirties and forties and none—according to family and friends, at any rate—had any previous history of sadomasochistic behavior. I gather that was true of your Dr. . . . Wayne, wasn't it?''

"Wade. And yes." She hadn't been talking loudly, but her throaty voice cut through the room's cacophony, and Branch felt everyone inclining toward them, having put on hold their conversations about casting calls and pilfered concepts. "Where were these murders?"

"Three were up north—Fort Bragg, Santa Rosa, Sacramento. One in Merced, one in Bakersfield. Five in the Los Angeles area, which is how I came to be involved with them. Two of those five were in West Hollywood, one in a rural area near Malibu called Solstice Canyon, two in the suburb of Manhattan Beach— Did I say something interesting, Mr. Samuels?''

"Manhattan Beach is interesting."

Kaplowitz nodded. "Because of the sex ring the cops busted up. There's a connection. One of the victims, a prominent local realtor, was on the periphery of the ring. That is, he frequented a prostitute who sometimes helped the madam out of an overbooking situation by taking on a customer for a little . . . light whipping, as she called it. Whores get very upset when you suggest they're into anything perverse, and she's adamant that that's the farthest it ever went. The point is, the gentleman who hired her for more ordinary activities may've gotten a whiff of her sideline. Some of my colleagues theorize that he was in love with the girl and couldn't stand the thought of her doing anything kinky; he got too noisy about his disapprobation and the madam had to have him shut up. I don't buy that: she wouldn't've approved a method that called attention to her activities; I think he got curious and ended up getting to know a man who was involved in autoerotic activities and who happened to be a killer. . . .

"The other Manhattan Beach victim bore many similarities to your Dr. Wade, who videotaped his exploits, didn't he? He was a respected professional—a lawyer, active in community affairs, and a sexual athlete with a long list of conquests; he didn't use video, he kept a diary, which he occasionally illustrated with Polaroid snapshots. . . . The two Manhattan Beach victims and one of the West Hollywood victims died by variations on the theme. They wore women's underwear and had collars around their necks of the sort you can buy at shops that cater to people who like some pain in their pleasure. They were asphyxiated, but they'd also had air injected into their veins with empty hypodermic needles, probably while they were choking to death and unable to resist. . . . You look a little pale, Mr. Samuels.''

Because his lucky streak unnerved him a little, but more than that because across the crowded room he'd just spied Jeff Derry, with a woman on his arm who wrenched attention away from Kaplowitz and her delicious anecdotes, for she was one of those women who seem to be not wearing clothing as much as shedding it. Her beige linen suit was modest enough for a nun's mufti, but underneath, the action was all carnal. A step behind them, like a duenna, was Eve.

27

Derry reached for the brim of his Dodger cap, but of course he didn't have it on. He had put away childish things since taking on the job—nay, the duty—of escort for Maria de la Luz.

She called herself Petulia Corazón now (adding to the pseudonym given her by *Goddess* magazine a surname of her own devising), and she was . . . well, in the words of the *Goddess* pictorial (words Derry had memorized), "a dusky latin whose doe eyes ask of every man if he's really the man he thinks he is. This sultry *señorita* makes no apologies for her demanding nature: 'I'm not satisfied with just one orgasm when I make love. If a man can't give me at least three, I ask myself, "What's his hurry? Is there someplace he has to be that's more interesting to him than in my arms, between my thighs?" ' "

Derry could imagine no place more interesting, for the moment, than at her side, although it pained him to think of all those who had been elsewhere. Notwithstanding his efforts to examine his life, he entertained, as do so many men, the neurotic wish that every woman be that oxymoron the experienced virgin—someone who'd been around, but only on a small scale, and who would blossom under his ministrations. Not only was Maria (Derry thought of her as Maria) not a virgin, she had spread those "willowy limbs to the ardent caresses" (*Goddess*'s prose) of another woman on the pages of a national magazine and, she matter-of-factly recounted when pressed for her curriculum vitae, had appeared, as well, in a number of pornographic movies. (She called them, not in search of exculpation but to be clear, "soft *equis*," meaning that she had not been penetrated—or at least not on camera.)

Derry had looked into those doe eyes for the first time—in real life—on the doorstep of One Loma Largo, *chez* Hawkes, where Eve had taken him after their peek into the closet of Mayor Aura Quivers and Dr. Patrick Wade. On the way, she'd tried to prepare him for her latest surprise:

"Once upon a time, her mother worked for the Hawk-eses—before the rancho even existed. Maria was like a daughter to them, and a baby sister to Portia. When Fletch—when Admiral Hawkes—was taken prisoner in North Vietnam, Mrs. Hawkes had a breakdown, and got rid of all her servants. Maria's mother moved to the city and worked for some rich folks there for a while, but she got caught in an immigration crackdown and was deported—but not before she managed to hide Maria with some friends. So-called friends. The man of the house was a child-abuser and Maria was U.S. Prime. To get away from him, Maria hit the streets—hard. Drugs, prostitution, small-time larceny—she was an adept. . . .

"The Admiral was released, Mrs. Hawkes came out of her neurasthenia, the rancho was being built, and the whole family wanted the de la Luz women back. Portia went looking for them. She found the mother in Mexico, dead of shame—she'd heard about Maria's new life-style—and tracked Maria down in San Ysidro. They got her into an expensive drug clinic for a while, but she was hooked on the underworld. When she went down again, it was for

the last time—or so the Hawkeses thought: they got word
that Maria was dead. So the name was meant to be a
memorial, and a reminder to the Hawkeses of the limitations of their largesse. . . .

"It was Bobby, the Admiral's chauffeur, who found out
Maria was alive. He ran around with some bad company
after Nam, before Fletch took him in—they'd been prison-
ers together and Bobby'd become a kind of surrogate
son—and he knew some people who it turned out knew
Maria. Bobby told the Admiral and the Admiral got word
to her that she was welcome back aboard anytime she
wanted. Maria wasn't interested, at first, but about a month
ago she called Fletch to say she'd heard something she
knew he'd want to hear—that there was a contract out to
kill Felix. I know: Felix wasn't murdered. But we've been
right in thinking that someone wanted him killed. . . .

"Maria's source was a onetime boyfriend of hers who's
being sought by the feds for his part in a major caper to
launder narcotics money. Among the other things he knows
is the identity of the hit man known as El Bozo—in other
words, the guy Mularky worked for. Mularky being dead,
El Bozo—he's not a Mexican, apparently; he lived there
once, though, and picked up the name—El Bozo knows
better than anyone who wanted him to kill Felix. The
boyfriend—his name is Joey Finn (sometimes this is like
something out of Raymond Chandler, sometimes it's like
something out of Damon Runyon)—is willing to give us El
Bozo's name if we can help him make a deal with the
feds. Fletch went to Annapolis with the father of the U.S.
attorney in L.A. Maria, well, she's thinking about reform-
ing herself. She wants to get into modeling, maybe do
some dinner theater."

"Who's we?" Derry had said.

"Up to now, it's been Fletch and I."

"Meaning I'm coming aboard?"

Eve had laughed. "Yes and no. Yes, because you're

already aboard; no, because Fletch seems to've jumped ship.''

''Meaning what?''

She had shrugged. ''He's gone. Bobby, too, He arranged that I pick Maria up at the airport—she's been living in New York—but when I brought her here, there was no sign of them. The Admiral's car's gone, but it's not at the Yacht Club, but neither is the *Esmé's Wish,* his modest ocean liner. So take your pick of their means of escape.''

''Escape from what?''

''What, indeed?''

''You mean there's something you don't have the answer to?''

''Yup.''

''Mind if I join you?'' Derry already had his elbows on the table. ''You must be Lieutenant Kaplowitz.''

Kaplowitz looked at Branch. ''Friend of yours?'' She turned toward the bar, where the two women stood, giggling about something. ''Just in from Vegas?''

Derry laughed. ''Lieutenant, I'm sure you're unaware that the gentleman across the table from you is a fugitive on a murder charge. Sam Branch? Rancho Maria de la Luz Police Lieutenant Sam Branch? Maybe you've read about him?''

Branch pushed his chair back. ''Spare us the hard-boiled routine, Jeff. Let's just—''

''Sit, Sam. I want to make sure the lieutenant here understands the situation.'' Derry took out his shield and showed it to Kaplowitz, who flicked her eyes at it fractionally, then resumed boring with them into Branch's forehead. ''The situation, Lieutenant, is you've been had. I got a tip that Branch was up here to see you, posing as a reporter. Your office told me I'd find you here. Don't worry, I didn't tell them who your lunch date was. Sam,

maybe I better relieve you of your heat. Give it to me in
your napkin under the table, nice and slow. We don't want
to give anybody indigestion.''

Branch did as he was told. He could feel Derry's enthusiasm, although his monologue needed work.

Kaplowitz leaned over the table. ''You jive muthah-
fuckah.''

Derry put a hand on her arm. ''Now, now, Lieutenant. I
know it's embarrassing, but it doesn't have to be. The
collar's yours, if you want it, although I won't honestly be
able to say that when I arrived on the premises you were in
complete control of the situation. I may have to say that,
in fact—''

Kaplowitz put her mouth close to Derry's ear. ''Take
the jive muthah*fuckah.* An lock up yo *lip,* boy. It go down
I was fucked *ovah* by this muthah*fuckah,* I be done go
make sho fuh *suhtin* you fuckin *ass* ain't wuth *nuthin* in
this *town.* You heah *what* I say?'' She sat up straight and
dropped the rap. ''This is your story: You got your tip,
you found out where I was meeting Branch, you got here
before I did and made the collar. All I know is I was stood
up for a lunch date by someone calling himself Samuels. I
never laid eyes on the muthah*fuckah.* Don't worry about
the waiters and the customers; they're all coked up.'' She
stood and shouldered her bag. ''Don't forget to pay the
check.''

Eve looked at Branch in the rearview mirror. ''I've
never known a murderer before. Oh, I guess my father
killed a couple of guys. The first was in his rookie year—a
junkie, although I don't think they called them that then;
they called them hopheads, or something. He slugged
Harry with a plank full of nails; two of them went through
the back of his hand. The second was in his last year
before he went downtown—do you think he thought he
might never get another chance?—an Attica parolee who'd

been on the street two days and already robbed two liquor stores and a checkcashing place. I don't think he lost any sleep over either of them. How about you—any other notches on your gun?''

A cabbie blocking a crosswalk; a deli counterman who buttered only half of a corn muffin; a woman talking in a movie; a newscaster using *hopefully* to mean "let's hope''; a guy handing out massage parlor leaflets; Mayor Koch several times; a cashier in a Korean market who rang up twelve items in four seconds; a jogger who could talk only about jogging; a woman in a supermarket express line with fifteen items, a handful of coupons, a bagful of empty bottles and her checkbook out; a man urging a dog named Heathcliff to pee on the sidewalk; a kid on the subway with his size fourteen Converse All-Stars up on a pole and Grandmaster Flash and the Furious Five on his blaster— and that was just in New York. In California, he'd killed a waitress on roller skates, a waitress dressed like a banana split, a waitress in a French maid's outfit . . . It hadn't occurred to him that he'd developed a thing about waitresses. ''Did Escobar tell you I'd come up here?''

''He was worried about you, Branch. He likes you. He said to tell you he visited the place you asked him to and found a needle missing. He said you'd tell us what that meant. What does it mean, Sam?''

Branch looked to Derry, who sat beside him, one hand on the top of the front seat, over which the dozing Maria's mahogany tresses cascaded. ''Where does Strock think you are?''

''Out with that back problem I get now and then.'' He leaned toward Maria's ear as he said it, intimating he could use a rubdown. ''Oh, yeah, and here's the key you gave Escobar. He said you might want it back.''

Branch put it on his key ring, mauling a fingernail in the process. Why did he have so many keys? What were they the keys to?

"We've been real busy on your behalf," Eve said. "Guess who Portia called the afternoon you, uh, killed Mularky."

He was too tired to play games with her, and to say so.

"Leah Marston." Eve smiled into the mirror. "Joseph Litvak's sister. She and Portia went to Berkeley together. I called the registrar, said I was doing a piece on the class of seventy-three—Where Are They Now? Portia Hawkes and Leah Litvak were classmates, lived in the same dorm as freshmen, at the same address for the next three years—2804 Webster."

Branch tried to count the cars going the other way on the Harbor Freeway. He got to twelve. *It wasn't till I went to Berkeley that I met a Jew,* Portia had told him, yet another example of the phenomenon he had observed over and over again in his two thousand years as a cop: people lie and lie and lie, but they want you to know the truth, and they tell it to you without telling you they're telling you. "Can I have my gun back, Jeff?"

"I thought I'd hold on to it, Sam. You won't be able to take it on the plane."

"What plane?"

"We're going to New York," Eve said. "You and I. Don't worry, I'll pay for it with plastic. And we've got to get you some clothes, too. What Maria and I were laughing at, back at the bar? We heard two guys arguing about who you and Kaplowitz were. One guy insisted you covered skiing for ABC and that Kaplowitz was an actress he'd seen on *Miami Vice.*"

28

Rain.

It began over western Pennsylvania—or rather, they entered its dominion, descending through the thunderheads on the declination of their transcontinental arc.

At Kennedy, it coursed down the terminal's plate-glass windows, making them feel like visitors to an aquarium.

On the Long Island Expressway, the eighteen-wheelers racketed down the center lane, sending up spindrift all around. Branch clung like a novice to the steering wheel of the rented car, trying to ignore the siren song of their speed.

"You want to hear a story? It'll take your mind off the driving." Eve slid down in the passenger seat and put her knees against the dashboard. "It's the rest of the story about how I found Texas and Bright and Just John. Remember who they are?"

"Charlie Fox's in-laws."

"Good. Being on the LIE reminds me of it because out here is where I found them. . . . Before I tell you the story, though, did I tell you I solved the Jitney mystery?"

"I didn't know there was a Jitney mystery. I thought that was about the only thing that wasn't mysterious."

"You're wrong. You see, we know Litvak went out to Southampton on a Friday afternoon to visit his sister and brother-in-law. And we know Felix took the same bus. Litvak stayed overnight Friday and Saturday and got the Jitney back to New York on Sunday evening. But what about Felix? He caught a nine A.M. American Airlines flight out of Kennedy on Saturday morning and the night manager at the Carlyle insists he stayed in his room Friday night. How is that possible?"

"I assumed he flew back."

"Assumed? I thought you were a cop. I called every charter airline on the East End, and no Felix Beaufils did any flying that Friday night or Saturday morning."

"He took the Jitney back, then. They must have a late bus."

"The last one from Southampton's at five-thirty, except on Sundays. His bus got in at eight-twenty. And the last *train* out of Southampton, before you say, Well, then, he took the train, was at seven fifty-two."

"It *is* a mystery."

"Don't be sarcastic. The solution is, Felix didn't go to Southampton—not all the way, that is. The bus was a local—the express was full up, being a Friday night. It made its first stop at Westhampton at seven-fifty; at Quogue at seven-fifty-five; at Hampton Bays at eight-oh-five. Meanwhile, the train—going the other way, you understand—stopped at Hampton Bays at eight-oh-four—one minute be*fore* the Jitney, assuming everything was on time; however, the train got to Quogue at eight-twelve—seventeen minutes *after* the Jitney—and to Westhampton at eight-nineteen—almost half an hour after the Jitney, oodles of time, time for a sandwich. . . .

"After Westhampton, the bus goes north, toward Manorville, to get on the LIE; the train goes more southerly, through Speonk and other garden spots, to Babylon. At Quogue or Westhampton, therefore, either one, Felix got off the Jitney, caught the train and was back in New York at ten-fourteen. Twenty minutes by cab—or even forty, being a Friday night—and he was at the Carlyle before eleven, a little dusty and tired, probably, but able to be up to catch his plane. Admit it, Branch—it's clever. It's like one of those problems you do in high school: If the good news left Ghent at noon, traveling at twenty miles an hour, how long did it take to get to Aix, given that Aix was approaching Ghent at the rate of three inches every two hundred thousand years?''

''Very clever.''

''The only thing is, Felix Beaufils on the Long Island Rail Road? There's no parlor car on that train, and almost no passengers. It's a milk run. So why did he take it? Because whatever Litvak told him was something he had to do something about right away. Maybe not that night, maybe not in New York, but the next day certainly, in California.''

''And what did Litvak tell him?''

Eve shook her head. ''That's why we're going to see Leah Marston.''

''Née Litvak.''

''Née Litvak.''

''. . . How do you know so much about Long Island?''

Eve laughed. ''That's what I started to tell you—about how I found Charlie Fox's in-laws. To refresh your memory, Charlie's ex-daughter-in-law, Texas, ran off with a carpenter named Just John, taking her daughter, Bright, with her. I found out that before Just John came to Nashville, he lived in Vermont, so I called Motor Vehicles up there and got his old phone number. A woman answered, with whom he'd lived and whom he'd run out on, and she was understandably uninterested in talking about him, but she did say that before Vermont he'd lived on Long Island

and had sometimes talked about settling down there. I said Long Island was *long* and could she do better than that, but all she could remember was that it was farther from New York than it was nearer and that it had a funny name. 'You mean, an Indian name—like Ronkonkoma, or Wyandanch, or Amagansett?' 'No. Just . . . a funny name . . .'

"Well, Long Island *is* long, but after a while, it's skinny. Once you're east of Riverhead, there're only two main roads, one on each fork, and anybody who lives there has to travel on one or the other of them most of the time. And anybody with a kid would have to send her to one of a very few schools. I figured the thing to do was just drive up one fork and down the other, showing pictures Charlie gave me at gas stations and supermarkets and schools. As it turned out, I didn't have to, because a couple of days after I called the woman in Vermont, she called me, said, 'Fireplace,' and hung up.

"It reminded me of a game I used to play with a sportswriter for the Boston *Globe*. Whenever we ran into each other, one of us would say the name of a fifties baseball player—not a star, a journeyman. The other had to have a name ready to match it, or had to buy dinner. I'd say, 'Cass Michaels,' and he'd say, 'Andy Pafko.' 'Dee Fondy,' 'Eddie Joost.' 'Irv Noren,' 'Eddie Waitkus,' 'Ferris Fain,' 'Phil Cavarretta.'

"She wasn't playing the game, of course; she was telling me the place with the funny name where Just John used to live. Fireplace. It's part of East Hampton. Sort of the low-rent district, up on the Sound side—or Gardiners Bay, actually. . . . It was easy as pie. I drove out to East Hampton and took the Springs–Fireplace Road and found an IGA and showed the store manager the pictures and, sure enough, Texas and Bright were regular customers— and Just John had been, but he hadn't seen him in quite a while. He even knew where they lived, out at the end of a spit of land with the picturesque name of Louse Point. . . .

"Yaphank"—Eve pointed at the exit sign. "There was once a Charles Addams cartoon in *The New Yorker* about this exit: the sign said, 'You may skip Yaphank.' . . .

"I found Louse Point and found the house and knocked on the door and found Texas. She wasn't as pretty as the picture I had, but she looked pretty good—like that Marlboro woman a few years back: the blonde in the blue work shirt?—and I could understand why a man would feel the need to hole up with her out in the middle of nowhere. She said, 'Lost?' which was a pretty funny thing to say—or maybe you had to be there—and I said, 'Not anymore,' meaning her, and she said, 'Hunh?' and I said, 'Yup,' and she said, 'Charlie?' You couldn't have such an inarticulate yet lucid conversation with an eastern sophisticate; they're always wanting you to spell things out.

"Texas asked how I found her and I told her and she asked what Charlie wanted and I said he wanted to be a granddaddy and she said she liked Charlie, the problem was he wasn't just Bright's granddaddy, he was Ben Fox's daddy, and she never wanted to lay eyes on Ben again. I said no one was asking her to. . . . She thought about that for a while, then said, 'You want a Schmidt's?' A Southerner will always use a proper noun where we Yankees use a common one. Old Zabriskie never called beer beer, he called it whatever brand he was drinking at the time, which depended on what part of the country he was in: he drank Oly when he was out west and Rolling Rock when he was back east and Pearl when he was in West comma Texas.

"One Schmidt's led to another and I asked where Bright was and Texas said, 'Over to Napeague, horseback riding,' and I said, 'Where's Just John?' and she said, 'He just up and left,' and I laughed, but I could tell she had a hurting heart and was going to be a pushover for Charlie.

While we could still move our lips, I got on the phone and tracked down Charlie, who was on the road in Alabama or something, and Texas got on the phone and talked to him and he said he was going to charter a plane to come up and get them, and when they were through, I got back on and Charlie said, 'Thanks jess a ho lot,' and I said, 'Don't minchin it,' and he said he'd send me a check first thang and if there was ever innathang he could do for me— innathang at all, innatime, innawhar—I should let him know. I never took him up on it . . . till now. Which is really the point of this whole story.''

The traffic had thinned and the rain let up and Branch had been relaxed for a while, comforted by the lilt of her voice and glad not to be hearing the buzzing of the questions that had swarmed in his mind even in his sleep on the flight from Los Angeles. He glanced at Eve, who was smiling giddily, waiting for him to prompt her. "All right. *What*'s the point of the whole story?''

''Well, when you disappeared, Jeff and I, uh, broke into your house—on the chance you were hiding in the attic, on the chance there was something lying around that might tell us where you'd gone. There *was* something lying around, and I sent it to Charlie. Your song—'Lord, Lord, Lord, You Make Good Coffee.' ''

29

"Mr. Henry?" Derry stepped over a yellow and blue Fisher-Price bus at the foot of the flagstone walk beside the privet.

"Hiya. Hey, come on in." He tore off a golf glove and came at Derry as if he were not only expected but anticipated. His handshake was a politician's, firm but fleeting. An unlit cigarette was fitted in a holder clamped between his back teeth. "Not selling something, are you? Got everything I need." He waved a seven iron at his fifty-by-two-hundred-foot domain, his adobe ranch, his Olds 88, his McCulloch hedge trimmer. He wore a white Andy Williams Open sun visor, a lavender Jack Nicklaus shirt, bright yellow slacks and two-tone golf shoes, oxblood and white. "Or soliciting?" He put the glove back on and addressed a Wiffle ball. "I gave at the office. Just let me have one more whack at this pill, will you? I played eighteen at Capistrano this morning and my short game smelled from here to Frisco." He stroked the ball onto the roof of the house. "Easy come, easy go. Had nice loft to it, though. Now, what can I do you for?"

"I'm thinking about buying the house down the block.
The colonial."

He put the club in his red and white Wilson bag and
propped it against the Olds's rear fender. "The Milford
place? Damn nice house. And you want to know what kind
of area this is."

"In particular, what it's like having a hit man for a
neighbor."

He leaned against the fender, took off the glove, tucked
it in a back pocket and removed the cigarette from the
holder. He fieldstripped it and rubbed the tobacco flakes
from his fingertips, looking like a chef garnishing a dish.
"I didn't get your name."

Derry looked toward the house. Music filtered through
the screen door—an easy-listening station. On the porch
were a pink plastic hobbyhorse; a bicycle with training
wheels, one missing; a rubber raft with one plastic oar, a
half-dozen patches and almost no air in it; a croquet set, its
wickets bent and rusted, the balls scuffed, two mallets
decapitated; a badminton net, but no racquets or shuttle-
cocks; a small left-handed baseball glove and a larger first
baseman's mitt, right-handed. Except for the music, and
the desuetude, it could be his house, his and Maria's. The
music would be progressive rock; the bike would glisten
and wouldn't have training wheels, for the boys would
learn without crutches; the raft would be plump and ship-
shape; the badminton net in place, the court lined, all the
accoutrements accounted for. There would be no croquet—
too passive, too fussy—although maybe horseshoes. And
he wouldn't spend his Saturday mornings golfing; he'd be
throwing a ball—round or oblate, depending on the season—
with the boys, while Maria, her hands floured from frying
chicken for their afternoon outing, paused at the screen
door to admire her men. "This is a nice place you've got
here, Mr. Claude Henry, also known as Claudio Enrique,
also as El Bozo. Funny choice of a nickname, El Bozo—or

maybe you didn't have a choice. I mean, I know it means peach fuzz, like on your chin, but there can't be too many people who know that; the rest must think you're some kind of fuckup instead of the last of the great contract killers. Nice place, nice neighborhood. It'd be a shame if it all went down the tubes.''

Henry took a pack of Merit from his shirt pocket and fitted one in the holder. ''You from around here?''

''Down south a ways.''

''P.I.?''

''Nope. I've got a badge and everything.''

''But you're not here on orders. Your superiors don't know what you're up to.''

''Not at the moment.''

''And you're after—what?—money? Or just fame?''

''I want the name of a client. A recent client.''

Henry searched in his pockets for a matchbook, then unzipped a compartment of the golf bag and took out a small green plastic tin. He twisted off the lid and held it out to Derry. ''Care for one?'' He chuckled as Derry drew back. ''It's not a controlled substance, pal. It's snuff. Smokeless tobacco. You've seen the commercials: 'Take a pouch instead of a puff.' '' He took out one of the small packets, an inch by half an inch, and slipped it into his cheek. ''I've tried everything to quit smoking short of sewing up my lips. Not lighting up, not carrying matches, using the holder when I do light up, sucking on one of these instead. They're probably just as bad for you in the long run, but they give you a nice little buzz and your lungs get a break. Sure you won't have one?''

Derry took one, juggled it in his palm, then put it in his pocket. Maria was a glutton for cigarettes; maybe he could use these to lure her down the path toward abstinence. She'd have to be clean when she was pregnant; he didn't want sons about whom it would always be wondered how far they'd've gone if they hadn't been stunted. "I don't have a whole lot of time."

Henry put away the tin and studied his calluses. "Does it really seem reasonable, my friend, that someone in the line of work you're suggesting I'm in would know the names of his clients? Think about it a minute and I think you'll think again."

Flatter him, Branch had advised. *There's not a professional criminal in the world who doesn't think he's the best. Let him think you're as impressed with him as he is with himself.* "Look, Henry. An asshole like Mularky running your business, making big decisions? Don't make me laugh." Derry kicked softly at the golf bag. "You're playing skins, you have to make a putt for a bird, who reads the green, you or your caddy?"

Henry smiled. "Suppose I were to give you the name. How can I reasonably expect to continue in business— since you've got a badge and everything?"

"Because in this case the guy the client wanted murdered died before he could be."

Henry shifted his pouch of snuff and smiled. "I see." He turned the smile up even louder and waved at a neighbor who was backing his Bonneville down the next driveway. "What the hell would Tom think if he knew what we were talking about, hey, pal?"

"What do they think you do?"

"I have a little office in a professional building at a mall down the road. The sign on my door says I'm an insurance adjuster."

"I guess you sort of are, aren't you?"

"I thought it was clever, yeah. A little private joke . . . There's a concept in the insurance racket, pal. Exposure. It refers to the extent of your liability. In this particular case you mentioned, it doesn't look like I have any exposure—or very little. One person's word against mine, if it ever came to that."

"That sounds right."

"On the other hand, if it were to get around that I'd fingered a client, I could say sayonara to my reputation and my livelihood, not to mention maybe my life—the same as if my exposure were complete and I was nailed by the law. What assurance do I have that the client won't suspect I'm the stoolie, pal, because that's what we're talking about—a violation of trust?"

"I'll tell them I got the name from Mularky."

"His dying words?"

"Something like that."

He laughed. "I like you, Derry. Officer Jeff Derry of the Rancho Maria de la Luz Police Department. I'm glad you don't look surprised, because you shouldn't be. I spend a lot of time in my office, for appearances' sake, I get a chance to read the papers. The stuff going on down your way's made great reading—even if I weren't interested in it because of my, uh, limited exposure. I make a habit when I read anything to match the names with the faces in the photographs—when there are any; it's frustrating when there aren't—and I remarked on your, uh, youthful features. You could be called El Bozo yourself. You're right, it's a lousy nickname. I got into this racket in Mexico. I wasn't all that young, but I looked it, the way you do, and, well, names have a way of sticking. Are you working with this guy Branch or against him? No, you wouldn't want to say. I don't suppose you'll tell me who fingered me, either? No, you wouldn't want to do that. . . .

"Listen, I can see my wife peeking out the window— the one with the pink curtains there—wondering what the hell's going on. She's probably thinking I'm working on an excuse not to pick the kids up at the pool and take them to McDonald's, the way I said I would, so she can have some down time. That's what she calls it, down time; she read it in *Cosmo,* or one of those magazines." He poked with a foot at the hedge trimmer. "Then I'm supposed to give the bushes a haircut. We pay a guy to take care of the yard, but for some reason he doesn't do bushes. It's a hell of a world, isn't it? You want something done right, you have to do it yourself, but the compensation is never what it should be. . . . Do you have something to write on, Jeff? I'd rather not say the name out loud, just so I can, you know, look at myself in the mirror and say I didn't *tell* you.''

Derry turned on the radio and punched the button for the all-news station to hear the scores. Phillies 8 Cardinals 4. Expos 2 Mets 1. Cubs at Pittsburgh rained out. Braves 4 Dodgers 3, in eleven innings.

"Shit."

He punched up KSUN. Don Henley sang "The Boys of Summer."

Those had been the days: The top rolled back, the radio on. The brown-skinned girls, their Wayfarers on. The way they drove him crazy, the way he made them scream.

He honked at a Camaro ahead of him in the fast lane and passed on the right when it wouldn't give way. The driver gave him the finger and mouthed *asshole*.

He supposed he was. Everything he did lately, he overdid. Except eat and sleep: food didn't interest him, when there was Maria to be consumed; sleep was out of the question, with her dancing inside his eyelids, not a girl just for the summer, but for eternity.

He was passed on the right by a stretch limo with vanity plates: H_2O. Trailing it, a little breathlessly, was a shabby Caprice. Derry got in line. The two cars got off at the next exit and so did he. They turned onto the Corniche and so did he. They turned into the parking lot at La Ermita Beach and so did he. A girl he knew waved at him, but he kept on going down to the end of the lot, where the surfers parked their vans and buggies. He got a Coke—Classic— from the vending machine and sat on the hood and pretended to study the waves while using his Ray-Bans as a mirror to keep an eye on the limo and the Caprice.

He finished the Coke and flipped the can at a garbage pail. Swish. He got back in the Cobra and got back on the Corniche, but he could've gone faster without a car. He was flying now, flying back to Maria. He would have thought he would never go to La Ermita again to check out the girls of summer, but now that he had, he realized that it had been the perfect test. He hadn't been tempted to look at a one, and it wasn't just that he'd been preoccupied, wondering what Howard Maddox and Warren Cable were talking about in the back seat of Cable's car.

30

Leah Litvak Marston's stuff proclaimed that she was her brother's sister: a Ralph Lauren navy and white cotton shawlcollar cardigan (against the chill a sea breeze brought to the terrace of the Meadow Club) over a Chanel ivory chiffon T-shirt; Calvin Klein loose white jacquard linen trousers; navy and white Newton Elkin spectator pumps; a Gucci burgundy pressed-alligator tote in which she'd half-stuffed her Fila tennis dress, her Fred Perry sneakers and her Snauwaert racquet. She swiped at her damp black hair with a Tek Italian wood comb, displaying a Baume & Mercier watch—four strands of finely woven gold linked to a diamond-encrusted case—while from her lips a pair of Vuarnet sunglasses dangled by an earpiece. She jammed the comb in a pocket of the tote, seated the sunglasses, took a Schimmelpenninck cigar from a Mark Cross leather case, lighted it with a gold Dunhill lighter, lifted a Galway crystal highball glass and took a sip of Glenlivet. "Now. How may I help you?" Her perfume was Raffinée by Houbigant.

"Where's Portia?" Branch said.

A discreet puckering of her nostrils was the only hint of

distress. "I was misinformed, then. The club secretary said he received a phone call from my maid to the effect that two representatives of the insurance company were on their way to see me."

"We lied," Eve said. "We saw the scratch on the Jag in your driveway. Pity."

". . . Ah. You're Sam Branch. And you?" She didn't wait for an answer, for she was a woman for whom women held no interest unless they were as eloquently caparisoned as she. "You're not as young as I imagined, Mr. Branch. Or perhaps it's the beard. But I can see why Portia was once attracted to you."

Branch duly recorded the adverb. "Where is Portia?"

"How would I know?"

"She called you a week ago yesterday. To say what?"

"To commiserate. I had lost a brother, she a husband."

"She told me she didn't know a Joseph Litvak."

"Perhaps she saw no point in telling you."

"The way you saw no point in telling me, when you and I talked on the phone, that Rancho Maria de la Luz, where your brother died, wasn't some exotic dateline to you, that it was founded by your college roommate's family? The way you neglected to tell me that your brother's quest wasn't quite as aimless as I thought at the time, that he was looking for a man named Schatz?"

She cocked her head. "Did you ask Portia if she knew this . . . Schatz?"

"Yes, but if she did, she saw no point in telling me."

She smiled. "No. She wouldn't."

"Who's Schatz?"

"If Portia wouldn't tell you, you can hardly expect me to."

"Have you heard from her, since Tuesday?"

Leah Marston twirled the ash off the end of her cigar.

"Who killed your brother, Mrs. Marston?"

The corners of her mouth drooped. "Do you really not

know? How sad. How pathetically sad. And what Portia admired most about you was your intelligence, your—''

He slapped her, pulling his blow at the last instant, and so swiftly that Eve wasn't sure it had happened and none of the club members on the terrace had an inkling. But it got her attention, and opened a floodgate.

She put the tip of her middle finger against the corner of her mouth, glanced at it, flicked at it with her thumb. ''Portia and I met in college, yes. We were more like allies, at first, than true friends, being both of us proponents of the Vietnam war, which was deplored nearly unanimously on the Berkeley campus. Portia's father was fighting the war, of course, and I was a professional soldier—I'm a few years older than she and had already done my military service—and believed that wars should be fought only to be won. In time, we came to share other interests.

''After Berkeley, we took a flat together in New York. Portia was doing graduate work and I was pretending to be a painter. What I did was sleep with painters, one of whom took me to Paris, where I met Eugene, my future husband, an American, who was working there for Chase Manhattan Bank. He called it Chase, with a very particular inflection that I have never been able to duplicate but that was meant to indicate its importance in the scheme of things. He no longer works for Chase; he works for Lazard, which he says in the same fashion.''

Branch didn't ask how it was that her husband had sounded on the phone as though he'd never heard of Rancho Maria de la Luz; the Marstons' marriage could have survived only if he was as oblivious as she was contemptuous.

Leah Marston waved at a couple of her peers who passed beneath the terrace on their way to one of the grass courts; it hadn't rained on the Meadow Club, the front having stopped just to the west, as if it might be asked its pedigree. "In some way that I have forgotten, Portia became interested in wine and came to study at the University of Bordeaux. We saw each other quite often while she was in France, but when she returned to the United States it was to California, with the result that for several years we saw each other hardly at all, although we talked on the phone a couple of times a month—which is how I know about you, Mr. Branch. . . .

"Portia came to Paris for a visit four years ago, just before my husband and I moved to New York. It was then that she met Felix, whose account Eugene managed. She was smitten by the paternal quality of his affection, since most of the men in her life up to that point—forgive me, Mr. Branch, for speaking frankly—had tended to be preoccupied with her face and her physique, and since her own father was more in love with his country—and later with his utopian community—than with his family. She did have one last passionate fling, however, before surrendering to life with a father figure: with a much younger man—younger than Felix, that is—who had come to Paris in the footsteps, more or less, although from a different direction, of his sister, determined to do as she had done—fuck all the right people. His name was Joseph Litvak. . . . I suppose I should pause there, while you take a moment to digest that."

Branch just waved a hand; he'd asked to be fed it, he'd have to chew it. Eve, for her part, was remembering a story told her by the man who cut her hair about a customer who as he was about to start snipping took the scissors from his hand, pointed them at him, and said, *There's something very important you should know—I'm an Israeli.*

Leah Marston took a sip of her drink and granted her cigar a touch of her lips. "My brother. For all his acquired sophistication, Joseph was a *yenta.* He collected gossip the way people collect paper clips or pennies—not because it was valuable, but because it was there. As Portia got to know Felix, Joseph did, as well—everything about him. I suppose she confided in him the way one does in a stranger on an airplane; she never thought she'd see him again. She was particularly concerned that her father not find out about her prospective husband's Jewishness, so perhaps to prepare herself for the necessary subterfuge, she had an affair with a Jew behind the back of another. By the way, I had met Portia's father and gotten along well with him, in spite of *my* Jewishness; but then, I wasn't a Semite in his eyes, I was a soldier. Did I say something to shock you, Mr. Branch?''

Nothing shocked him any longer. Or rather, everything did; he was a naïf in a land of artifice. "Felix was Schatz."

"Hunh," Eve said.

Leah Marston had her head tipped back and smiled the smile of a veteran watching tyros make their error-filled way. "He was born Felix Schatz, in the Alsace; the family changed its name in anticipation of the Holocaust and managed, perhaps because of that, to avoid its ravages. I say perhaps because . . . Well, I do not mean to impute collaborationism, but the family made a number of quite successful business ventures during the Vichy regime, one of which was the acquisition of considerable land in suburbs of Paris where, today, land is rare and dear. Felix was little more than a teenager at the time, but he was very active in the family's enterprises—and in some other activities, not quite as legal, having to do with the black market, smuggling, the usual wartime exploitation. In these sidelights, he had a partner, a man as young as he, named Simon Rafelson, who also took a new surname, calling himself de la Chance—"

"Lucky," Eve said.

"Baruch," Branch said.

A brusque nod was all she gave it, she to whom it was all so simple. "At the war's end, Felix Beaufils and Simon de la Chance had a falling out and went their separate ways. Felix had had enough of the underworld, and dedicated himself to becoming a legitimate financier. Simon, once again calling himself Rafelson, emigrated to Israel, seeing in that brand-new nation any number of voids to be filled by one of his talents. He founded a gang, the Baruch Gang—they like to be thought of as mobsters, but I fear that's overstating their ferocity—using as a front for its activities several legitimate businesses, including his own liquor exporting company. . . ."

She paused to consult her watch, but reacted not at all to what it told her; perhaps she simply needed to be reminded from time to time of its worth. "Felix never met my brother. I took care to see that there was never an opportunity; Joseph couldn't truly savor deceiving a man unless he let him know that he had. When Felix left for America with Portia, Joseph exacted his pathetic version of revenge by getting a job in the European operation of Simon Rafelson, with whom he knew too well Felix had broken. He was little more than an office boy, but his talent for duplicity and underhandedness was such that he came to the attention, in time, of Rafelson himself, who made him into a kind of spy; his duties were to keep Rafelson abreast of any untoward opportunism manifested by his European lieutenants. . . .

"That brings us, more or less, to the present. Rafelson did very little business in the United States. He had an idea that a way to gain a modest foothold would be by exporting Israeli wines—in particular a champagne that would have been directly competitive with the champagne Felix Beaufils was producing in his vineyard. Your faces say that you doubt that the stakes in such a competition would be very high, and you're correct. No, something else was at stake, a question of honor—something to do with that something that happened very long ago between the two former friends—something even Joseph was not able to find out. A remarkable achievement, to keep something from Joseph, for as you can see, he was as adept at ferreting out secrets as he was incapable of keeping them; everything I have just told you I know from him—and I never had to ask. . . .

"Whatever that something was, it was sufficient to motivate Rafelson to abort Felix's new enterprise. The plan, at first, was very simple: Rafelson would invest a large amount of money, using not names but numbered accounts in Swiss banks, in Felix's mutual fund, inflating its value, then would withdraw it more or less overnight, bankrupting the fund and imperiling Felix's entire empire—especially its newest element, the vineyard. Again, your faces express some disbelief in what I'm saying."

Branch shook his head. "We knew about the withdrawals—and the juggling act Felix devised to deal with them. We had an idea someone else was behind them."

"Oh? Who?"

"Someone else."

"I see. Yes. Well. In any case, there seemed to be nothing for it but to kill Felix. The problem was to make it look as though he was killed over something other than the champagne. Joseph—it was the finest moment of his sordid career, to hear him tell it—Joseph remembered hearing about Felix's property in the Paris suburbs and came up with the idea of inventing the story that a piece of land in Neuilly belonging to Felix was in the way of development whose backers were prepared to pay twenty million dollars for it. The million would be a down payment. Joseph would make a public show of searching for a mysterious Monsieur Schatz, new identity and whereabouts unknown. Since Felix was strapped for money, the idea was that he would learn of the search for Schatz and be lured to a meeting at which Joseph—whom he wouldn't recognize, understand—would kill him. It would be a secret meeting, because Felix wouldn't want to admit publicly to being

Schatz—not an admission he could make before a community that has as little use for Jews as does Rancho Maria de
la Luz. It would appear that Felix had been killed—and
robbed of the cashier's check—after leaving the meeting,
by someone who had heard of my brother's search.

"One of Rafelson's men, pretending to be someone who
had known Felix in the old days, phoned him to say he
was in New York on business and had heard Joseph on a
radio call-in show, one of those despicable things that New
York cabdrivers always seem to be listening to—"

"Cab radios get only those shows," Eve said, and when
Leah Marston stared at her, said, "Never mind."

"Felix flew to New York and contacted Joseph. He was
wisely suspicious, since he didn't recall the man Rafelson's
associate claimed to be, and when he learned that Joseph
was planning to take the Jitney out here for the weekend,
proposed that the bus be the site of their preliminary
discussions. It was a safe place. Joseph wasn't in any
position to object, nor, when Felix got off the bus short of
its destination in order to catch a train back to New York,
could he do anything about it. Why do you smile,
Miss . . . ?"

"No reason," Eve said.

". . . The arrangement was that Joseph would come to
California to make the payment. He and Felix were to
meet in Los Angeles on the Saturday after the party celebrating the new Beaufils champagne. As with the jitney,
Joseph had permitted himself to be outmaneuvered, for he
could not very well appear on the radio in Los Angeles
saying he was looking for Schatz, as Felix might hear of it
and demand to know the reason. He thought to regain the
upper hand by going to Rancho Maria de la Luz, confront-
ing Felix, threatening to expose his Jewishness, insisting
that he take the check, then killing him— Now it is you
who are amused, Mr. Branch."

Indeed, he had to laugh. "Your brother traveled under

his own name. Was he crazy? And kill him with what? He didn't have a gun—he couldn't have taken one on the plane—or a knife or anything lethal.''

She had bristled just a little at the first question. "He was an egotist. Is that the same thing? And besides, his scheme was contingent on his appearing to be aboveboard. As for his choice of weapon, I didn't ask. I rather assumed he planned to kill Felix with his bare hands; he *was* insanely jealous.''

"He was crazy. It was crazy to tell you he was going to kill your friend's husband. Did he think you wouldn't warn them? You *did* warn them?''

Her cigar had gone out and she took a moment to rekindle it. In the lighter's flame, Branch saw that she was, in fact, older than Portia, older than he, old—that her apparent youthfulness was due to packaging and preservation.

"You have a secret, too, don't you? Like all the rest of them. Something your brother knows that could destroy your marriage, your reputation, your status in this community.''

She smoked concentratedly for a moment, shrouding herself in a gray swirl. "Do you want to hear it?''

Branch sat very still; he was a sponge of revelation— and about as passive; all he did was listen, look, listen some more; and yet he was never saturated, just soaked to the point of immobility.

Leah Marston sat forward in her chair and finished her Scotch. She spoke quickly now, as though she'd remembered that she had to leave soon, to go buy something. The offer, if it had been that, of a trip around to her dark side had clearly been withdrawn. "Indeed, I warned Portia— and Felix—of Joseph's plan. I phoned them the Monday after Joseph's visit. Felix appeared not to be overly concerned; he said he had suspected that Joseph was not who he claimed to be; Joseph apparently had been unable to resist asking about Schatz's wife, and Felix wondered how he knew Schatz *had* a wife. *He* had a plan, Felix; he was quite amused by it. He would arrange to meet Joseph in some out-of-the-way place, but instead of keeping the rendezvous himself, he would send someone in his place, someone who would rob Joseph, take the check, and force him to return to his employers with whatever explanation he could devise for its loss. I gather something went awry.''

"Hold on. I thought you said you knew who killed your brother.''

"I was being snide, Mr. Branch. You came on belligerently, and I reacted in kind. I am an Israeli.''

Eve turned a shoulder to them, and laughed into it.

Branch stared at nothing. Sponges don't think. And he'd lost his absorbency; he'd sucked up too much. "Here's my number in California, Mrs. Marston.'' He took out his notebook and tried to write it, but his ballpoint pen had gone dry; she handed him hers, a Mont Blanc Diplomat gold-covered fountain pen with gold nib: "If you think of anything, or hear anything, call me.''

She folded the slip of paper and put it in a pocket of her cardigan. "You have come a long way for very little, Mr. Branch.''

"It comes with the territory when you're dealing with someone like your brother. There aren't many traces of a worthless life; just shadows and echoes, a vague memory or two. Can you even remember what he looked like? I saw him cut open in a morgue, *Le*ah, and you know what? As far as I can recall, he was empty. Thanks for the beer.''

"I guess you told her.''

Branch just drove. After a while, he said, "What about Royal Worcester china?''

"*What?*''

"Tony Astin said to ask you about Royal Worcester china—apropos of his thinking highly of himself because he works for the *Times*."

Eve laughed. "God, I'd forgotten all about that. It wasn't he who thought highly of himself; it was me. I. I went to Altman's to buy some good china. I was a grownup; it was time I stopped eating off Pottery Barn plates. Tony went with me. We were watching the saleswoman wrap up the pattern I picked out—Royal Worcester. She wrapped it in pages from the *Post*. I was very offended. I insisted she wrap it in the *Times*. The joke was that the pages from the *Times* were pages with a story I'd written. . . . This isn't the way to Kennedy."

"The plane's not till four. It's not too far out of the way."

" 'It'?"

Branch just drove.

"Which house is it?"

"The white one."

"A big house, for three people."

"Her uncle lives upstairs. Her maiden uncle, I used to call him."

"Is he a cop, too?"

"Yes."

"What's this neighborhood called?"

"Kensington."

"It's nice. It looks like Iowa, or something. . . . Do you want to see if anybody's home? No—of course, you can't."

Branch turned the ignition key.

"It'll be over soon, Sam. Then you can . . ."

"Yeah."

31

"*Fe*lix?"

"Felix."

"*Fe*lix hired El Bozo?"

"His name's Henry, Sam. Claude Henry. He's a nice guy. I can't call him El Bozo."

"*Fe*lix hired El Bozo to kill him? To kill himself? To—" Branch tried a different voice. "El Bozo was hired by Felix to kill Felix?" It still didn't sound right, but he couldn't think of another way to say it. He slumped back in the seat. ARRIVALS, said a sign with a left-pointing arrow; DEPARTURES, said another, with an arrow pointing right. He wasn't sure which he was; it seemed years since he and Eve had flown to New York from this airport; it had been twenty-four hours.

Derry took a quick look over his shoulder. "You all right?"

"Tell it to me one more time."

Derry challenged a taxi for its right-of-way, and won. "It was some kind of setup. Felix wanted it to look like there was an attempt on his life. Maddox was the middle-man; he met with Mularky. We were right about that

248

much, at least. Only thing is, Maddox didn't say it was a setup and he didn't say he was fronting for Felix. He didn't say who he was fronting for, but according to Henry, Mularky had two meetings with Maddox and came away from them with the distinct impression Warren Cable was the man behind the scenes—''

''Maybe Annie was right.'' Eve turned to look at Branch. ''I mean, wrong but right. She was wrong that Cable was behind the Moneda monkey business; but maybe he was behind the plot to kill Felix. How is Annie, Jeff?''

''Haven't seen her. . . . It was more than an impression Mularky had; he followed Maddox after their first meeting —to the parking lot at La Ermita. Maddox got out of his car and spent half an hour in the back seat of Cable's stretch. Maddox and Cable had another meeting yesterday afternoon—same place—that I happened to see. I was driving by on the way back from El Boz—from Henry's. It's a stupid place to meet. I go there a lot—or I used to—and so do a bunch of guys from County. On their lunch hour, you know? To check out the local talent.''

''How did El Bozo know it was supposed to be a setup, if Maddox didn't say so?''

''Felix got in touch with him. Said he didn't trust Maddox and wanted to be sure for himself that El Boz— that Henry understood the arrangements.''

''Didn't trust Maddox why?''

''He didn't say.''

''How was he able to get in touch with El Bozo if so few people know who El Bozo is?''

''He didn't say.''

''Felix didn't say, or El Bozo didn't say?''

Derry shifted his shoulders. ''You're doing it again, Sam. You're asking questions that don't go anywhere.''

''See that County whitetop over there, Jeff? That cop would be justified, if he thought he recognized me, in pulling us over and sticking a gun through the window—in my face, not yours—and if I didn't do what he said, pulling the trigger. I'm trying to find out what the fuck happened."

". . . Henry said—"

"Let's call him El Bozo, Jeff. Just so we both know who we're talking about."

"Jesus, Sam."

"Right."

". . . El Bozo said Felix wouldn't tell him how he got onto who he was. But he said he figured Felix had someone tail Mularky the way Mularky tailed Maddox. Mularky and El Bozo mostly talked on the phone, but they met every now and then at the insurance office El Bozo has for a front."

Now that Branch knew what the fuck happened, he didn't know what the fuck it mattered. "When and where was the hit going to be?"

"After the champagne party. Felix was going to go out on the patio for a cigar and El Bozo was going to bust one of the flowerpots alongside his head with a Remington deer rifle, with a night scope. The cops'd find a cartridge and a slip of paper with Southland's logo on it giving directions to the house and a map of Portia's little golf course, which was where the shot'd be fired from—the left bunker. It's a hell of a note, isn't it? Felix *wasn't* murdered, but he wanted to make it look like someone tried."

"Let's find Maddox." Branch sat up and leaned his elbows on the front seat. "Just you and I, Jeff. Drop Eve off at your place. Did you bring my gun? Don't look at me like that, Eve. This could be serious."

"As opposed to what?"

Branch checked the chambers of the revolver Derry handed over to him.

"I solved the Jitney mystery."

"There is something you can do. Find out what happened to Hawkes. I think it's more likely he went by boat than by car. Check marinas up and down—"

"Hey. Branch. I found Texas and Bright and Just John—"

"Who?" Derry said.

"—So just let me do it my way, okay? How long do you think you can roam around here undetected by your fellow peace officers? You'd be better off turning yourself in, getting yourself a lawyer, getting out on bail. At least you could walk the streets—nobody walks here, do they? —*drive* the streets, even if you were a pariah."

" . . . I'll call Annie."

"No, I'll call Annie. I owe her an explanation of what's been going on and I'll ask if she'll help you out. . . . Don't worry, Jeff. Nothing's been going *on*. How come you stopped wearing your Dodger hat?"

Derry shifted to get at his side pocket. "Do me a favor, Eve. Give these to Maria, will you?"

Eve hefted the tin he handed her. "Skoal Bandits? Maria likes a chaw?"

"They're little pouches. You don't chew it, you just—"

"I know what you do. I covered baseball, for God's sake." She opened the tin and sniffed at the contents, then held it out to Branch. "Care for one, hoss?"

Branch lifted one of the pouches, an inch by half an inch, between his thumb and forefinger. "Jesus."

"Not very ladylike, are they? But then, Maria's not your average lady."

Branch read the lid: SKOAL BANDITS. WINTERGREEN SMOKE-LESS TOBACCO. THE LITTLE POUCH OF TOBACCO PLEASURE. EASY TO ENJOY. JUST PLACE A POUCH BETWEEN YOUR CHEEK AND GUM. YOU DON'T CHEW IT . . . YOU JUST ENJOY THE TOBACCO PLEASURE. "Where'd you get these, Jeff?"

"Seven Eleven."

"*Why'd* you get them?"

"Hen—El Bozo uses them, to cut down on smoking

cigarettes. I got some for Maria. She's trying to cut down—or I'm trying to get her to try.''

"I found one of these outside Strock's house, the day after Wade was killed.''

"Well, it wasn't Maria's; she just started using them.''

"I also found one in Escobar's car.''

Derry shrugged. "Maybe he's trying to kick the habit, too.''

"No.''

"What do you mean, no?''

"I don't know what I mean. I just know it wasn't Escobar's. And the other one wasn't Strock's.''

Eve turned to face Branch. "You don't think El Bozo. . . ?''

"No. I don't know what I think.''

"Funny,'' Derry said. "I never thought of Maddox as having his own place—and certainly not in the H el R. I think of him spending all his time at Kallistos, curling up with the computers whenever he needs a little shut-eye.''

What was funnier was that Maddox hadn't been at Kallistos. A weekday. Not even six o'clock. It wasn't like him to knock off early. Funnier still, he hadn't been in all day, and hadn't called in sick or otherwise. Not so funny to the secretary, maybe, who said Maddox had been doing a lot of work at home lately, "what with all that's been going down,'' but she didn't know the half of it.

"You don't like it, do you, Sam?''

"Nope.''

"Me, neither. I especially don't like sitting out here on El Centro. Somebody's sure to drive by and wonder what I—who's supposed to be flat on my aching back—am doing with you, who's the object of an intensive manhunt, as they say on the evening news. How're we going in—ballsy or sneaky?''

They were a little of each. Branch got down behind the

front seat while Derry parked in the driveway, showed the doorman his shield, and said he was doing a fire inspection of the building; County Fire and Rescue was shorthanded and had enlisted off-duty cops to lend a hand. The doorman said okay, but Derry couldn't leave his car out front; he'd have to put it in the Hacienda el Refugio's garage. Which was where Branch wanted to be, for from there they could ride the elevator unseen up to Maddox's apartment.

"How come you know the layout in this place?"

"Portia used to live here. Before your time."

"Hunh. Why'd Portia kill Mularky, Sam? You figured it out?"

Branch shook his head. If he shook it enough, maybe something would fall into place.

"You thought about how we're going to get in? I didn't bring my picks."

"The locks in this place're locks in name only. I once opened Portia's door by accident with my house key. I doubt if things've changed that much."

"Must've changed a little if Maddox lives here. I can't wait to see his decor."

Stainless-steel racks; modern versions of colonial stocks; handcuffs of metal and wire and leather; leather masks and gloves and collars and codpieces and chastity belts; whips, flails, prods, canes, pincers, nails, needles, knives, scalpels, mallets, screws, chains, manacles, hobbles; garter belts, silk stockings, G-strings, teddies, merry widows, crotchless panties, crotchless tights, crotchless body stockings; maribou slippers, stiletto heels, jackboots, motorcycle boots, combat boots; a hockey goalie's mask, a welder's mask, a Navaho tribal mask, a Lone Ranger mask, a gas mask, a fencing mask, a kendo mask, a knitted ski mask, a full-contact karate helmet; rubber heads of Frankenstein's monster, a *Planet of the Apes* creature,

Richard Nixon, Ronald Reagan and John Kennedy, Steve
Martin with an arrow through his head.

The last was on the head of Maddox, who was espaliered
by a pair of handcuffs on one of the racks, a prosaic noose
around his neck, wearing a satin nightgown encrusted with
lace and embroidered with pastel appliqués. A trocar lay at
his feet, like a remembrance.

"Get out real slow, Strock."

"The hell . . . ?"

Branch kept the barrel of his gun behind Strock's ear
until he was out of the Mercedes. "Spread 'em."

"Branch?"

"Pat him down, Jeff."

*"Der*ry? Hell're you doing here? I thought you were
laid up."

Derry stepped back with Strock's revolver. "He's clean,
Sam."

"Get his keys and let's go inside. Did you change your
locks recently, Strock?"

"The *hell*'re you talking about?"

"Did you?"

"No . . . Why?"

"Let's go inside."

"This yours?" Branch laid a towel on the coffee table
and unwrapped the trocar. "Or this?" He opened the lid of
the Carr's Table Water Crackers tin Derry had unearthed
from the base of Branch's weeping willow on the way over
from the H el R, removed the waterproof pouch and shook
out the trocar he'd found beneath Patrick Wade's deathbed.

Strock took a step back and looked sideways at the
needles. "Hell'd you get those?"

Branch sat in Strock's leather recliner and leaned way
back. "You're fucked, Tom."

"I'm fucked? *You're* fucked." He whirled on Derry,

who reached inside his sport coat. "The hell're you doing mixed up in this, Jeff? You've just flushed your entire goddamn career down the goddamn toilet."

Derry kept his hand on his gun butt. "Have a seat, Chief. We've got a lot of talking to do." He took a tin of Skoal Bandits from his pocket—they'd stopped at the 7 Eleven on the way, as well—and held it out to Strock. "Care for one, Chief?"

Strock's eyelids fluttered, as if it were something that might explode.

"*Mad*dox?" Eve said.

"With one of Strock's needles. Strock swears he didn't do it. We left him locked up in a storeroom in his basement, but I believe him. I think someone's trying to set him up, using the Manhattan Beach connection. That grand jury turned in a no true bill, by the way, so Strock's clean. Did you talk to Annie?"

"I can't find her, Sam. Her car's at her office, but she's not, and her neighbors haven't seen her since Monday morning."

"Monday? What about her kids? Today's Wednesday." Wasn't it? Could he really have flown to New York on Tuesday night and be back home—if home this was—on Wednesday evening? *As you go to the East, the time doth increase; as you go to the West, the time doth grow less.*

"They're up north—up the coast, as you say around here—visiting friends. Annie was supposed to call last night, and didn't. The last person to see her was Warren Cable."

"How do you know that?"

"I told you, I'm good at this. I solved the Jitney mystery. I thought: Annie was so sure Cable and Southland were behind the Moneda monkey business, maybe she was pugnacious enough to confront him and tell him so. She had an appointment with him Monday morning."

"About what?"

"The dam committee. Cable'd offered Portia a seat on Southland's board. In view of her departure, could Annie think of anyone else from the committee who'd be suitable?"

"Could she?"

"Cable says they left it at that. They were going to talk again after the committee had a meeting. . . . He said Annie was acting funny, Sam."

"Funny how?"

"He said she was dressed funny—in jeans and a T-shirt, that she was hostile, that she didn't concentrate on what he was saying. He put it down to events, but . . ."

"But what?"

"He said he wondered if Annie'd been involved with Wade—if she was on one of his tapes and concerned that it'd get out. . . . She wasn't, was she, Sam?"

"No."

"He's smooth, Cable. I'm not saying I didn't believe what he said, but I got the feeling it was . . . rehearsed."

"Like Leah Marston?"

"Now that you mention it. Do you think that means anything?"

Branch shook his head, as if she could see him. "Any luck with Hawkes?"

"Not yet. Maria's helping me make phone calls. She was getting antsy. She and Jeff're in love, did you know that?"

Branch felt jealous, not of the couple, but of their capacity to have the emotion.

32

The town was called Pesadilla—nightmare. Whose, and about what, had escaped history—unless it referred to the place itself, which brought to mind Tony Astin's *half a dozen 'dobe huts and half a hundred hounds;* in this case, two bars and four whores. Somewhere beyond the dark at the edge of town was Mexico.

Though far from full, the jai alai *frontón* was the noisiest place Branch had been in in years. (Californians didn't like to clump together, and when they did it was in cantilevered stadiums that diluted their enthusiasm.) It smelled of olive oil and beer and tobacco and marijuana.

"*¿Está este asiento ocupado?*" Escobar was about halfway up in the stands, a vantage Branch liked to watch things from because it offered the possibility of neutrality. Any closer and you had to be partisan, had to have an opinion about every strategy, every judgment; any farther and you risked losing interest.

". . . Sam?"

"*¿Qué tal*, Ray?"

"You are a free man, Sam? You have cleared your name? Did you find the woman you were looking for? You understand why I told Jeff where to find you. I could not let you—"

"Is there someplace we can talk?"

"*Momentito*, okay? I have twenty on the Big Q."

"Which one is he?"

Escobar laughed. "Not he, Sam. It. The Big Quiniela."

"That's first and second, right?"

"The first two teams, no matter what order, in two consecutive games. I had three and six in the last game, three and eight in this. Eight is leading, three has a strong chance for second."

Branch watched a long rally, the players climbing the side and back walls, hurling themselves full-length on their follow-throughs, scrambling to their feet and retreating to a defensive position. They reminded him of kids at Columbia, or outside Whitehall Street, stoning cops, stoning him, making him try harder than ever to get out of uniform and into clothes. "The court's called a *frontón*, right?"

"The building is the *frontón*. The court is *la cancha*." Escobar was sweating, but so was Branch, and everyone else.

"And what's the object?"

"As in handball. A player from one team serves the ball—the *pelota*—against the front wall—the *frontis*. It must land in the service box without touching the red areas, the screen overhead, and without going outside the foul line—where the judges are sitting. An opposing player catches it in his *cesta* before it bounces twice and returns it. The catch and the throw must be in one continuous motion. After the serve, the *pelota* may be played off the side wall—the *lateral*—or the back wall—the *rebote*—before it reaches the front wall."

"And you bet on what—a point, the final score, what?"

"In Cuba—and in Spain, of course—they play *partidos*, singles or doubles, a game of between ten and forty points, depending on the level of play. You bet on the outcome of the game, at any time in the game. In America, the betting has been altered—some would say perverted—to accommodate the pari-mutuel system. Eight teams—they are identified by their post position, as if they were horses—play a game of five points. The first two teams play a point and the losers leave the *cancha;* the winners continue against the next team, and remain on the *cancha* until they lose a point or win all five points; then there are playoffs for place and show. If three positions reach three points, the others are eliminated and those three play off. There is straight betting—win, place or show; *quiniela* betting—the first two teams, in either order; *perfecta* betting—first and second in that order; the daily double—first in two successive games; and the Big Q—the *quiniela* in two successive games.''

You could probably learn anything at all from a man with his back to the wall and out of room to do anything but talk—medicine, law, history, car repair, computer programming, macramé. ''Three missed, so they're out, right?''

''They still have a chance.''

''But basically, you're a loser.''

Escobar laughed too loudly. ''Hey, *hermano,* do not lecture me. I have a good time. It is a night out on the town. I do not get drunk. I do not get the clap.''

''Let's go someplace and talk, Ray. This object in your ribs is a gun.''

''*¿Qué pasa, hermano?* Why a gun?''

''*A causa de las mentiras.* Why the lies, Ray? And why Maddox?''

''*Yo no*—''

''You do . . . *hermano. Vámanos.*''

They sat in Derry's Cobra, looking out the windshield at a billboard whose tattered message advertised condos in a community called Rancho Ensueño—which was what it had been, an illusion built squarely in the path of the Arozbispo Mountains' annual forest fire.

"What was it you said that day in the morgue, Ray, when you were cutting up Litvak—that I always have a theory in the absence of a suspect? Well, here's my theory: You killed Patrick Wade. You made it look like a murder made to look like a case of autoerotic asphyxia—like, in fact, one of Kaplowitz's serial murders. The trocar would be traced to Strock. Manhattan Beach, S and M rings, end of Strock. It was elegant, Ray: you commit a nearly perfect crime—a murder an ordinary pathologist would think was a suicide, or, if he knew his stuff, an arcane accident—then you, no ordinary pathologist, see the imperfection, see it as a murder masquerading as an accident. You'd've been the star. There'd've been interviews, profiles. The Miami thing would've had to be put in a different perspective. . . .

"I fouled things up by pocketing the needle, then unfouled them to some extent by asking you to find out if it *was* Strock's. You didn't have to find out, of course. You already knew. You'd taken the needle from the case of needles and scalpels in Strock's den—taken it and the needle you used to kill Howard Maddox. That key I gave you, Ray, wasn't the key to Strock's house; by mistake, I gave you the key to his office at headquarters. . . .

"It was a fluke, an accident, bad luck—yours. I never suspected you. Oh, I wondered, that morning at La Ermita, why you didn't push me to turn myself in—or at least give you a good explanation why I wasn't turning myself in. You stayed too quiet, Ray; you should've been more upset when I said Strock'd told me the story about you in Miami, about the teeth. Strock knew you were up to something, but he didn't know what; he told me that story thinking I'd tell you—he knew we were getting to be close—and that it'd spook you. And of course I wondered about the pouch of chewing tobacco I found under the seat

of your car, since I'd found the same kind of pouch
outside Strock's house. I now know they were dropped by
Aura Quivers, who's more a litterbug than a mayor ought
to be. . . . By the way, here's the money you loaned me.''

Escobar just looked at the envelope Branch laid on the
dashboard. "What now, Sam?"

Branch read the tattered billboard: THE DREAM IS A REAL-
ITY. THE FUTURE HAS ARRIVED. YOUR CASTLE AWAITS. "This
has all been a freelance effort. Strock and I both have a lot
of explaining to do to the DA. It's going to take a couple
of days to get it straightened out to the point where we can
start getting warrants and making arrests. Tell me everything, Ray, and I'll do what I can to make things easier on
you. Maybe you can cop a plea to a conspiracy charge.
You didn't actually kill Wade and Maddox, did you, just
devised the method? Quivers killed them, didn't she, and
planted the needles she stole from Strock? She was having
an affair with Strock and I don't know what to call it with
Wade and maybe Maddox and maybe you. Or was she into
you for something else—something about your gambling?
Not that it matters.''

Escobar picked up the envelope and tapped it on his
knee. "And if I get out and walk away, Sam? You are still
a free lance. You have no authority to arrest me.''

"Walk where? To your car? Then what? Mexico? Central America? South America? Tierra del Fuego?'' He
snorted. "That's what they should've called Rancho Ensueño.
. . . If you mean will I stop you, no. You can run if you
want, Ray, but there's no freedom down the road.''

"*¿Y aquí?*'' Escobar gestured at their view. "This
might be the parking lot at the gateway to Hell. Long-term
rates available. Are there free men in Hell, *en el calabozo*?''

"There're no free men outside the law. The law doesn't
only punish, Ray; it's also merciful. Part of its mercy is
that it makes deals.''

Escobar put the envelope in an inside pocket. When his

hand reappeared, it held a gun, which he pointed at Branch's
face. "You're pathetic, Branch. A *marico*. That anyone
could have suspected you'd killed a man . . ." He turned
his head and spat out the window. "Pathetic, too, is that a
man like Warren Cable is finishing a good dinner right
about now, drinking a good brandy, smoking a good cigar,
talking of this and that with good friends and family. Is it
an accident of birth, or is choice involved? And if so, at
what juncture in one's life? When did I make the decision
that brought me here, to *este estación a la puerta del
Infierno?* . . . *Su pistola, hermano.*"

Branch drew his gun between thumb and forefinger and
held it out.

Escobar shook his head. "No. Shoot me, Sam."

"Ray—"

"I cannot do it, Sam."

Branch put his gun on the dashboard. "Ray—"

"Do it!"

"No."

"Do it!"

"No!"

So Escobar did it, the barrel in his mouth.

33

Branch lay on the *cancha* of an open-air *frontón* in Ixtapa, Portia in his arms. A doubles game whirled around them. Escobar was one of the players and Leah Marston was another; her *cesta* was made of peacock feathers. The ball struck Escobar in the mouth and his head exploded.

"Sam?"

Branch opened his eyes. "Yeah?"

Derry had his elbows on the windowsill of his neighbor's GTO, looking through binoculars up at Warren Cable's house, perched on stilts on the side of Rancho Maria's only notable elevation, known on maps as Bellavista Dome and irreverently as BVD. The adobe glowed pink in the dawn's light. "They're moving. I see Cable . . . and his driver . . . and a woman."

"Annie?"

"No. Too hefty."

"Quivers?"

"Could be. She's got a hat on. Or a scarf. But it could be . . . Yes, it is. It's Quivers." Derry tossed the binoculars on the back seat and started the car. The radio came on with the engine and the Beach Boys sang "She'll Have

Fun, Fun, Fun Till Her Daddy Takes Her T-Bird Away.''
He missed the Cobra, which fit like a glove, but it had
been used as an ambulance to take Maddox and Escobar to
the morgue (they'd used the latter's keys to get in), and
there hadn't been time to clean Escobar's brains off the
upholstery.

Bellavista to Roble Rojo, Roble Rojo to El Látigo, El
Látigo to Esmeralda, to Calle Verde, to Sequoia to El
Centro to Rancho Maria de la Luz Boulevard—past the
dozing guard and the dozing dogs (on the way in, Branch
had assumed his favorite position on the floor of the back
seat)—to the Beltway. Then east.

Derry lowered the visor against the rising run. ''It's a
little early to be tailing anybody. I don't want to get too far
back.''

''Jeff, thanks for everything you've done. I couldn't've
done it without you. That includes the lecture over my
spaghetti.''

''Your world-famous spaghetti.''

''In New York, we had a little time before the plane and
swung by the neighborhood in Brooklyn where my wife
and kids live. I hoped I'd get a look at the kids, playing in
front of the house or something. I'm glad I didn't, because
it would've been hard to just drive away without giving
them a kiss and a hug—and I couldn't've done that, made
them accessories. It made me realize, though, that for five
years that's how I've been thinking of my relationship with
my kids: I was a criminal and they were always in danger
of being associated with me. Megan's partly responsible
for that; she's long on guilt and short on forgiveness. But
I'm responsible, too, and I want it to change.

''As someone with one of your character disorders, I've
never felt that need. Megan'd been gone only a few months
when I met Portia, and I thought if I was attractive to a
woman who looked like a movie star then there was

nothing wrong with me, there was something wrong with Megan, who looked like a housewife with two kids. After Portia, there was Annie, and again I thought that there was nothing wrong with me if I was attractive to a beautiful woman who was also a mother and a professional; any problems I'd had with Portia were her problems. Then Eve showed up, and the problems Annie and I were having seemed to me to be Annie's problems; she was always wanting me to always say what I was thinking and feeling, wanting me to say what I wanted. If I was attractive to a woman who'd come to terms with our society's absence of commitment, who'd built her life around irresponsibility—her own and others'—then there was nothing wrong with me—They're getting off, Jeff.''

"I see. Las Pasas. This is the way to the reservoir. I guess that makes sense. There're a couple of buildings up there where they could be keeping her. You don't think they killed her, do you, Sam?"

"I think they're rigging an accident. I hope they haven't already rigged it. Let me finish what I was saying. I want to say it out loud and it'll keep me from worrying about Annie that much longer. . . . I have to go back to New York. I have to work things out with Megan and the kids. I don't mean get undivorced, remarried, whatever; I mean really work out what being divorced means—what it means for us and for the kids. I guess that'll mean therapy or family counseling or whatever. To Megan, it'll mean seeing a priest, and I guess I can do that if I can also convince her there's a secular route we should explore, as well. . . . What's so funny?"

Derry put out a hand to clarify his laugh. "I'm glad to hear you say this, Sam. It sounds like a good idea. It was me I was laughing at. What a jerk I've been. Maria. Maria de la Luz. What the hell was I thinking—that I'd reform her, show her the way? That I was the only man in the world who could possibly understand her? Talk about character disorders. It's not the first time I've tried that line. I tried it with Annie. I'm ashamed to say it, Sam, but the night Annie walked out on your world-famous spaghetti, I went by her place—to make sure she was okay, that sort of thing. I was hoping . . . well, I was hoping to score. It was pretty clear Eve was interested in you and pretty clear I wasn't going to get anywhere with her, and . . . well, shit, I'm sorry, that's all. I hope I get a chance to say that to Annie, too. I don't know what I'll say to Maria. I'm afraid she's buying what I've been selling. The bill of goods according to Saint Jeffrey.''

"Maybe it's not such a bill of goods.''

"Come on, Sam. She's a porno star.''

"And you're a ladies' man, and how important has it really been to you who the lady was? No more important than it is to some actor, if that's the word, in a porno movie. Maybe you'll teach each other something.''

Derry shook his head. "This is a hell of a conversation to be having while tailing some bad guys.''

"Bear left at the fork, Jeff.''

"There's their dust. They went right.''

"Left'll put us on higher ground. When I don't know what the fuck I'm doing, I like to be on higher ground.''

Derry reached for Branch's hand and gave it a squeeze. "It's good to be working with you again, partner.''

Branch shifted his grip, so he could return the pressure.

Derry shaded his eyes with a hand, wishing he had his Dodger cap. "That's Annie's car. I thought it was in the lot at her office.''

The purple Rabbit was parked behind the concrete pumphouse at the edge of Las Pasas Reservoir; in front of the pumphouse were Cable's limousine and a silver Jeep Cherokee. "They're going to use it to rig the accident.

Someone must've brought it up during the night. You know the one standing guard?"

"Looks like a biker. That means there're at least four of them—Cable, Quivers, Cable's driver, and the guard. Why've they waited this long, Sam? This is the fourth day they've had Annie."

"She must have something they want but don't know where it is. And I'd say there must be six—somebody to stay with Annie, somebody to drive the Cherokee down, somebody else to drive the Rabbit back. Plus Quivers and Cable and the driver. Watch the sun on those binoculars."

"Six is crowded. Be nice if we had a chopper and an outboard and at least two more cars. And maybe a couple of ORVs."

"What're ORVs?"

"Off-road vehicles."

He *should* go back to New York; he'd never be a Westerner. "I think it's just us, Jeff."

"Then we ought to hit them now. If they all get out in the open we're going to have a tough time. Unless, of course, you were planning on shooting to kill."

"How long do you figure it'll take you to climb down this bluff?"

"What're you going to be doing?"

"Working my way down through those trees. They left the gate open and I want to lock it."

"Two minutes. Three minutes. We're downwind, so I can be kind of noisy."

Branch turned on his back to look at his watch. "Let's sync up. I've got— Morning."

The man had a shaven head and a rose tattoo on his right bicep; he waggled the barrel of his UZI at Branch's midriff. "Take out your piece real easy, slick. Fella, you stay on your belly and I'll relieve you of yours." He bent over Derry and took his revolver from the hip holster he wore in the small of his back. "Never did like the idea of carrying a gun back there. Too easy for other folks to get at and kind of awkward for you. And ain't it uncomfortable when you're driving? Now get up nice and slow, both of you fellows, and let's go down below and join the party.''

What kind of party wasn't hard to imagine, for besides the UZI and the bands of ammunition across his chest, the man carried a Beretta 9 mm in a holster belted around his waist, a paratrooper's knife in his combat boots, and a bullwhip. He didn't need to snap it; he was above effects.

34

Dark.

A motor. Pesky. Irritating. Like a lawnmower.

Or an outboard.

Laughter. Men high on beer and pills and evil. Three of them. Maybe four.

Maybe more.

A skittering in the corner. A water bug. Or a rat.

A rat.

Branch hissed at it.

Derry sat forward, or so it felt. "What?"

"Nothing."

Somehow, Annie slept. Branch watched over her—Saint Sam, her errant knight errant.

Derry gave up trying to contort his legs between his manacled wrists—or his wrists over his legs; he wasn't sure—and lay panting on his back on the cold stone floor. "Isn't this the part where the bad guys tell the good guys what's been right in front of their faces if they weren't so fucking dumb? Right before they kill them?"

"I think I've figured it out." It had been something to do.

"I'd love to hear it." Aura Quivers stood in a doorway they hadn't known was there, hands on hips. A hooded light on the ceiling of the room behind her put a highlight on her mane of hair. Aura's aura. She wore her western clothes, and sounded mean. "Really, Sam. Go ahead. It'll be a sort of satisfaction."

For him, Branch knew she meant. He didn't need that sort of satisfaction and didn't want to give her any, but it just poured out of him, as if the sponge were being squeezed. "You and Cable wanted Felix out of the water picture. You bribed Maddox to work from inside Kallistos to sabotage the dam committee. At the same time, an Israeli mobster named Rafelson with an old grudge against Felix was also trying to ruin Kallistos by pulling money out of Moneda Investing. Felix thought Cable was behind the pullout and he dreamed up a fake assassination attempt that would be pinned on Cable. He had Maddox make the arrangements, not knowing Maddox had sold out. That was okay with your side; Maddox simply didn't tell the assassin to leave clues pointing to Cable and didn't tell him it was just pretend.

"Meanwhile, Pat Wade found out about the Moneda withdrawals and also mistakenly concluded Cable was responsible. Wade dropped a hint about it to Eve Zabriskie and maybe to others. He had to be shut up. You had Escobar by the balls, knowing about his gambling problem, and you squeezed him to come up with a way to kill Wade—a way that would point the finger at Strock, who was an easy mark because of the Manhattan Beach thing and who would've caused you trouble in the long run. Maddox was a problem in the short run; he knew far too much. So Escobar killed him, too—or rather, thought up the method. You did the dirty work. Except I guess it was fun for you, wasn't it? What drives you, Aura? What makes you tick? Is it just that you can't stand men?"

She had shifted to stand against the doorpost, her arms

crossed under her breasts. "This is all so trite, Branch.
The ritual attempt to induce remorse."

He laughed. "You're good, Aura. I'm just paying hom-
age. . . . What kind of games do you play with Cable?"
He could see better now and saw how she clutched her
arms. "You're the boss and he's the secretary? You're the
mistress of the house and he's the maid? I can't see him in
a dress, but I couldn't see Pat Wade, either—until I did."

A pause, for effect, and then he was talking to Derry,
making Quivers the acolyte in search of enlightenment.
"Escobar would've been next, and knew it, which is why
he killed himself. He was going to get it last night. Aura
here had somebody following him. They followed him to
the *frontón*, then followed me. While we were watching
Cable's, they were watching us. So now we're next—you
and I and Annie, Annie who's Wade's lawyer and who
presumably came across some documentation of his suspicions about the Moneda monkey business, as Eve calls it.
Aura here forgot about Eve. She didn't know till now that
she's going to have to kill her, too, since she has the
tape."

Another pause. Quivers was standing straight, her arms
at her sides, one hand fiddling with the seam of her jeans.
"I left something out, Jeff. When Wade found out about
the Moneda monkey business, he told Aura here. She
already knew about it, obviously, but she saw in Wade's
knowing a way to solve a problem. Whom to pin Felix's
death on? Cable mustn't be suspected, so how about Wade?
The scenario would be that Wade threatened to blow the
whistle on Felix. But Felix had something on Wade—a
videotape of Wade and Aura here playing *General Hospital*,
with Wade as the nurse, down to his white stockings. Of
all the tapes, it was the one most damaging to Wade's
reputation; if anyone ever found out about the others,
they'd say, 'What the hell—he's a gynecologist.' So Aura
here *gave* the tape to Felix. Well, not gave it exactly; she

planted it in his house. The cops would find it and see it as Wade's motive for killing Felix.''

''Why would I do that, Sam.'' Quivers's voice was pitched high. ''Wouldn't it be damaging to my reputation, as well?''

Good. To be incredulous is to be off-balance. He answered her question, but not to her. ''Since the tape was hidden, in effect, it isn't likely that we'd've found it—not you or I, Jeff, anyway. But Aura here was going to make sure Strock found it. Aura here had Strock by the balls, too. He'd've destroyed the tape, to protect her reputation, and looked for another way to nail Wade. But Felix *wasn't* murdered, which meant all signals were off, all the scenarios had to be torn up—all but the scenario that required that Wade be gotten rid of. Since Aura here didn't need Strock anymore, she set it up to make Strock look like Wade's killer. Like I said, she's good. Not perfect, though. It was stupid of her to think the tape was safe where it was, just because she was the only one—''

Quivers was gone, slamming the door behind her.

''—who knew it was there.''

Derry chuckled. ''It's crazy. It just goes round and round.'' He resumed his squirming, then gave it up for good. ''Annie *is* alive, isn't she, Sam? She didn't stir when they brought us in and she didn't stir through all that blabbling.''

Branch watched the rise and fall of her chest. *20 Years of Women on Top*, indeed. ''She's alive. She looks real weak.''

''And who're these bikers?''

''Cable's strong-arm men, I guess. Maybe Cable's into narcotics, too. A lot of Angels've gone that route.''

''You sure have figured it out, all right. Fucking lot of good it does us.''

Branch sat back against the wall and shut his eyes. ''Try and get some rest, Jeff. Whatever we're going to do, we're going to have to be sharp to do it.'' But Branch couldn't rest. It just went round and round. Shadows and echoes. Echoes and shadows.

There's dust in the corners, holes in the screens,
Dishes piled high in the sink.
I'm out of clean socks, there's no food for the dog,
I've drunk all the booze I can drink.

Shadows and echoes. Echoes and shadows.
They're all that you left behind.
Echoes and shadows. Shadows and echoes.
They're driving me out of my mind.

The phone it don't ring; no cars stopping by.
I smoked my last Lucky last night.
My boss said don't bother to come in no more.
Ain't been in a bar where I ain't had a fight.

Shadows and echoes. Echoes and shadows.
They're all that I have of you.
Echoes and shadows. Shadows and echoes.
The echoes are hollow, the shadows are blue.

''Sam?''

''Umm?''

''You asleep?''

''Nope.''

''There's one other thing.''

''Yeah?''

''Who killed Litvak?''

The sponge wasn't dry. Another squeeze. ''Litvak was sent to deal with Felix, who'd temporarily, at least, found a way to deal with the Moneda monkey business. He told his sister he was going to kill Felix, but I think he was just going to lean on him. Leah Marston tipped Felix, who dreamed up another of his setups. Things would've turned out very differently if Felix hadn't been so addicted to charades. . . . The setup was: Felix arranged to meet Litvak and get the check; Felix didn't show up, somebody else did—somebody who was supposed to mug Litvak and take the check, leaving Litvak to go home with his tail between his legs.''

"Somebody else who?"

"Bobby Lucas."

"Who the fuck is Bobby Lucas?"

"Admiral Hawkes's driver. I was in Yosemite with my kids when he killed that guy last year. What do you know about it?"

Derry gave his sponge a squeeze. "He killed a drifter. In his room at the Admiral's place. Lucas said he came home and found a window forced and the drifter passed out drunk on the floor. Said he'd never seen him before. He dumped a bucket of water on him and he came up swinging and went for Lucas's throat. Lucas slipped him and got a gun out of a drawer—a Bren ten, if you can believe that; I mean, we're talking half a grand—and shot the drifter in the face. Exactly how the drifter got back on the bed, in a sleeping position, and how most of his head got on the wall right next to the bed, was something we couldn't get out of Lucas. Some money and a watch of Lucas's was in the drifter's pocket, a bottle of his bourbon in his stomach, and, like I said, a window'd been forced, so it wasn't much of a stretch to make it into self-defense in the course of an attempted burglary. Admiral Hawkes knew somebody in the Defense Department who knew somebody at Justice who convinced the DA to do the stretching.''

Branch went on: "Lucas killed Litvak. He was supposed to mug him, but he overdid it. Sounds like it was his way. He also forgot to take the check. . . . This is where it gets complicated—''

Derry laughed.

"—When Felix died accidentally, Mularky saw a chance to make some big money from Warren Cable, who he still thought was behind the plot to kill Felix. Cable, Quivers and Maddox told Mularky he had it wrong, that Portia was the brains. They set up a meeting between them that I was to witness. But when Mularky told Portia he knew about her people, she misunderstood him and thought he meant the people plotting, such as they were, to kill Litvak. She killed him to protect Bobby and, more importantly, her father, who could've been implicated."

"I thought her father didn't like Jews. To be in on the Litvak scam, wouldn't he have had to know Felix was Schatz? And don't forget—he told Eve about the Moneda monkey business, too."

"He told her thinking Cable was behind it. He thought it because it was what Felix and Portia thought."

"Jesus. Everybody thought something different, didn't they? Jesus. Round and round."

I can't sleep for dreaming, can't walk but I fall;
I'd run but there's nowhere to go.
Something mean's eating what's left of my heart.
The face in the mirror's a face I don't know.

Shadows and echoes. Echoes and shadows.
They're driving me out of my mind.
Echoes and shadows. Shadows and echoes.
The echoes are deaf and the shadows are blind.

35

Annie stirred, moaned, woke.

"Annie. It's Sam. Sam and Jeff." Mutt and Jeff.

She wept.

Branch made it onto his knees and walked on them to her and bent over her. "How are you? Did they hurt you?" *Did they get physical?*

Where had that come from? Oh, yeah—Eve. Eve's Olivia Newton-John shtick.

"Oh, Sam."

"It's okay. We'll get out of this okay."

The boom of metal on metal.

Annie startled and whimpered.

"It's okay." His shtick. A dried-up sponge.

A band of light beneath the door—not the door Quivers had opened; the door they'd been brought through, the door to a hallway.

"Sam."

"I see it."

"If I can get behind the door, I can kick it back in their faces when they open it. Maybe hurt somebody."

"Yeah."

276

Derry began to move. His shtick. A man of action. No echoes and shadows in his life. Just adrenaline and testosterone.

Then, where there had been a door there was nothing but light. And laughter.

Derry was frozen by the light, his face turned away from it.

A man moved to kick him in the face, but another, the one with the shaven head, grabbed his shoulders and threw him aside.

"You fucking asshole. They gotta look like they bought it in a wreck, you scumbag."

"Fuck 'em."

A third man hauled Branch away from Annie. He grabbed her hair and wrenched her head back. "I want the girl. I waited all this fucking time, I want the girl."

"You fucking shithead. They do an autopsy, man, find out she was reamed, the whole fucking thing's blown away."

"What autopsy, man? The fucking coroner's on the fucking payroll."

Branch arched his back and pushed off with his shoulders and kicked at the shithead's crotch. He missed, and the one with the shaven head saved him from retaliation. It occurred to Branch that he should've taken aim at him, whom the others wouldn't stop, or who wouldn't be able to stop the others, from beating him, so that it wouldn't look like a wreck, so that, so that . . . Should he tell them the coroner was no longer on the payroll? Should he tell them he'd figured it out, show them his scorecard? What was the score?

Litvak, Felix, Wade, Maddox, Escobar. Bad Guys 5, Good Guys 0.

But of course, Felix *wasn't* murdered. Bad Guys 4. Litvak, well . . . Litvak was caught, in a sense, in the crossfire. Bad Guys 3. Escobar? They should have Escobar.

Bad Guys 3, Good Guys 0. Bottom of the ninth. Not an insurmountable lead. A pitcher's battle, sort of.

No—top of the ninth. Derry, Annie, him. It would be Bad Guys 6, Good Guys out of guys. A laugher, sort of.

Then they were hauled up—Branch by the shithead—and quick-marched out the door and along a narrow hall lined with oozing, scummy pipes and through another door and out into the night.

Bullfrogs. Crickets. A nighthawk. A fish jumped. The Wonderful World of Nature.

The headlights of Cable's stretch turned the gravel yellow. Branch remembered a midnight picnic on some nameless empty beach, with Portia. She had draped her scarlet blouse over one of the Porsche's headlights and his blue shirt over the other and they had made love to Beatles music on the radio, like hippies. Why the Beatles? Ah, yes—it was the night after John Lennon died. There was nothing else on the radio. They should have John Lennon, too. Bad Guys 7, Good Guys 0. And all the rest: Janis and Jimi and Elvis and Hank and Buddy and Richie and the Big Bopper; the Kennedys; Judy and Marilyn and Princess Grace; Bill Holden and John Belushi; Martin Luther King; Lassie and Smokey the Bear and Elsa the lioness; Jesus. Who had played Phil on *Hill Street Blues?* Something Conrad. *Michael* Conrad. They should have him, too.

Bad Guys 27, Good Guys 0.

Hey, give the Good Guys Joe McCarthy and Hitler and Attila the Hun.

You can have Hitler, but we get six million Jews.

That's fair. Six million Jews and Harry Chapin.

Bad Guys 6,000,028, Good Guys 3.

You give up?

We got last licks.

Last licks, shit, man. We just ate the bats.

Manson. The Good Guys get Charles Manson.

Manson's not dead, you stupid fucks. But thanks for reminding us; we get Sharon Tate and them other assholes.

Bad Guys 6,000,028 and Sharon makes 29 and them other assholes, Good Guys 3.

We get Stalin.

Take him. We get all the suckers in the Goo-lag.

Mussolini.

Take him.

Hirohito.

Take the fucking Nip. You're up to six and we got 6,000,029 and them other assholes and all the suckers in the Goo-lag. You give up?

. . . Ho Chi Minh.

You want Ho Chi Minh? I'm surprised. I thought you were one of them Commie-lovers. Take him. We'll take the women and kids and old farts they wasted at My Lai.

. . . Göring.

No doubles. You already got Hitler. Taking Göring's like having doubles. You get Göring, we make it twelve million Jews.

. . . You give up?

. . . The Joker.

Who?

Forget it.

Take him. Fuck do we care. Okay, Bad Guys 6,000,029 and them other assholes and all the suckers in the Goo-lag and the women and kids and old farts they wasted at My Lai. Good Guys 6, and Ho Ho Ho Chi Minh is 7 and The Joker is 8. Nice game, suckers. Anytime you want to play again, you know where to find us.

Cable and Quivers stood at the perimeter of the pool of light, just watching. He wasn't wearing a dress, but a white cotton boatneck shirt, madras patch slacks, Bass Weejuns with no socks. The cowgirl and the superannuated preppy, dressed to kill.

Branch tried to writhe free; he wanted to tell them just
how well he knew the score. But the shithead was strong.
The shithead pumped iron. The shithead thrust Branch into
the passenger seat of Annie's Rabbit. The nameless biker
put Derry in the back seat. The one with the shaven head
put Annie behind the wheel.

"It's going to be hard to drive like this, asshole."

The bikers walked away. There would be no repartee.
They wouldn't talk their way out of it. They were in it
forever. And the bad guys wouldn't be telling the good
guys what had been right in front of their faces if they'd
had a fucking scorecard and weren't so fucking dumb. The
game was over. The score was history.

Cable met the bikers and talked to them, staying out of
range of their beery breath and the stench of their colors. Quivers turned her back on the parley and got in Cable's car.

"Sam?"

"It's okay, Annie. It's going to be okay."

Derry was moving, twisting, turning, rocking the car.
"Annie, does this seat open down into the trunk?"

"I-I think so."

"You have a tire iron or something back there?"

"Yes. I think so."

The shithead was at the Cherokee, removing something
from the back seat.

"Jeff, they've got some kind of black bag—like a doctor's bag. I think they're going to try their injection trick
again."

"I can't hear you, Sam."

The wind had come up suddenly. A loud wind. Like
the wind a forest fire makes. That would be handy. That
would save them the trouble. They could just leave them
there to roast. Bad Guys 6,000,029 and them other
assholes and all the suckers in the Goo-lag and the women

and kids and old farts they wasted at My Lai and one
forest. Good Guys 8, one of them a comic book character.

"Sam."

"It's okay, Annie."

"No, look."

"A chopper." Derry laughed. "Didn't I say we needed
a chopper?"

A County chopper with every spotlight known to man
and a bullhorn and a guy who'd seen all the movies and
TV shows and practiced at night in the basement and had
been waiting for years to do *his* shtick.

*"You there on the, uh, ground, this is the, uh, county
police. Kindly step away from those vee-hicles and put
your hands in the air. This is your only warning. Failure
to comply with my instructions will be construed as—
Say, you with the, uh, Yul Brynner haircut, I said away
from the vee-hicle. You're going to be mighty unhappy
with a load of twelve-gauge buckshot up your asshole. Uh,
you folks in the VW, you want to get out nice and slow,
and keep your hands where I can see them. That means
up, fellow, not be— Hunh. Okay. Well. That's the way
it is, you just stay real still till we can get down there
and see what's what and who's who. . . ."*

And so on, right down to the ground. He kept the bullhorn in one hand even after he disembarked—the shot-
gun was in the other hand, the butt against his hip, just in
case some deer or bear came down to see what was up,
perhaps. *Uh, you there with the hatrack on your head,
would you, uh, step out where I can get a look at you?
And bring your, uh, furry friend with you.*

Then he got stupid, and turned his back on them to signal to the pilot to cut the chopper's engine. The one with
the shaven head went for the Cherokee and was in it before the cop turned and back out with the UZI just as
he did and then the cop was dead and the pilot was probably little better behind the windshield that had ex-

ploded into diamonds. He'd never touched the switch, for
the rotors still whirled. Bad Guys 6,000,031 and them
other assholes and all the suckers in the Goo-lag and the
women and kids and old farts they wasted at My Lai
and one windshield.

Branch ran at Annie and put his shoulder into her chest
and knocked her behind the Rabbit and lay on top of
her. Under the car, he saw Derry, cringing as enfilading
bullets sprayed the gravel around him. "Get under it,
Jeff! *Under* it!"

The rotors splattered his shout all over the place.

Other sounds. Screams. Shouts. No gender. The an-
drogyny of fear. An engine. Another. But through,
above, around all the sounds still the belches of the UZI,
the farts of the UZI, the UZI's mad diarrhea.

Then only reverberations. Then nothing. Or so it seemed.
Nothing but gravel crunched by cars that had got to
where they were going, that were no longer hurrying, the
calls to one another of men who had done what they'd
set out to do, the sudden bursts of static from two-way
radios. Then really nothing. Nothing but heartbeats.

"Howdy, folks. Everybody just dandy?" A gaunt man
in a baseball cap, shooting glasses, a black turtleneck
under immaculate khakis, the trousers tucked into gleam-
ing boots, stood over them, slipping his pistol (coincidentally, a Bren 10 mm) into the shoulder holster he wore
exposed. "Beamon's the name; rescue's my game. Let
me see if this here's the key—" He bent over Annie, fit-
ting a key into the cuffs on her wrists. "Yup. You're
next, fella. You must be Branch."

"Is Derry—"

Derry appeared, a little wobbly, his hands held out to
his liberator. "I'm all right, Sam. You?"

"I'm all right. Annie, let me see that."

She had her hand to her cheek. "It's from when you
knocked me down."

"I'm sorry."

"If you're sorry, you're crazy." She hugged him. "Oh, Sam."

The final score was a little less lopsided: Bad Guys 6,000,031 and them other assholes and all the suckers in the Goo-lag and the women and kids and old farts they wasted at My Lai and one windshield. Good Guys 14, one of them a comic book character.

The Good Guys had had help, however, for the shithead, the nameless biker, Aura Quivers, Warren Cable and Cable's driver were all determined to have been victims of the UZI, the one with the shaven head having presumably decided that if he was going to make a getaway he would leave no one behind who might enlighten his pursuers as to his possible whereabouts (even bikers have homes and haunts). He had almost made good on his flight, for rather than use the Cherokee or one of the other vee-hicles to run the gauntlet of county cops who had sneaked, under Beamon's leadership, up the road to the reservoir as the helicopter was making its approach, he'd made for the outboard whose motor Branch had heard in the night, only to be stymied by the knot that held the painter to an iron eye in the wall of the reservoir; while he'd worried over it (either the shithead or the nameless biker, apparently, had had some nautical skills and had tied a knot that was meant to stay tied), a County sharpshooter had added him unequivocally to the Good Guys' side of the ledger.

36

Dolly Parton sang "Send Me the Pillow You Dream On."

Ashburn lined up bottles of St. Pauli Girl on the bar. "S'all on the house, I reckon, though I ain't real sure what we're celebrating."

"Domestic tranquillity," Eve said.

Derry reached over her shoulder for a bottle. "I'd still like to know why Portia killed Mularky. And where she is. And Hawkes and Bobby."

"Don't start, Jeff."

Ashburn came out from behind the bar and sat on a stool. "Sitting on the sidelines the way I been doing, that ain't but one of the questions I got. Reckon I'll have to wait for your book to come out, Eve."

Derry froze, bottle upraised, looking like a bugler. "Book?"

"Reckon you'll be giving yourself a nice fat part, too, since Jeff tells me it was you who decided it'd been too long since you'd heard from the Lone Ranger and Tonto, it was time for some heavy hitters, called up County. Got any idea who might could play you in the movie?"

"Anouk Aimée," Eve said. "One reason I'm not writing a book is everyone around here talks alike—like a god-damn cowboy. Maybe you should write a song about it."

Ashburn snorted. " 'Felix Wasn't Murdered, But a Bunch of Other Folks Was, and Who the Hell Done It, and Why'd They Go to the All-Fired Fuss?' Number nine thousand nine-hundred ninety-nine with a bullet."

Waylon Jennings sang "The Old Mother's Locket Trick."

Derry sucked on his beer and looked up and down the aisle. "Thought there'd be more people here, Rol."

"Yeah, well. Word ain't out yet that the hunters're home from the hill. 'Sides, lot of folks're still lip-reading their way through the afternoon papers, trying to figure out what the hell happened. Not that *I* know, despite my being on speaking terms with a few of the principals. Heard on the radio they're planning a big press conference in the city tomorrow—to clear Sam and Strock of assorted suspicions and generally explaining who did what to who. Reckon I'll have to wait till then to find out—unless you'd like to tell me about it now."

Eve slipped off her stool. "I don't want to talk about it, Rollie. In a week, maybe. Or a month. Thanks for the beer."

Ashburn put a hand on her arm. "Hey, now, little lady. What's the all-fired hurry?"

"I want to pack."

"Pack what?"

"Hey, Eve." Derry hemmed her in.

She pushed at his chest. "Let me out of here, you two."

"Pack what?"

"My suitcase, you assholes."

"To go where?"

"Home."

"New York?"

"It'll be restful after this godawful place."

Derry pulled the stool around so she could sit on it.

"Weren't you the one saying you could get to like California, the one who was bragging about leading the pack on the Beltway?"

She spun the stool, but didn't sit. "This is a nice place to visit, Jeff. But I feel far away from what's important to me."

"I'm not talking about living in Rancho Maria. But the city's got restaurants, discos, everything."

Eve smiled.

Hank Williams Junior sang "Queen of My Heart."

Ashburn and Derry took simultaneous swigs and Eve slipped between them. "I'll say goodbye before I go."

Ashburn played with a coaster for a while. "Well, shit."

"What?" Derry said.

"I don't know."

"Well, hell, Rollie. If you're interested in her, don't just let her walk out like that."

"I'm a paunchy old coot, Jeffrey. She ain't seen the grisly side of forty."

"I think she's older than you think, Rol."

"Well, that's a fine thing to say about a lady. 'Sides, who ain't?"

"Well, Branch."

"Well, Chief."

"Thank you, Sam, for never quite going so far as to think I was a killer. If you had, well, it would've taken some doing for me to prove I wasn't."

"Tom, I want to take some time off. I have things to look after back in New York—things I should've looked after years ago. I have some vacation time and if I could get some unpaid time off, I'd appreciate it."

"Well, you know, we still got a killer to catch. Two killers—if you're right that Bobby Lucas killed Litvak."

"I don't know that I think that anymore. Anymore meaning today. I might think it again tomorrow."

"Well, what do you think today?"

". . . I think Portia killed Litvak—for whatever it was that he knew about Leah Marston that kept her from estranging herself from him years ago, and for whatever it was that he knew about Felix's feud with Rafelson."

Strock pinched the bridge of his nose. "I'm trying to remember everything you told me about your talk with Litvak's sister. It's hard to keep it all together, isn't it? Just goes around and around." He blinked until the phosphenes cleared from his eyes. "You got any thoughts about where she is?"

Branch shook his head.

"You're not holding out on me, Sam, are you?"

"No."

"You're not planning to use this time off to track her down? I mean, you do have a knack for doing things on your own."

"If I looked for Portia, I'd find her. She expected me to find her. It's not easy to say, but that's how much contempt she had for me: she killed a man with my gun, and ran, and expected me to run, too—run away, but also run after her. I'd find her, and we'd live on the run together."

"Well, what about the Admiral? It's not like him to run from a fight."

"There's nothing left for him here—nothing but ghosts and memories"—and echoes and shadows. "What was with Quivers, Tom? What I mean is, did she mean something to you? If she did, I'm sorry."

Strock waved backhanded at her shadow. "She did strange things in bed, Sam. Wild things. Don't most men like the idea of having a woman like that at one time or another? I never went as far as these other fellows, I want you to know." He cocked his head, listening to her echo. "What was with her? I'd be guessing. She liked money. She liked power. The power she had in Rancho

Maria wasn't enough for her; she liked to maneuver, to manipulate people behind their backs. From what I know about her background, she was an orphan, brought up by an aunt and an uncle who was always trying to get in her pants. She got married real young to a guy who beat her up regular. I suppose the shrinks'll make something out of all that. I think she was the way she was because she liked being that way. You don't go to the lengths she went to kill two men without liking it more than a little. . . . What's this?''

"An extra key to your office."

"What's this?'' Branch said.

"A key to your place,'' Derry said. "Eve found it in your desk that time we broke in. She took it in case we needed to get back in. She went back to New York, Sam. Said to say goodbye—and to give you this."

Branch propped the envelope against his typewriter and handed Derry a slip of paper. "That fellow Beamon from County called to confirm your lunch date. What's that all about?''

"Don't say anything to Strock, Sam, okay? But it looks like he might be offering me a job. I thought it might be time to do something different."

"Something real?"

"I remember you telling me a story once about your kid, your son, when he was two or so and thought fire engines and ambulances and police cars were putting on a show for his benefit. You said you always told him that it was serious business, that they were going to help some-body. I thought that was a good thing to teach him. I guess that's why I became a cop. I mean, it was be a cop or be a lifeguard—or a lifer in the Marines—and it's all sort of the same thing, isn't it? People around here, well, they don't exactly need that kind of help. There're peo-ple in the county who do."

"How's Maria?"

"She got a job in the city. A place that makes TV commercials. She's just a receptionist for now, but she thinks it might lead to some acting work. We're sort of, uh, living together. I'm glad you said what you said, Sam, before the shooting started."

"It was my stupidity that got us in jeopardy, Jeff. I should've seen that someone would be watching Escobar, then watching me. And that wasn't the only stupid thing I've done in my career. But if you need a reference, even a dumb one, I'll be glad to give it to you."

"Well, if you're not doing anything, maybe you could type something up right now."

Before he did, Branch read Eve's note:

Dear Sam,
    Well.
    I can't say it wasn't, occasionally, fun.
    Whatever I can say it was, I can't say it to your face. Call it unfriendly. Call it irresponsible. Call it fear. Let's just say I think it's the friendliest, most responsible thing I can do for Annie, with whom, after all, I go farther back than I do with you, even though you and I have certainly done a lot of hard traveling—in record short time.
    Hasta luego, Sam. *Felice navidad*. That's the extent of my Spanish. I'll probably have dinner with my folks when I get back home and I wonder if I'll tell Harry that the escapades he's surely read about in the papers had me as a protagonist. I don't think I'll tell him we almost got physical.
    There's one loose end, Sherlock. Why did Maddox tell you about Felix's trip to New York? Because he wanted you to ask Portia about it, then start suspecting Felix killed Litvak, or had something to do with it? Who the fuck cares, right?
    Good luck.

You know what's really funny? (I don't seem to be able to just end this, do I?) What's really funny is I make lousy coffee. I always have. Old Chuck Zabriskie from West comma Texas said it tasted like I scraped it offa the insahd of a John Deere's crankcase. Fuck him.

E.

"For how long?" Annie said.

"I don't know," Branch said. "A month. A couple of months."

"Where will you stay?"

"Not with Megan, if that's what you mean."

"Actually, I was thinking of Eve."

"I'm sorry, Annie. Nothing happened between me and Eve, but I'm sorry that I thought it might. I'll probably stay at a Y."

"Nothing happened. That's what Eve said, too, when she came to say goodbye. Then, to her credit, she had to laugh and say everything happened—or a whole lot, anyway. You don't fly back and forth across the country together without stuff happening. What fools we all are."

"Some of us."

"I've been thinking about going back to Carmel. Or maybe to San Francisco. I think the kids could use some city life. I think they should learn to walk around and stumble onto things—a good bookstore, a little restaurant, a park that's not on any map. There's nothing like that here. I know there're no bums or bag women or drug pushers, either, but you can't have everything. I look at the things in the garage sometimes—a stroller, a trike, a bike with training wheels, a bigger bike—and I think that next there'll be a moped, then a Harley and a car, and then they'll be gone. Maybe I could hang on to them a little longer in the city. We could take those walks together— some of the time, anyway. . . . I'd probably meet a better brand of man in the city, too—or aren't there any straight men left in San Francisco?''

"Annie—''

"Don't say it, Sam. Don't say you won't be gone all that long and when you come back you'll be different. . . . I finally know what happened to you in New York and the reason I know is I read it in the newspaper and I read it in the newspaper because . . . Well, you know why. It's a horrible way to find out something essential about a man you thought you knew something about. I take part of the blame for not having pushed you sooner to tell me everything. I thought . . . I don't know—that it made you mysteriously attractive or something. But the next time you meet a woman, I hope you'll sit her down as soon as it's appropriate and tell her a whole lot more about yourself than you told me. . . . There's some stuff of yours at my house.''

"Just . . . throw it out.''

"You see, Sam? You walk through all this shit, then you want someone else to clean it up or throw it out. It doesn't work that way. You come get it. Use your key, and then leave it when you go.''

Creedence Clearwater sang "Proud Mary.''

"Well, well, Well. The notorious Samuel Branch.''

"Hello, Rollie.''

"A Bud?''

"Let me try one of those, uh, St. Pauli Girls.''

"Well, well, well.''

"You've got a right to be pissed off, Rollie.''

"You do that to people, motherfucker. You don't have a lizard on a highway's idea how much they care for you.''

Branch poured some beer and sipped it. "Annie's talking about moving back up the coast. Eve's gone back to New York. Derry's trying to get a job with County. I feel like people're slipping away.''

"I ain't going nowhere. Well . . .''

"What?"

"I've been thinking of taking a drive over to the ocean. You may be right it's time I had a look at it. You recommend a good spot to commune with the waves?"

"It might be best if you find your own. Beaches're like beer. What tastes fine to one tastes like piss to another."

Ashburn laughed. "Eve was right. Everybody 'round here does talk like a cowboy. . . . I got to be straight with you, Sam—I kind of took a liking to her. I drove her to the airport and thought a long time about suggesting we keep on going, down to San Clemente, maybe, or Mexico, even. Couldn't get up the nerve. Did get her phone number, though, case I'm ever back east. First one of those I've had in a while.''

". . . This isn't bad beer."

"It's good to see you, Sam."

Kenny and Dolly sang "Islands in the Stream."

"Hello?"

"This Sam Branch?"

"Uh, he's out. Can I take a message?"

The man laughed. "Howdy. Name's Fox. Charlie Fox."

". . . Hello."

"Listen, I reckon you're going more different ways than a bronc with a burr under his saddle blanket, but I just wondered if you had any music to go with them words Eve sent me."

"Music?"

"It's a song, ain't it?"

"Uh, yeah, but, uh, I can play 'Buttons and Bows' on the piano, and that's about it."

"That's gonna make it a tad hard for you to make a career out of this, hoss. Unless you got yourself a co-lab-oh-rator."

"Uh, no, I don't really."

"Well, let me just say this, hoss. I don't butt into other folks' business as a rule, but you could do a lot worse than to hook up with Rollie. I like the words, is what I'm saying, 'cept it's a mite complicated. I find that making the words fit to the line of music has a way of simplifying things. You ought to consider having someone strum some chords while you write. . . . You wrote anything else?"

"Uh . . ."

"What's it called?"

". . . 'Echoes and Shadows.' Or 'Shadows and Echoes.' I'm not sure."

"Sing me a couple of bars."

"Sing it?"

"Look, hoss, you must have some idea what it's going to sound like."

". . . Hum hum humhumhum, hum hum humhum. Humhum hum hum humhumhum—"

"That's called humming, hoss. I said singing."

". . . 'There's dust in the corners, holes in the screens, Dishes piled high—' I don't know about the dishes. I'm just trying to give the sense that someone's, you know, lonely."

"I don't mind dishes, hoss. Dishes is life."

". . . 'Dishes piled high in the sink. I'm out of clean socks, there's no food for the dog, I've drunk all the booze I can drink . . .' And, uh, it goes on like that."

"Lemme hear the chorus, hoss. Lemme hear 'bout the shadows and echoes."

". . . 'Shadows and echoes. Echoes and shadows. They're all that you left behind. Echoes and shadows. Shadows and echoes. They're driving me out of my mind.' "

"Hunh."

"It's real rough."

"It sure is, but that ain't to say it's bad. Look, Sam, if

I can call you Sam, it ain't my way to string somebody along just to do a friend a favor. Eve sent me your song and a letter saying you and Rollie was pals, and Rollie's someone everyone in Nashville misses just a whole lot and hopes he might someday bust out of that writing block he built round himself. I read a little about the fix y'all got yourself into out there and I reckon it'll be a while before you have time to do any more songwriting. There's a million fellows and girls out there trying to make it big in this business. 'Bout a quarter of them're camping on my doorstep even as we speak. But some of them do make it. If you want to be one of them—I don't know that you do, but if you do—then you'd be a goddang fool to pass up the opportunity to get a little help from someone like Rollie. And who knows, you might light a fire under him and for that alone you'd at least get yourself a lifetime pass to the Opry."

Branch laughed. "Thanks for calling, Mr. Fox."

"Charlie."

"Charlie."

"You ever get out to Nashville, you stop by, you hear?"

"I will."

"Say hello to Eve."

"Eve's gone back to New York. The West kind of wore her out."

Charlie Fox laughed. "Like I said, I read about the fix y'all got yourself into. Lordie."

"Yup."

"Be seeing you."

"Be seeing you."